Critical acclaim for the marvelous romances of
JUDE DEVERAUX

TEMPTATION

HIGH TIDE
A *Romantic Times* Top Pick

BOOKS BY JUDE DEVERAUX

The Velvet Promise

Highland Velvet

Velvet Song

Velvet Angel

Sweetbriar

Counterfeit Lady

Lost Lady

River Lady

Twin of Fire

Twin of Ice

The Temptress

The Raider

The Princess

The Awakening

The Maiden

The Taming

The Conquest

A Knight in Shining Armor

Holly

Wishes

Mountain Laurel

The Duchess

Eternity

Sweet Liar

The Invitation

Remembrance

The Heiress

Legend

An Angel for Emily

The Blessing

High Tide

Temptation

The Summerhouse

The Mulberry Tree

Forever . . .

Wild Orchids

Forever and Always

Always

First Impressions

Carolina Isle

Someone to Love

Secrets

Return to Summerhouse

Lavender Morning

Days of Gold

Scarlet Nights

Scent of Jasmine

Heartwishes

Moonlight in the Morning

Stranger in the Moonlight

Moonlight Masquerade

Change of Heart

Jude Deveraux

The Temptress

Pocket Books

New York London Toronto Sydney New Delhi

Pocket Books
An Imprint of Simon & Schuster, Inc.
1230 Avenue of the Americas
New York, NY 10020

This book is a work of fiction. Any references to historical events, real people, or real places are used fictitiously. Other names, characters, places, and events are products of the author's imagination, and any resemblance to actual events or places or persons, living or dead, is entirely coincidental.

This Pocket Books paperback edition July 2016

POCKET and colophon are registered trademarks of Simon & Schuster, Inc.

For information about special discounts for bulk purchases, please contact Simon & Schuster Special Sales at 1-866-506-1949 or business@simonandschuster.com.

The Simon & Schuster Speakers Bureau can bring authors to your live event. For more information or to book an event, contact the Simon & Schuster Speakers Bureau at 1-866-248-3049 or visit our website at www.simonspeakers.com.

Manufactured in the United States of America

30 29 28 27 26 25 24 23

ISBN 978-0-671-74384-0
ISBN 978-0-7434-5939-6 (ebook)

The Temptress

Prologue

The tall, lean, dark-haired man left Del Mathison's office, shutting the door behind him. He stood there, muscles in his jaw working, as if he were contemplating what he'd just heard. After a moment, he left the hallway and went into Mathison's richly furnished parlor.

In that room a man was leaning against the mantel of the empty fireplace. He was also tall, but he had the soft, cared-for look of a man who'd lived inside a house all his life. His blond hair was perfectly trimmed, his suit of clothes perfectly cut.

"Ah," the blond man said, "you must be the man Del hired to take me to his daughter."

The dark man merely nodded. He looked a little uncomfortable and his eyes constantly strayed to corners of the room, as if he thought someone might be hiding there.

"I'm Asher Prescott," the blond man said. "Did Del tell you about my part in this mission?"

1

"No," the dark man said in a voice that was felt as much as heard.

Prescott removed a cigar from a box on the mantel and lit it before he spoke. "Del's daughter has a penchant,"—he stopped and gave the dark man a quick look up and down—"I mean, she has the capacity for getting herself in trouble. For the last few years, Del's allowed her to have her head and she's been in one scrape after another. I guess you've heard of Nola Dallas the reporter." He paused. "But then maybe you haven't."

He took a draw on the cigar, waiting, but the dark man didn't answer. "Well, her father is tired of it and he's decided to force her to come to her senses. She's north of here now, staying with some friends of friends." He made a grimace of disgust. "Poor girl is convinced that Hugh Lanier, the man whose family she's visiting, is inciting Indians to massacre missionaries. The charge is ridiculous and Del's right that it's time she ended this folly."

Prescott studied the dark man as he stood looking out the window. Del had said this man could guide them through any part of Washington Territory. In fact, Del had said he even knew how to get through the rain forest—a place that was said to be impenetrable.

"The plan," Prescott continued, "is to take Mathison's daughter from Lanier's house, by force if necessary, and return her to her father. You're to lead us through the rain forest so it'll give me time alone with Miss Mathison. I plan to be engaged to her by the time we return."

The dark man turned to stare at Prescott. "I don't force women."

"Force her?" Prescott gasped. "She's a twenty-eight-year-old old maid. She's traveled all over the world writing those ridiculous bleeding-heart stories of hers and no man has ever wanted her.''

"But you do."

Prescott clamped the cigar between his teeth. "I want this," he said, looking about the room. "Del Mathison is a rich and powerful man and all he has to leave it to is one horse-faced, sexless daughter who thinks she can save the world from all its evils. Now, I want it straight between us from the beginning. Are you going to help me or fight me?"

The dark man took a while answering. "She's yours if she wants you."

Prescott smiled around his cigar. "Oh, she'll want me all right. At her age, she'll be glad to get any man she can."

Chapter One

Christiana Montgomery Mathison put her hand in the tub of water to check the temperature and then began to disrobe. It was going to feel good to bathe after a day of hard riding and hours of sitting huddled over a desk writing. She had her story finished now and tomorrow she'd start the arduous journey back home.

When she was nude, she realized that she didn't have her dressing gown and went to the big double-doored wardrobe to get it.

When she opened the right hand door, her heart seemed to skip a beat, for there was a man standing inside the cabinet, his eyes wide, his mouth open as he looked at Chris's pretty little body in its unclad state. Chris, alert from years as a reporter, slammed the door shut and turned the key in the lock. Softly, obviously not wanting to be discovered, the man began to pound on the inside of the cabinet door. Chris had one foot toward the bed where she planned to take the spread off and cover herself, but then things happened too quickly for her to react.

The left side of the wardrobe opened behind her and out stepped another man, and he had her in his arms before she could even take a breath or see his face. Her face was buried in his chest, his arms around the back of her, one hand on her bare shoulders, the other resting just above the curve of her buttocks.

"Who are you? What do you want?" she asked and was appalled at the fear in her voice. The man was large and she knew she'd have no chance of success if she tried to escape him. "If it's money you want—" she began but his arms tightened on her and she didn't finish the sentence.

His left hand began to stroke her hair as it hung halfway down her back, gently tangling his fingers in its soft blondness, and even through her fear she found herself relaxing somewhat. She managed to turn her head sideways so she could breathe more easily, but he didn't allow her to move the rest of her body as he kept her pinned close and intimately to him.

"Let me out of here," hissed the man locked in the wardrobe.

The man holding Chris didn't react, he just kept stroking her hair, his right hand inching down her back toward her buttocks. She'd never had a man touch her bare skin before and his rough, calloused hands felt good.

She recovered herself and began to struggle against him, trying to get free, but he held her firmly, not hurting her, but showing no signs that he ever intended to release her.

"Who are you?" she repeated. "Tell me what you

5

want and I'll see if I can get it for you. I don't have much money, but I do have a bracelet that's worth something. Release me and I'll get it." When she again tried to move, he held her fast.

With a sigh of frustration, she relaxed against him again. "If you plan to take me by force, I warn you that I'll put up a struggle such as you've never seen before. I'll take some of your skin to replace what you take from me." She tried to twist her head to look up at him but he didn't allow her to see his face. Am I saying the wrong thing? she thought, wondering if what she'd just said were words that were inflammatory to a . . . a rapist, she finally said the word to herself. In spite of her brave words, she began to shiver and his arms tightened around her in a way that, had the circumstances been different, Chris might have found protective.

"We've come from your father," he said in a voice that Chris felt through her cheek. It was a very deep, very rich voice. "There are two of us and we've come to take you home."

"Yes, I'm ready to go home. But first I have to—"

"Ssssh," he whispered, snuggling her against him as if they were lovers and familiar with each other's bodies. "You have to go home now whether you want to or not," he said, obviously not listening to her. "You can fight it out with your father later, but now we take you home to him. Do you understand?"

"But there's a story that I—"

"Chris," he said and the way he said her name made her try to look up at him, but he still wouldn't allow her to see his face. "Chris, you have to return to your father. I'm going to release you and I want you to get dressed, then I'll let Prescott out of the wardrobe. I'll meet you outside with the horses. Pack only what you'll need for the trip. We'll be going through the rain forest and it'll take a few days so take rain gear if you have it."

"Through the rain forest! But no one can travel through that."

"There's a way and I know how. Don't worry your lovely little self about that, just get ready to leave."

"I have to take my story to John Anderson," Chris said. She didn't seem to be in all that much of a hurry to move away from him and sometime during the past few minutes, her hands had moved to his waist. She wasn't exactly hugging him but she wasn't pushing him away either.

"Who is John Anderson?"

"My friend and the editor of a newspaper. He's the one who first suspected Hugh of selling rifles to the Indians."

He moved his head so that his face was buried in her hair and she could have sworn she felt his lips against her scalp. "We'll talk about that later, but now we have to go. We've taken too long as it is. You'll have to get dressed so we can leave."

Chris waited, but he just held her, his hand now stroking gently across her shoulder blades. "Are you going to release me or not?"

"You aren't cold, are you?"

"I am not in the least cold. What I am is being kidnapped by a man who may or may not be from my father, but knowing him, you probably are, and I am standing here in my birthday suit being smothered by a man I've never even seen, much less been introduced

7

to. Now, will you please let me go so I can put on some clothes?"

"Yes," he said in that voice of his, but he made no effort to release her.

Chris made a sound that was half a cry of rage and half a scream of protest.

"If you hurt her, Tynan, you'll answer to me," came the voice of the man in the wardrobe who had been surprisingly quiet for the last several minutes.

The man called Tynan held her for a few more minutes, then with what seemed to be a heartfelt sigh, he released her and turned away toward her bureau all in one motion.

Chris grabbed the corner of the spread on the bed but she didn't need it since he stood with his back to her, toying with the items on the bureau top. With the spread wrapped around her, she edged toward the wardrobe, opened the left side and withdrew a clean riding habit.

"I need my other garments from inside the chest," she said to the back of him. From what she could see of him she could tell that he was big, broad-shouldered, had dark hair and that his clothes were completely new. From his boots to the gun and holster slung low on his hip, to his brown leather vest and his blue chambray shirt, all of it was new. He hadn't spoken since he'd released her and now he merely stepped aside, staring at the wall as if it were of great interest.

Chris withdrew undergarments from a drawer, all the while trying to see his face but she couldn't, and when she moved back into the room to put on her clothes, he went back to the dresser. She dressed as quickly as possible, tightening her corset strings with such speed that she knotted them and had to spend extra minutes untangling the laces.

"All right," she said when she was dressed, expecting him to turn around.

But he didn't turn toward her, going instead to the wardrobe and unlocking it. Out stepped a tall blond man who did nothing but look at Chris.

"Help her get packed. I'll meet you outside," Tynan said and before Chris realized what he was doing, he was out the window and she was alone with the blond man.

It was an awkward moment, but the blond man stepped forward, smiling. He was very good-looking, with bright blue eyes that looked as if they were accustomed to laughing and a smile that Chris was sure had melted the hearts of many women.

"I'm Asher Prescott. I'm sorry about what happened there," he said, motioning toward the wardrobe, but he didn't look sorry at all. In fact, he looked quite happy about everything. "We really are from your father and our assignment is to bring you back no matter what excuse you give. He is very worried about you."

She gave him a weak smile. "That sounds just like my father. I'll go, I was ready to leave, but I do need to pack a few things," she said as she walked in front of Mr. Prescott to pick up the toilet articles on the bureau top. As she did so, she saw that one of the items Tynan had been toying with was her hand mirror. And, as she looked from the mirror to where she had been dressing, she realized that Tynan had been watching her while she dressed.

A quick surge of anger ran through her but then she smiled, dropped the mirror into the carpet bag she'd taken from the bottom of the wardrobe, and went to the desk to take the papers of her story on Hugh Lanier.

After a second's thought, she sat down and wrote a quick letter to Hugh, explaining the purpose of her visit, and telling him why she had to do what she must.

Chapter Two

Chris followed Asher Prescott through the window, where, at the edge of the trees, two horses awaited them.

"Miss Mathison," Mr. Prescott began, "may I say what a pleasure it is to—"

"You can do your courting later," came a voice that Chris recognized instantly. She looked up at the man on horseback hidden in the shadows. "We have to get out of here, so let's ride."

Both Chris and Asher obeyed that voice without delay.

Chris and Asher rode close to each other all night and all the next day, through trees as big around as horses, past small villages, both Indian and white, past logger camps, past saw mills. Always, they stayed away from people, moving southeast and allowing as few people as possible to see them. They traveled across paths that were so narrow that they had to lead the horses. Tynan always stayed far ahead, leading them, scouting the trail, looking for places where too many people watched. Only once did they stop. Tynan gave a low whistle and Mr. Prescott put up his hand to halt Chris, then went ahead to see what Tynan wanted. He came back to say that ahead was a party of loggers taking their noon meal and so they had to rest until the men were gone.

Asher pulled jerky out of his saddle bags and a canteen and gave a piece of the dried meat to Chris.

Chris leaned back against the trunk of a tree, her body feeling weak with exhaustion. "I think there's something wrong with that Tynan of yours," she said to Asher, watching him from under her lashes. Sometimes the best way to get information from someone was to pretend to not want it. "I think he must be scarred or disfigured in some way or else he wouldn't be afraid to show his face."

"He's not *my* Tynan," Asher answered, looking affronted. "If he belongs to anyone, it's to your father. He hired him."

"Do you know why we're going through the rain forest?" Chris asked, trying a new tact. "It seems like such a long way around."

"It is," Asher answered, gazing off into the trees.

Chris had been a reporter for several years and she was used to interviewing people and she'd developed a sixth sense about when someone was lying. Perhaps this man wasn't exactly lying but he certainly wasn't telling the whole truth.

Before Chris could ask another question, there was a whistle from within the trees and, as obedient as a dog, Prescott rose from the ground and started packing.

"Tell me, does anyone ever *see* this Mr. Tynan?" Chris asked as she mounted her horse.

Asher looked startled. "Why are you so interested in him?"

Chris watched as Asher heaved himself into the saddle. He acted as if he were more used to the comfort of a buggy than being on horseback. "Professional curiosity. Do you know why my father hired this man? What are his qualifications for leading us through the forest?"

Asher shrugged as he mounted. "He's been there before, I guess, but he's an odd one. Doesn't seem to like people at all, always puts his bedroll outside the campsite, never wants to ride with anyone, and he doesn't like to talk. Ask him a question about himself and he refuses to answer. I'd like to know where your father got him too."

"Knowing my father, you probably don't want to learn the entire truth of whatever he's done," Chris said under her breath. When she got home, she was going to give her father a piece of her mind about this ridiculous kidnapping.

At sundown, they heard the whistle again and Asher halted her as he went ahead into the trees, returning minutes later with two fresh horses.

"Did you suggest to him that we might like to rest?" Chris asked as she mounted the horse.

"I most certainly did," Asher said. He looked more tired than Chris felt and she thought she was probably more accustomed to riding long hours than he was. "But we have to go on. Ty wants to get to the edge of the forest before we halt. But he says we'll have an entire day of rest when we get there."

"Ty," Chris murmured as she mounted. She spent

the next several hours as they jogged along wondering about this mysterious man who came into her room and held her, watched her dress, then disappeared to lead them through a forest that was said by the Indians to be haunted. And why had her father hired him? And who was Prescott? He didn't seem to know much more about traveling through this land than she did, but he'd been chosen as half of the rescue team. What in the world was her father up to?

Chris had plenty of time to puzzle over the facts since they continued riding all night. Her questions kept her mind alert and kept her from feeling the absolute exhaustion that ran through her. They'd had no sleep or rest for two days and two nights now.

When Chris was beginning to weave in the saddle and twice she had nearly fallen off, she thought she saw a light through the trees. Blinking several times to clear her vision, she began to be more sure of what she saw. Somehow, she knew it was a fire built for them. "Otherwise, Ty wouldn't let us get so near," she murmured to herself.

"Mr. Prescott," she called and succeeded in waking him from where he slumped forward in his saddle. "Look ahead."

There was renewed energy as they urged the horses on toward the fire and all Chris could think of was finally being allowed to stop and sleep. Even as she was still moving, she began to unfasten the straps at the back of the saddle that held her sleeping roll.

When they did halt, Chris dropped her bedroll onto the ground, then fell on top of it and was asleep in an instant.

She had no idea how long she slept before something woke her. She opened her heavy eyelids. It was still dark but there was a faint hint of early morning light and in it, she could see outlined a man wearing a wide brimmed hat moving almost silently as he unsaddled the horses and gave them food and water.

Chris half slept, half waked as she watched him and even when he began to walk toward her, she still didn't awaken fully.

He knelt by her and it seemed perfectly natural when he pulled her into his arms. Like a sleepy child, she just smiled and snuggled against him.

"You're on top of your blankets," he said in that voice that seemed to rumble through her. "You'll get cold."

She nodded once while he straightened the blanket under her, then put the other one on top. For just a moment, as he covered the far side of her, she thought his lips were near her forehead and she smiled, eyes closed. It was like a good-night kiss from her father. "Good night, Ty," she whispered and fell asleep again.

When she woke again, it was full daylight and at first she thought she must be dreaming, for around her was a place of fantasy. Tall, tall trees towered overhead, blocking the sun, everything covered with gray-green moss or ferns, everything so soft. It was as if she were at the end of the earth.

Near her, Mr. Prescott slept soundly. It felt to Chris that she was the only person alive on earth.

Slowly, she got up, stood and stretched. The eerie forest seemed to be utterly and totally silent. In front of her was what passed for a path, little more than a rut in the greenery. They'd come in from the right so now she took the left path.

She was no more than a few feet from the camp but, as soon as she turned a bend, she felt alone. She may as

15

well have been a hundred miles away from another human. She kept walking, no more than a few yards on the springy forest floor, and she thought she heard water ahead of her.

Another few yards and she could see a rushing stream below and to her right, with big boulders in the water covered with patches of black moss. Suddenly, the only thought that Chris had was of the bath she'd missed two days ago. She thought with regret of the tub full of hot water that she'd had to leave behind. Why couldn't the men have stayed inside the closet until she'd finished bathing? Of course they might have if she hadn't opened the door to the wardrobe. Stayed in there and watched her, she thought with a grimace as she ran down to the water.

Now, all she could think of was getting clean again and she had her clothes off in a second and was wading into the water. It was icy and took her breath away but she wanted to be clean more than she wanted to be warm. She washed while standing behind a cluster of boulders so that if either of the men came from the camp, they wouldn't be able to see her, and she was close to the edge of the forest so she could make a run for it if necessary.

She was just finishing her bath and regretting her impulsiveness because she didn't have a towel with her when she thought she heard a man whistling and looked up to see Mr. Prescott coming down the trail. Quickly, she ran from the water, grabbed her clothes and ran into the forest—only to run smack into the hard chest of Tynan.

For a moment they were both too astonished to speak. The lush, abundant greenery of the forest deadened all sound and two people could walk into

Chapter Three

Chris sat there looking at the top of his hat and thought how utterly bizarre the situation was. This man had made her look like a fool twice, he'd held her in his arms three times—not to mention that two of those times she'd had no clothes on—he had kidnapped her, telling her that it didn't matter at all what she wanted, yet here she was feeling as if she should comfort him. She put out her hand to touch his and as she did so, she saw a red, raw place on his wrist, just barely visible beneath his shirt cuff.

"You've hurt yourself," she said, immediately concerned.

He was on his feet instantly, and before Chris could say another word, he walked, half ran actually, to the edge of the stream and called to Prescott.

Chris was left sitting on the moss and wondering what she had said to offend him.

"Here she is," she heard Tynan saying before he reappeared, leading the man as if he were herding a maverick. As little as she knew of Tynan, she was sure that the voice he was using was a false one. "You've introduced yourselves, haven't you, Miss Mathison? This is Asher Prescott. He's a friend of your father and will be with us while we slowly make our way through this forest. Ash, why don't you take Miss Mathison fishing? We'll need fresh food. And later, you two can gather firewood." He gave Ash a little push in Chris's direction.

Asher smiled down at Chris and offered her his hand to help her stand. "Shall we go fishing, Miss Mathison? I hear there are salmon in these waters."

Chris was confused by what was happening. She didn't want to spend the day with Mr. Prescott but it didn't seem as if she had any choice. It seemed to be already arranged. She glanced at Tynan but he had his head turned so that she couldn't see his face.

"Why, yes, fishing sounds like a delightful pastime," she answered as she accepted Mr. Prescott's hand. By the time she stood, Tynan had disappeared into the trees.

She and Asher walked back to the camp together to find that there were supplies and two mules that Chris had not seen before and Mr. Prescott was already handing her a fishing pole.

"Shall we go, Miss Mathison?"

He led her back the way she'd gone that morning, over rocks, past the place she'd bathed, but not far from the camp. "I think this will be a good place to try," he said.

"Is that your idea or Mr. Tynan's?"

He smiled at her. "I don't think he's *Mr.* Tynan. I'm not sure he has but the one name. But let's not talk about him. I hear you worked on a newspaper. Is it true that you're the infamous Nola Dallas?"

"Nola Dallas is my pen name," she said stiffly, as she expertly tossed the fishing line into the water. She'd always lived in Washington and she'd fished since she was a child.

Asher looked stricken. "I didn't mean to give offense, it's just that, having read your articles, I thought you'd be a much older woman—or maybe even a man. Did you really do those things you wrote about?"

"Every one of them."

"Even appearing as a chorus girl? Wearing pink tights on stage?"

Chris smiled at the memory. "And getting myself thrown out during the second act. I'm not much of a dancer."

"But then who cares about dancing when you can implement the reforms that you have?"

Smiling, she felt herself warming to him. "Tell me, Mr. Prescott, why did my father choose you to help in this rescue mission? I would have thought he'd choose a man who knew this forest."

"That's Tynan's job. He's to take care of the animals and the food and look after our safety."

"And what are you to do?"

Ash smiled at her in a very pleasant way. "My only job is to make your trip enjoyable."

"I see," Chris said as she looked back at the water. But she didn't see at all. "What do you do for a living, Mr. Prescott?"

"Please call me Ash. It's not as if we first met in a drawing room."

Chris tried to control the redness in her cheeks as she

remembered the first time she'd seen this man inside the wardrobe in Hugh's house.

"Until last year I had my own lumber mill south of here but there was a fire and I lost everything."

She glanced at him quickly and saw the way the muscles in his jaw twitched. Having lost his business, he was obviously not over the hurt of it. "But you've started another business?" she said with much sympathy in her voice.

"Everything I had was tied up in the mill and when it went, I had nothing left." His voice lowered. "Not even credit." After a moment, he turned to her and gave a little smile. "But I have every hope that my fortunes will change for the better very soon. Look! I think you have a fish on the end of your line. Shall I bring it in for you?"

"I can manage," she said as she began pulling and reeling in the line. There was indeed a salmon on the end and within another hour she'd brought in half a dozen good-sized fish, while Ash had two small ones.

He laughed good-naturedly about her being the breadwinner and they walked companionably back to the camp.

There was a small fire going, built for them by Tynan, Chris thought, but the man was nowhere to be seen.

"I'd like to discuss something with you, Mr. . . . Ash," Chris said as she expertly cleaned the fish and spitted them with a stick. "I wanted to talk to both you and Mr. Tynan but I can't seem to get you together. The reason I was at Hugh Lanier's house was that I was investigating a rumor that Mr. Lanier was involved in something quite evil and—"

"Evil?" Asher said, leaning back against a tree. "Perhaps evil is too harsh a word."

22

"I don't think so and I don't believe my readers will think so. Hugh Lanier wanted some land that had been settled by eight missionaries. But they wouldn't sell so he bought guns and hired white men to dress as Indians and massacre the missionaries. If that isn't evil, I don't know what is." As always, when she thought of injustice of this magnitude, her temper began to rise.

"But if it's only a rumor—"

"It *was* only a rumor. I have proof that he did it. Among other things, I have a bill of sale for rifles. I even heard him talking to one of the 'Indians' and—"

"Heard him?" Asher said. "Do you mean you eavesdropped?"

"Of course I did. I wore a green dress and hid among the cornstalks. But the point is, I have to get my evidence to the newsman who sent me on this mission and, by my calculations, we're due west of John's office. We need to leave tomorrow morning."

She watched Asher as he held his hat in his lap and played with the hatband. "Chris, I don't believe your father would want you traipsing across the country accusing men of . . . of what you're accusing Lanier of. Perhaps when we return to your father's house, he can send your information to this newsman. Until then I think it best that you stay here in safety."

Chris just looked at him for a moment. She'd grown up with a man like this one, and she'd worked with men like him. He was perfectly sure she was wrong and nothing she said or did was going to change his mind. "I think the fish are done," she said softly, then watched as he smiled at her in a way that men who'd just won always smiled at women. She returned his smile but it didn't reach her eyes.

She made light, ladylike conversation with Asher

while they ate, not once referring to her plans for getting her story to John Anderson. But as soon as they were finished, she stood.

"I think I'll go and see if I can find Mr. Tynan," she said absently as she started down the path toward the river.

"I wouldn't do that if I were you, Chris," Asher said. "I'm sure the man would be here if he wanted to be and I'm quite sure that he can feed himself. I think you should sit down and share your lovely company with me."

Chris didn't know what she hated more in life than being told what she *should* do. It was the source of all her problems with her father. He never tried to reason with her, but just told her what was best for her and expected blind obedience.

She smiled sweetly at Asher. "I think I'll look for our host," she said and moved so quickly down the path that she didn't give him time to voice a protest. Within seconds, she heard him thrashing about through the forest as he searched for her. Thanking her mother and her ancestors that she was small, she jumped over a fallen log and hid in the ferns until she saw him go by. When she could hear him no more, she walked a short way through the underbrush before finding that it was impossible to go any further due to the fallen logs and the heavy curtain of moss hanging from every possible surface. She went back to the trail again and started toward the water, essentially following Asher. At the top of the little ridge that overlooked the water, she could see him below, frowning and looking annoyed. Smiling to herself, she continued down the trail.

She'd only gone a few feet when all sound was gone. The rain forest gave one the oddest feeling of being totally alone. All around her was green—gray-green, blue-green, green that was almost black, a lime-green, hundreds of shades of the color. And everything was soft. She ran her hand over a fallen log that was covered with a forest of its own in miniature and smiled at its softness.

Ahead were odd formations created of moss and rotted tree trunks. She couldn't hear her own footsteps as she walked.

As she rounded a curve, she gasped, for lying just inches off the path was Tynan, fast asleep. There was a pack near his head and a rumpled blanket under him. He slept as bonelessly as a child and he looked very young. Again, Chris was amazed at the sheer beauty of the man and she had an enormous desire to just sit down and look at him—a desire which she indulged.

She had been sitting there for just moments when he stirred and opened his eyes.

"Chris," he said with a little smile, then closed his eyes again. A fraction of a second later he sat bolt upright, grabbed his hat and put it low down over his face and looked at her. "Miss Mathison, I thought you were fishing with Prescott."

"I was until I caught so many more fish than he that he suggested we return to the camp. After that I managed to escape down the path and I found you. Did you enjoy your nap? You certainly deserved it after the way you stayed awake and took care of us."

Looking like a sleepy boy, he began to rub his eyes and this time, Chris saw that both his wrists were sore. There was also a bruise under his right cheekbone and a half-healed cut above one eye.

"Why don't you come back to the camp and join us? We have more than enough fish. Have you eaten?"

25

"Yes, thank you, but you ought to go back to the camp. Prescott's probably worried about you." He stood. "Besides, I need to get to work. I have to scout the trail ahead. I'm sure there're logs that have fallen across it since the last time I was through here."

"And when was that, Mr. Tynan?"

"Just Tynan, nothing else and certainly no mister," he said as if he'd said it a hundred times.

Chris rose and moved to stand closer to him. He turned his back to her, removed his hat and ran his hand through his hair, which looked to be damp. She wondered if he'd been bathing. His shirt cuff was unbuttoned and as it fell back, she saw that all the muscles in his forearm, along with the veins, were prominent under his skin. He looked as if he had been starved for a while.

"I don't want to be a troublemaker because I know that you're only doing what my father has hired you to do, but . . ." She hesitated over using his name. "But, Tynan, I think you could use a few good meals and I insist that you return with me. If you don't, I promise to make this journey very uncomfortable."

He opened his mouth to speak but then closed it and grinned instead—and Chris felt her knees go weak. His entire face lit up and it flashed through her mind that he could get *any* woman anywhere to do whatever he wanted.

"I can't resist an invitation like that. I'll follow you."

"No, we shall go together. Tell me, why were you in the forest before? Who made this path?"

"Did you enjoy your fishing expedition with Ash? He seems to be a pleasant man. All the way here he was a great help, nothing was too much for him to do. And he's great with horses and everyone we met liked him. I guess you did too."

"Well, yes," she said hesitantly. "How did you meet my father?"

"Ash has known your father for years. It's a wonder you never met him. Ash's father worked his way up and made a lot of money in the east. I'm sure Ash is the same kind of man."

Chris looked up at Tynan in bewilderment. What in the world was he talking about? But he just smiled at her and, this time, instead of being dazzled, she wondered if he often used that smile to get women to stop talking about whatever he didn't want to hear—or from asking questions that he didn't want to answer.

She smiled back at him but, if he'd known Chris better, he would have known that her glittering eyes showed that she'd just accepted a challenge. She was going to find out who this Tynan—no last name, no first name—was.

Chapter Four

"I need to talk to you," Chris said as soon as Tynan was seated in the camp and eating one of the fish she'd cooked. She told him just what she'd told Asher, about Lanier being responsible for killing the missionaries, but Tynan didn't interrupt her, didn't say a word, in fact.

When she'd finished speaking, he licked his fingers. "Now tell me what you've left out," he said.

Chris was startled for a moment. "All right," she said, smiling. "The truth is, Mr. Lanier was very good to me while I was his guest and his wife is very sweet, so I've felt some twinge of conscience about telling the world what Mr. Lanier did. Of course every word of it's true, but, when the story comes out in print, I'm afraid Mr. Lanier's life could be . . . ah, changed."

"Not to mention the length of his neck," Tynan said, looking at her.

"So I left him a letter telling him what I planned to do."

There was a long moment of silence from Tynan. "So, if we step out of this forest, no doubt Lanier's men will be waiting for us with rifles, or maybe cannons, anything to prevent that story from going to press."

She gave him a weak smile. "Yes, I guess so." Her face changed. "But they are things I *had* to do. I *had* to give Mr. Lanier a chance to flee and I *have* to give this story to the press. Don't you understand?"

Tynan stood. "I understand that a man has to do what he must, but you, Miss Mathison, need help and I'm not in a position to give it. Prescott's in charge of this expedition. I'm just the guide. I follow orders and that's all. Thank you for the fish, ma'am, and now I need to go scout the trail ahead." He turned back.

"And I wouldn't consider going alone if I were you," he said as he picked up a piece of wood and tossed it to the right of her head onto what looked to be solid ground. The log fell through vines and hit the ground a full second later. He didn't have to say another word. One could leave the trail and walk into deep holes that were concealed by a tangle of greenery.

With that, he left Chris alone.

She stood there for a moment cursing all men everywhere. "*Women* must do what they must, also, Mr. Tynan," she said to no one and set about gathering wood for the fire.

Chris stayed in the camp, talked to Asher when he returned, and didn't mention Hugh Lanier again. When Tynan returned, she glanced at him, but he didn't look at her. Chris kept her head turned toward Asher, pretending to find every word he said fascinating. But in truth, she was planning how she'd escape these two men. John Anderson's newspaper office was on the edge of the rain forest, not four miles from where they'd entered the forest last night. If she could get a horse, ride like blazes down the trail, then into town, she could be there and back by sundown. If luck were with her, she could be back before she was missed.

She stood. "I think I'll take a walk," she said to Asher.

"I'll go with you."

"No thank you," she said, giving him her prettiest smile. "I have things I have to do." She widened her eyes. "Female things." The mysteries of womanhood always stopped men like Asher Prescott.

"Of course," he said politely.

She walked away from him, past Tynan, then hid in the undergrowth until both men had left camp. Nobody ever slapped a saddle on a horse faster than she did. The poor animal pranced around, lifting its legs. "Be a good boy now," she coaxed. "We're going to have a good run."

"And where would that be, Miss Mathison?"

Chris whirled on her heel to face Tynan, her jaw set. "I'm going to take my story to John Anderson and if you plan to stop me you'll have to tie me here—and you'll have to watch me night and day. You'll have to give up sleep and—"

"I understand," he said and Chris saw amusement in his eyes. "How far away is this Anderson?"

Chris held her breath. "With hard riding, I can be back by sundown."

"And what did you plan to do about Lanier's men? What if they're waiting on the edge of the forest?"

"Run just as fast as I can and pray I don't get shot."

He stood there looking at her for a while, then withdrew his gun from its holster, making sure it was loaded. "Maybe I can help some. Which way is this town?"

Chris mounted her horse. "Southeast from the edge of the forest. John's office is the third building on the right."

Tynan saddled his horse. "As soon as we drop it off, Lanier pulls a gun and takes it. You got more paper? Why don't you drop a package off at the freight line—if there is one—then stop and say hello to Mrs. Anderson?"

"Why . . . yes, that might work," she said, looking at him in wonder. "There is no Mrs. Anderson but his sister is married to the town doctor."

"Even better," Ty said, mounting. "You know how to ride?"

"I can go anywhere you can," Chris said arrogantly but soon wondered if she were telling the truth. Tynan led a pace that scared her—and her horse. She had to use all the muscles in her arms to control the animal as they ran through the dangerous forest.

At the edge of the trees, Ty didn't slow down but kept pounding down the road. Chris half expected gunshots over her head but all was quiet. When no one shot at them, Ty halted his horse and turned back to her. "We're going in the back way. No doubt they're waiting for us in town. I'm going to drop you off at the freight office and I want you to stay there until you see me. I'll take the story to the doctor's wife and leave your horse in back of the freight office. When you see me ride past the front, run out the back and get on the horse and ride like hell. I'll be right behind you. Think you can do that?"

"Yes," Chris answered, controlling her horse. "But if they catch you with the story—"

"Don't worry about me, worry about obeying my orders. My temper's worse than Lanier's bullets."

"Yes, sir," she said, smiling and he winked at her as he turned his horse and continued southeast.

They paused outside the new, rough little town, the single main street a rutted tract. Tynan sat still for a moment, looking at the town, then turned to her. "I think they're here."

"How could you know that?"

"Too many men doing nothing but looking, their hands on their guns. They're watching for somebody. Give me your story," he said, and when he had tucked it inside his shirt he looked at her. "You ready? You remember what you're to do?"

"It's not exactly complicated."

"But vital. Come on."

He led her through the back of the town, skirting in and out of shadows, staying close to the buildings, keeping her inside as he rode protectively on the outside. Once, a wagon came around a building and instantly Tynan pulled her halfway across his saddle into his arms. "You still sick, honey?" he asked loudly. "It's always that way with the first baby."

As soon as the wagon was gone, he pushed Chris back. He certainly is a fast thinker, she thought.

"Wait here," he said as they came to the freight building. There was a big loading platform and ramp in back and a hook suspended over the doorway. Chris sat on her horse and waited, jumping at every little sound. With Tynan gone, she suddenly didn't feel so brave.

"Here she is," she heard Tynan say, as he walked up on the dock with another man beside him. "She just can't go another step." Before she could speak, Ty pulled her up from the saddle onto the dock. "It's her first one and she's not used to the sickness yet, so mind if I leave her here while I fetch the doctor?"

"Sure thing. I got eight of my own, but I don't know what the doc can do. She'll just have to wait it out."

Tynan practically smothered Chris in his protective embrace. "If it'll help her rest easier having the doctor, then I'll do it."

"Sure. Here, little lady, just sit right here."

"How about by the window so she can watch for me? It'll make her feel better."

"Sure," the man said.

Ty escorted Chris to a chair in front of a window looking out onto the main street. "Don't forget to look sick and give him something to deliver for you."

Chris nodded as she looked up into Tynan's beautiful blue eyes. He hesitated for a moment then kissed her forehead. "I'll be back in a minute, honey."

When he was gone, Chris lounged against the chair, trying not to show how intently she was watching the street. Across the road were two men, both holding rifles, both wearing guns, their right hands resting on the handles as if they meant to draw at any moment. Chris saw that her hand was shaking as she withdrew from her pocket a sealed letter addressed to her father. She didn't have to do any pretending to the freightman as she was sure she looked as scared as she felt. And she realized that at least half of her fear was for Tynan. He wasn't involved in this, had no reason to risk his life on her behalf, but he was.

The minutes passed and Chris began to grow anxious. What was taking him so long? Maybe John's sister wasn't there. Maybe—

Her thoughts stopped as she heard gunshots from the end of town where Tynan had gone. She stood.

"There's no need for you to get upset," said the freightman from behind his big desk. "Somebody's always shootin' at somebody in this town. You just sit there and rest."

But Chris couldn't rest as she leaned toward the window to see farther out.

Her breath stopped as she saw what she feared: Tynan was riding hell bent for leather down the street, two men on horseback chasing him, their guns blazing. With wide eyes, she watched him approach, then turned to the freightman. "May I borrow this?" she asked, taking a rifle from a cabinet on the wall.

Before the man could grasp what she was doing, Chris walked out the door, fell to one knee on the porch, propped her left arm on her raised knee and took aim. She dropped the first man behind Tynan with a shot in his shoulder, and was aiming for the second when Ty turned his horse and rode straight for her. There was a ramp in front of the freight office for rolling barrels and now Ty rode his horse straight up it.

Chris stood, stepped back a bit and when Ty bent and stretched his arm out to her, she caught it, put her foot on his in the stirrup and hauled herself up into the saddle behind him. Ty didn't slow his pace as he went thundering through the freight office, past open mouthed workers, and out the back, down the ramp.

It took longer for the men following to go around the freight office, and Chris heard the scream of the horse as the one man who tried to follow them misjudged the distance and went flying off the side of the freight dock.

Chris hung onto Tynan with all her might, her hair coming unpinned and flying out behind her, her body plastered to his. He leaned forward on his horse and she went with him. There were bullets coming at them but they were traveling too fast to be in range—and the men were shooting from the back of horses so their aim wasn't that good—or at least Chris hoped it wasn't.

When they reached the edge of the rain forest, Tynan didn't slow down, but kept on at a breakneck speed for a few hundred yards. Suddenly, he halted the horse, turned, grabbed Chris and lowered her to the ground. He dismounted behind her.

"Now we disappear," he said, taking the horse's reins and Chris's hand. He motioned for her to climb down into a tangle of vines. She clambered down so fast, she skidded half the way. "Persuading" the horse was another matter and Ty did it with a series of quiet-voiced threats that made Chris's eyes widen. No sooner had he gotten the animal into the ravine and pulled vines over their heads to cover them than three men came down the trail after them.

Ty held his hand on the horse's nose to keep it from making a sound while Chris stood close to him, both of them looking up through the vines at the men.

"We've lost them," one of the men said.

"Yeah and we lost four of our men on the way in. Lanier's not gonna like this."

"Let's get out of here. This place gives me the creeps. If they went in here, they won't come out alive. Ain't nothin' but ghosts in this place."

The first man snorted. "Lanier pays you to shoot ghosts. Come on, let's go back to the freight office. Maybe the girl left somethin' there."

Chris held her breath as the men left and only released it when she could hear them no more. With a sigh, she leaned against the bank and looked at Ty. "How did they know you?"

"Somebody saw us leaving Lanier's house and she recognized me."

"She?"

"I think she's a maid of Lanier's. Anyway, she told Lanier I was the one who took you, so when he found your letter, he was looking for me too. But I did get the story to the doc's wife."

Chris grinned. Now that they were safe, she was beginning to feel euphoric. "I wonder if those freight men have closed their mouths yet? I couldn't believe it when I realized you were bringing that horse straight on through the building."

Ty's eyes twinkled. "I could have taken a paddle to you when you walked out there and started shooting. You should have stayed inside, then when I was out of town, with everybody following me, you could have ridden away, safe and sound. Where'd you learn to shoot like that, anyway?"

"My father. That poor freight man. One minute I'm so ill I can barely sit up and the next—"

"And the next you're leaping onto a horse behind me. Chris, you were great!" He laughed, taking her shoulders and giving her a hard kiss of joy on her mouth.

Blinking, wide-eyed, Chris looked up at him. When he'd kissed her, a spark of pure, undiluted fire had run through her. "Oh," she whispered and moved toward him.

He released her shoulders as if they burned him, then turned his back on her. "I got to get this horse out of here and we'd better get back before Prescott misses us," he mumbled.

Chris felt a little lost, not sure what she'd done wrong. He'd seemed so pleased with her, so happy a

36

moment ago, and he'd kissed her. Not a kiss of passion, but one of friendship, between two people who'd shared a great deal, but when she'd shown interest in him, he'd moved away.

Glancing down at her body, she wondered if maybe she wasn't appealing to him. All her life she'd been told she was pretty, but her curves were subtle, not exaggerated as was the fashion.

"The maid at Mr. Lanier's who recognized you, was her name Elsie?"

"Yeah," he said under his breath, his back still to her. "You leave first and I'll come later."

With a sigh, Chris began climbing the steep bank, pushing vines away as she climbed. Elsie was the same height as Chris but weighed thirty pounds more—and all of it equally distributed above and below a twenty-inch waist. If that's the kind of woman he liked, no wonder he moved away from Chris.

She sighed all the way back to camp, fastening buttons that had come undone in the fracas.

"Are you all right?" Asher greeted her. "You were gone an awfully long time."

"I'm fine," she said, pouring herself a cup of coffee. "And you?"

"I'm all right and I'm glad you got some rest. Tomorrow will probably be another hard day of riding."

"Yes," she said, looking at him over her cup. "I am glad to rest. Is there anything to eat? Long afternoon naps make me ravenously hungry."

Chris didn't see Tynan until the next morning. Twice, she tried to catch his eye, to smile at him, but he wouldn't look at her. It was as if he wanted to pretend yesterday hadn't happened.

Yet, the more he ignored her, the more she watched him. They stopped to make camp in the afternoon and Tynan immediately put Asher and Chris together. Chris sat and watched Ty as he took care of the horses and as he walked past her, she was sure that once she saw him limp. Could he have hurt himself yesterday? He kept that blasted hat pulled down over his face so far that she couldn't really see his face, but as she watched, she saw him grimace as he lifted one arm to take the reins of the horse. Asher looked annoyed once, but Chris kept on watching every move Tynan made—and the more she saw, the more she was convinced that he was in constant pain.

Chris gave a big yawn. "I think I'm rather tired and if no one minds, I'll go down the trail and take a nap."

Tynan turned around and, briefly, his eyes met Chris's, but he looked away almost instantly. "Don't go too far," he mumbled as he passed her and went down the trail into the forest.

"Are you sure you wouldn't rather take a walk with me, Chris?" Asher asked. "I would so like to hear more about your newspaper work."

"I really am very tired. Perhaps another time," she said as she took up her sleeping roll and carpet bag, and, acting as if she could barely move, she started down the trail behind Tynan.

As soon as she was out of Asher's sight, she opened her carpet bag, removed her medical kit and started running down the path, hoping she could catch Tynan before he disappeared.

She seemed to have gone a long way and there was no sign of him when she thought she heard a horse neigh. Doing what she knew she shouldn't, she left the trail to walk to a place where she hoped she could see what was below her.

The area off the trail was frightening to her, she was afraid of the covered drop-offs that Ty had shown them, and who knew what lurked beneath the layers of greenery?

She made it to the base of an enormous tree, parted the hanging moss and looked below. Tynan was standing several feet below in a rocky clearing, his shirt off, rubbing down one of the horses. When he turned and she saw his back, she let out a little gasp. She had been horribly right when she thought he moved as if he were in pain. Even from several feet away, she could see that the gashes that crisscrossed his back were only half healed. And she was sure the wounds had been made by a whip. What he'd done yesterday, tearing about on his horse, hauling her up, her clutching his back, must have caused him untold amounts of pain.

She waited until he'd turned again, so that he was facing her, and then she moved back into the forest, acting as if she were just coming out of it. She made a lot of noise and called his name.

When she emerged and could see him, he'd put his shirt on and was just pulling on his boots.

"Here," he called up to her.

"How do I get down there?"

"You don't. Go back to the camp."

She smiled at him and took a tentative step forward, as if she meant to go straight down the side of the drop off.

"No!" Tynan yelled, but it was too late.

Chris had meant to only pretend to go down that way but, what she'd thought was ground wasn't and she went sliding down the hill on her back.

Tynan ran across the clearing and leaped on top of her to keep her from sliding any farther.

Instinctively, Chris's arms went around him, clutching him close to her. When he lifted his head and looked at her, she was aware of his body on top of hers with every fiber of her being. For a moment, she thought he was going to kiss her—and she welcomed him.

He was a half inch from her lips before he jumped up, leaving her lying on the steep bank. For just a moment, he turned away from her and she had the distinct impression that he was trying to control his emotions. When he turned back, his eyes were alight, but he seemed calm otherwise. "I told you to go back to the camp. And I thought you were too tired to go anywhere and needed to rest."

"I lied," she said with a smile.

"And do you often lie, Miss Mathison?"

"Not nearly as often as the other people in this party," she said, blinking her eyes innocently. "You tell me the truth and I'll tell you the truth. I think that's fair."

He seemed to start to say something, but changed his mind because he turned away from her and went back to the horse. "There's a trail over there. You can use it to get back to the path that takes you to the camp."

She stood, straightened her skirt and retrieved the medical kit that had come down with her. "Actually, I was searching for you because I wanted to have a look at your back."

"My what?!" he said, turning toward her with a face full of fury. "Look, Miss Mathison, I don't know what you're after but I've had about all I can take." He was moving forward, pointing the horse brush at her, and

Chris was backing up. "Maybe you think I'm going to be one of those people in one of your stories but you've got another think coming. I was hired by your father to take you and Prescott through this forest and to take you home to him. I did *not* bargain for you following me everywhere I go nor did I expect for you to keep leaping out at me without a stitch of clothes on. Under different circumstances, I'd enjoy your entertainment, but on this trip I got a job to do and I plan to do it no matter what you do to tempt me. You, lady, are Satan in one beautiful package. Now get out of here and leave me alone. I don't want to see you until I wake you in the morning—and I might even get somebody else to do that."

He closed his mouth abruptly, turned his back on her and went back to the horse.

"All right," Chris said. "I'll return to camp and tell Mr. Prescott that your back is a mass of lacerations that look as if they may become infected and also tell him that something is wrong with your feet. I'm sure the mutiny will be over and done with in no time and you will no longer be our leader and you can return to wherever it is that you refuse to tell anyone. Good day, Mr. Tynan," she said as she started toward the path he'd pointed out.

She'd gone no more than three feet before she heard a muttered oath behind her and what sounded like the horse brush being thrown down with some force.

"All right," he said loudly and Chris turned toward him. "What am I supposed to do?"

"Remove your shirt and boots and lie down on your stomach there on that patch of moss."

"I guess I should be glad you don't want anything else," he mumbled sulkily but did as she asked.

As Chris knelt beside him and looked at his back, she saw that the wounds were worse than she'd thought when she'd seen them from a distance. Most of them were healing well but a few had broken open yesterday. She imagined that they were very, very painful. Taking a deep breath, she opened her case and withdrew some salve.

"This will help ease the pain," she said softly and began to soothe it on his skin. His back was broad and he was quite muscular but there was little more than skin covering his muscles, hardly any fat. He looked as if he'd been worked very hard and fed very little.

When she felt him begin to relax under her fingers, she said, "How long were you in prison?"

"Two years," he answered quickly, then whispered, "Damn!"

"Mr. Tynan, I am a newspaper reporter and I work hard at observing. I don't know anywhere else that a man can be worked at hard labor, starved and beaten— at least not in America."

"And if there was such a place you'd get yourself thrown in there so you could write a story about it, right? Am I going to be your next story? 'I went through the rain forest with an escaped prisoner.' Something to that effect?"

"*Did* you escape? Somehow, I thought my father had you released."

When he didn't reply, she knew she'd hit close to home. "You see, Mr. Tynan, I know my father quite well. If he wanted someone to take me through an impenetrable forest, he wouldn't hesitate when people said it couldn't be done. He'd just find out how to do it. My guess is that he found that you'd been through the

42

forest and it wouldn't matter to him if you were on your way to the gallows. He has enough money and power to cut any ropes, even if they're hanging around someone's neck."

"He'd trust his daughter to a murderer?" Tynan asked, turning his head to look at her.

She was thoughtful for a moment. "No, I don't think he would. I believe that my mother and I are the only people he's ever really loved. I wasn't sure he was going to recover after my mother died, but I think he decided he still had me."

"But you're saying that he put you under the care of a criminal, someone rescued from the hangman's noose."

She paused in rubbing the cream into his wounds. "Mr. Tynan, you must be an innocent man. You're perfectly right that my father would never entrust my care to a villain. Yes, of course, that's it. You're either innocent or you did something that wasn't violent. Breach of promise perhaps." Smiling, she resumed smoothing the cream on his back. By now, she was as much massaging his muscles as doctoring him.

"How close am I to the truth?" she asked and when he didn't answer, she laughed. "You see, Mr. Tynan, we all give clues to ourselves, no matter how hard we try to conceal them. I'm sure Mr. Prescott has no idea that you are in pain every time you move, but if you watch, you begin to see things about people."

She kept rubbing his back, greasing her hands and running them over the curves of muscle in his arms, massaging until she felt him relaxing completely. His breathing was soft and deep, as if he were asleep. All Chris's motherly instincts rose within her. How she'd like to take this man home and feed him and see that he rested. She wondered if her father's housekeeper, Mrs. Sunberry, had met him. If she had, Chris was willing to bet she liked Tynan.

Smiling, Chris lifted one of Ty's hands and began to massage it, being careful of his scarred, raw wrist.

"I'm not hurt there," he murmured sleepily but made no attempt to move.

"I was thinking about Mrs. Sunberry."

"Blackberry cobbler," Ty said. "With cinnamon in the crust."

Chris laughed. "So you did meet her. I thought she'd like you."

"Like adopting a stray dog?"

"You're a stray perhaps, but certainly not a dog. Ty, where were you born?"

He moved as if he meant to get up but she pushed him back down.

"All right, no more questions, but please don't get angry again. It's too nice a day to ruin with anger." She ran her hands in his hair and began to massage his scalp.

"Do you like being a newspaper reporter?" he asked.

"Yes, at least I did, but I think I'm getting tired of it. I'm twenty-eight years old and I started when I was eighteen. That's a long time. I think I want . . . I don't know what I want but it's something more."

"A home and kids?"

She laughed. "You've been talking to my father. Did he tell you how he got me back to Washington? How he lied to me? I was working in New York and he sent me a telegram saying he was at death's door. I cried from one end of the country to the other thinking he was dying and when I arrived home, filthy, tired and terrified, there he was atop a bucking bronco having the time of his life."

"You're lucky to have a father."

"You don't?"

"Not that I know of."

"Or mother?"

"She's dead."

"Ah," Chris said. "How long have you been alone?"

"Always. Are you going to look at my feet and get this over with? I need to check the trail ahead to see what's happened to it over the years."

Reluctantly, Chris removed her hands from his skin as he turned and sat up. For a moment their eyes locked and held. Chris never wanted to look away but Ty broke the gaze.

"I was safer in jail," he mumbled. "Here! Take a look at my feet. That should keep you busy for a while."

With a sigh, Chris turned away from his face to look at his feet—then gasped. There were blisters, and blisters that had been worn away to bloody patches and what wasn't actually blistered was about to. "New boots and no socks," she said, taking one foot in her hand. "Did you just put them on and wear them without breaking them in first?"

"I had to. I'd ruined my dancing slippers the night before," he said solemnly.

She laughed. "I'll bandage these places and then I'll see if Mr. Prescott has an extra pair of socks."

"No!" Ty said quickly. "I don't take charity."

Chris looked at him in astonishment. "All right," she

45

said after a moment. "No charity. But the first town we come to, we buy you socks. My father did pay you for rescuing me, didn't he?"

"Yes," he said, watching her as she began to bandage his foot. She ran her hands over his ankles which were as raw as his wrists. "Chains?" she asked.

He acted as if she hadn't asked. "What made you go after Lanier anyway?"

"I don't know. Somebody has to. John Anderson will have that story in print by now. People hate the Indians even more than they already do whenever they hear of them killing missionaries. This time they didn't do it, Hugh Lanier did, and I didn't think it was fair for the Indians to get the blame."

"Even though it meant that a white man, a man you knew, would probably lose everything?"

"The missionaries lost everything," she said softly.

"I've never seen a woman who handled being shot at as well as you did yesterday. Had some practice?"

"Some," she answered.

"I thought women like you wanted to stay home and raise babies."

"What does that mean, women like me? Besides, I've never been in love. Have you?" She held his ankle in her hands and had no idea how her fingers were tightening.

"A few times. Hey! Your little nails are sharp."

"Sorry," she mumbled, her head down.

"What does it matter to you if I've ever been in love?"

"It doesn't, of course," she said stiffly, easing the pressure on his foot. "I ask questions of everyone."

"Look, Miss Mathison, believe me when I say I'm not your type. I'm a drifter and if there isn't any trouble

I seem to make it. You ought to learn something from Elsie. She turned me in because she can't stand me."

Chris smiled at him. "You probably didn't pay enough attention to her."

Ty leaned back on his elbows and watched a bird overhead. "A man can't spend two years in jail and then not give something like Elsie every ounce of his attention."

She yanked on the bandage she was wrapping around his foot. "If you like women like her, that is. I doubt if you've seen a woman like her without her corsets."

Ty looked back at her, his eyes dancing with laughter. "Fat, are they?"

"Twenty-seven-inch waists at least and maybe they do have a lot on top but by the time they're twenty-two, they'll all be sagging and—" Chris stopped, aghast at what she was saying. "Put your boots on," she said rigidly. "Maybe you can get a fat woman to change the bandages in a day or two since you obviously like well padded women and I'm sure I'm too skinny for you."

She started to stand but he caught her arm, grinning at her, but she kept her head down. He was making her so *angry!*

He put his finger under her chin. "You don't think you'll be sagging in a year or two? As old as you are?" There was laughter in his voice. "You don't think I like skinny little girls who follow me around and ask me questions?"

"I don't know," Chris whispered and felt exactly like a little girl. She'd never wanted anything as much as she wanted this man to like her.

"Slim, pretty little blondes are my favorite," he whispered.

Chris looked up at him with eyes sparkling with tears

and, as he moved his head toward her, she knew he was going to kiss her, so she closed her eyes and parted her lips in anticipation.

"What the hell am I doing?" he said and pushed Chris so that she landed on her seat a foot away from him. "Get out of here right now! You hear me? Don't come near me again. You're right that I like a different type woman. Virginal nurses who follow me around are the type I like *least*. Now go back to camp and don't even get near me again!"

Chris, a little frightened by his temper, ran up the trail to the path back to camp.

Chapter Five

When Chris reached the camp, out of breath from running, Asher was sitting by a cheery fire, smiling up at her. He began to talk to her about the forest, but Chris was barely listening. She was wondering why Tynan had been sent to jail.

"Chris! Are you listening to me?" Asher asked.

"Yes, of course," she said, looking at him but not listening.

Later, when she was snuggled inside her blankets, she lay awake for a long time. She could barely see the stars through the trees but she watched the leaves and the blackness above. At night this forest was a frightening place.

She'd been awake for over an hour when she heard a soft sound to her right. She knew it was Tynan come to see that they were all right. She'd never seen a man take his responsibilities more seriously.

Her eyes were fully open as she watched him walk

about the camp, checking that Asher was covered, that the horses were properly tethered, that the food was covered and that the fire was out. When he came to Chris he started slightly to see her eyes open.

"You should be asleep," he said, standing over her. "You have to get up early tomorrow."

"How is the trail ahead?"

Asher stirred in his bedroll and Ty knelt beside Chris, lowering his voice. She raised on one elbow.

"It's all right, just some brush across it, but I cleared most of it."

"Did you get anything to eat?"

She saw the whiteness of his teeth as he grinned at her. "You are going to make some man a wonderful mother. Yes, I ate. Now go to sleep and I'll see you in the morning."

She lay down on the hard bedroll but he didn't leave.

"Miss Mathison, I'm sorry about this afternoon. I shouldn't have lost my temper. It's just that I think we should keep this trip on an employee, employer basis. As I pointed out to you, I haven't been around women for a while and there are things that are difficult for me."

"Do I make things difficult for you?" she whispered in such a way that there was no doubt of her meaning. She hoped he'd say she was making his life hell.

He rocked back on his heels and grinned at her again. "Not anything that I can't handle. Now, be a good girl and go to sleep."

"No good-night kisses?" she asked, a little angry at his laughing at her.

"Not from me," he said and she smiled because there was horror in his voice. As he walked away, she turned over on her stomach and went to sleep.

The first thing that greeted Chris the next morning was the sight of Tynan bending over the fire. His hair was damp and there were fresh fish frying in a skillet.

"Did you go fishing?" she asked, smiling at him.

He mumbled something but she couldn't hear what it was before he stood and walked to the horses.

All morning Tynan stayed away from her and the three of them rode in silence on the trail.

When they stopped at noon to eat, Tynan quickly told Asher to take Chris with him to gather firewood.

Asher took Chris's elbow and half propelled her toward the path they'd just traveled.

"I hear your father is in shipping, too," Asher said for the second time before Chris heard him.

"Yes, he is," she said distractedly. "Canning, shipping, cattle, a couple of saw mills, anything he can get his hands on."

"Yet you left it all to run away to New York to become a newspaper reporter. But now you're back."

"Not by choice. I plan to return to New York as soon as I get back to my father's house."

"Ah, I see. Somehow, I thought you had other plans."

"Such as?" she asked, turning to look at him. "Did my father tell you that I had other plans?"

"Only that you were ready to settle down, that you were still young enough and he had hopes that you—"

"Young enough for what?" she interrupted.

"Why, to start a family I would imagine."

Chris bit her lower lip to keep from replying hastily. "No, I don't think I'm over the hill yet, even at my advanced age. I assume women can still bear children at my age."

"I didn't mean to give offense."

Quickly, Chris looked at him and a wave of guilt ran through her. Here she was walking in the forest with a handsome young man who was trying to be polite and she, because of some imagined infatuation with a man she barely knew, was being almost rude to him. She smiled at Asher. "I'm sure that you didn't, Mr. Prescott. How did you meet my father?"

Asher returned her smile. "He and my father were friends and did some business together. I saw you once when you were a little girl. You were with your mother. I thought she was the prettiest woman I'd ever seen."

"So did I."

He began to gather firewood from the ground, making a stack of it at her feet.

"And why did my father choose you to go on this rescue mission?" She also picked up a few pieces of wood and added them to the pile.

"I think he took who he could get. There aren't many men my age who have no business, and, after working for myself for so many years, I can't seem to settle down to just being an employee."

"I know how you feel. My father continues to tell me what to do and how to do it, even sending men after me when I don't obey him."

"Yes, but you're a—" Asher took one look at Chris's sparkling eyes and stopped. "I almost put my foot in it that time, didn't I?"

She cocked her head to one side. "Would it matter if you alienated me?"

Asher gave her a big grin. He really was quite pleasant-looking, not anything like Tynan, of course, but very handsome. "I'm alone in the woods with a beautiful woman and you ask if it would make any difference if she's angry with me? Why, Miss Mathison, this time and place is a dream come true and I would as soon die as ruin it."

She laughed at his pretty speech as he picked a tiny purple flower from a bank of moss and gave it to her with a little bow. Chris stuck the flower behind her ear and smiled at him.

"Well," he said slowly, "I guess we'd better get back." He picked up an enormous pile of wood. "Put the rest on top of this."

"No, I'll carry my share."

"Miss Mathison, while I am around, no woman shall ever carry firewood. Now do as I say and put the rest of that on this pile."

"You sound just like my father," she said with a sigh.

"Thank you very much. I admire and respect your father and I take it as a high compliment that you consider me like him in any respect. Now, lead the way because I can't see a thing."

Laughing, pleased that he'd said that he liked her father and didn't complain about him as most people did, Chris led him back to camp. Asher said that not only could he not see but he couldn't understand her directions, so Chris "had" to hold two fingers of his left hand to guide him back to camp.

When they entered the camp, Tynan was bending over the fire frying fish dipped in cornmeal. He looked up when a laughing Chris and a laden Asher arrived, but put his head down again quickly.

Chris suddenly felt ridiculously happy. Holding the divided skirt of her habit out, she began to hum.

"I don't guess you'd care to dance, Mr. Prescott," she said, holding out her arms. Out of the corner of her eye, she watched Tynan but he didn't even look up.

With obvious happiness, Asher took Chris's extended hands and began a quick dance about the little clearing. It was a cross between the Virginia Reel and a square dance that was exuberant and happy. Chris followed his lead and no matter how fast he led her in the dance, even when her feet barely touched the ground, she stayed with him.

"Watch out!" she heard Tynan shout just before she and Asher tumbled into a foot-deep depression filled with ferns.

They lay there together, Asher's arms around her protectively, Chris's skirts around his legs, while Tynan stood looming over them. "Are you two all right?" he asked, his brows drawn together in a scowl.

"Never been better in my life," Asher said, then planted a hearty kiss on Chris's cheek.

Still grinning, she turned to see Tynan looking at her oddly.

"I think we can eat now," Tynan said before turning away to return to the campfire. "That is, Miss Mathison, if you are finished with your dancing."

"For the moment," Chris said and went to take a place by the fire.

Chapter Six

Asher was in rollicking good spirits after their impromptu dance and he did his best to entertain Chris, even singing to her. She joined in and they made an enthusiastic duo.

Tynan sat to one side of them, head down, whittling on a stick, not participating but not leaving them either. Once, as she was singing with her cheek close to Asher's, it occurred to her that maybe Tynan didn't know how to participate.

It was midafternoon before anyone thought of leaving and then it was Chris who stopped the laughter and suggested that they clear up and go.

Tynan tossed his stick away, put his knife in his pocket and slowly started toward the horses. As Chris was tightening the straps on her bedroll, he stopped beside her.

"That was nice," he said. "Real nice."

"Where did you grow up?" she asked quickly.

"Not where people sang," he answered just as fast. "You like the man?"

"Of course. You've pointed out what a fine man he is, haven't you? And you've told me to stay away from you so I should be pleasing you now."

He looked at her in a way no man had ever looked at her before. His eyes seemed as if they could burn her. "You do please me." Abruptly, he turned on his heel and walked away, almost crashing into Asher.

"What was that about? He looked angry. Is something going on that I don't know about?"

"Mr. Prescott, I have no idea what you know and what you don't."

"Chris, I must give you some advice. Tynan isn't the sort of man . . . well, I mean, a girl like you . . . I don't like the interest he's taking in you."

"Interest in me?"

"Your father told him you were a Montgomery and he asked what that meant."

"And did you know to tell him?"

"No, I didn't, except that they are your mother's people. People like him don't have relatives, they don't even have names."

"Mr. Prescott," she said icily. "You and I will get along a great deal better if you keep your opinions about Mr. Tynan to yourself. After all, I've known the both of you an equal length of time so I see no reason to trust you over him." With that she mounted her horse, and all the rest of the day, she felt Asher Prescott's eyes looking at her thoughtfully.

For two days they traveled hard. Three times the men had to cut away small logs across the trail, and once Tynan and Asher had to lead the horses across a log as wide as some boardwalks. Another time they spent hours on either end of a crosscut saw hacking a way through a tree down across the trail. At night they fell into their blankets and slept hard—at least Chris assumed Tynan did too since he slept apart from the camp.

On the evening of the second day, Asher kissed her again. They'd ridden together for a while during the day and he'd asked her more questions about her newspaper career. He also apologized for what he'd said about Tynan, saying he was only concerned about her safety. That evening he asked her to walk with him and, when they were a few yards from the camp, he told her how pretty she was and asked permission to kiss her. Chris said yes.

She'd kissed very few men in her life and wasn't exactly sure how to do it. Asher's arms went around her, holding her pleasantly and his kiss was warm and dry and comforting but nothing like the quick, happy kiss of Tynan's. No fire ran through her body. Nothing made her lean toward him wanting more.

"What the hell are you doing, Prescott?" came Tynan's outraged voice, making Asher release Chris. "I came out here thinking you'd gotten lost and here you are mauling Miss Mathison."

"I was not mauling. I asked permission—" Asher halted, his face angry. "What's it any of your business anyway?"

"My business is to return Miss Mathison to her father."

"And I don't believe that's *all* you've been hired to do either," Asher said.

"Go back to camp," Tynan ordered Chris. "Now!"

She scurried to obey him, leaving the two men alone. Later, Asher returned to camp by himself and grinned at Chris. "Sometimes employees forget their places and have to be reminded," he said with a wink.

Tynan didn't return to camp that night and in the morning he was quiet, always keeping his distance from Chris.

A part of her wanted to scream with frustration over the mystery of what was going on. What was her father's original reason for having her taken through the rain forest? He couldn't have known Hugh Lanier would be chasing them. Why had her father hired a man who barely knew how to build a fire outdoors to help in a place like a rain forest? Why was Tynan one minute pushing her toward Asher and the next acting like a jealous lover?

The day after Asher kissed Chris, Ty allowed them to stop in the late afternoon. As Chris helped Ty unpack, she tried to make converstaion but he only mumbled answers to her questions.

"What is wrong with you?" she hissed under her breath. "You haven't spoken to me since last night. Are you angry with me about Asher?"

"What you do is your own business," he said, unsaddling a horse. "I've been hired as your guide and nothing more."

"It's *you* who keeps pushing me off to be alone with him. It's 'Miss Mathison, go with Prescott and fetch wood,' and 'Miss Mathison, why don't you and Prescott go fishing?' Every minute you're pushing me toward him. So if I kiss him, isn't that what you had in mind?"

"Nothing's in my mind. Look, why don't you go over there and sit down? Why are you always following me? Can't you ever give a man a moment of peace?"

Quick tears came to Chris's eyes as she turned

toward the fire. He called her name but she didn't look back.

Once, she felt that Ty was trying to catch her eye but she didn't look up at him, and after a while she heard him leave the camp.

"I'm going to take a walk and write in my journal," Chris said to Asher, removing her notebook, pen and ink from her saddlebag. "I'll be back in an hour or so." She then went down the path in the opposite direction of Tynan.

Chris walked for longer than she meant to. Tynan's sharp, angry words had hurt her and she wanted to think about what she had been doing and what she wanted to do in the future.

It was odd how this man attracted her. Never before had she made such a fool of herself over a man.

After a while, the light began to fade and she moved just off the trail to sit on a log and write in her journal. Maybe if she put in all the facts of this odd trip, she could figure out what was going on. She wrote a good deal about the one man who was so kind to her as opposed to the man who seemed to hope that she'd fall into a deep hole.

She was sheltered under the tree branches and a particularly heavy umbrella of moss and didn't at first feel the cold drops of rain begin to fall. One minute she was warm and dry and the next she was sitting under what seemed to be a waterfall that began in the sky.

Gathering her things with haste, she dropped her pen. She was leaning over the log to get it, searching in the plants, when the entire side of the trail suddenly gave way and Chris went tumbling down. The log rolled out from under her and she caught at a tree root as she went flying down the side of the forest wall.

Hanging there, suspended, the icy rain coming down on top of her, her feet touching nothing and not being able to see anything below or above her, she prayed for help. "Tynan," she whispered, not able to hear herself above the rain crashing down.

"Tynan!" she shouted.

Her hands were beginning to slip. She tried to keep a cool head about where she was and how she could get out of this mess. If she could only see how far it was to the bottom of the drop. For all she knew, she could be six inches from the ground.

Twisting, she tried to look below her, but the rising mist made it impossible to see anything. One of her hands slipped.

After several long minutes of struggle, she got both hands back on the tree root. She could feel the skin begin to tear away. She tried to swing forward, hoping to get her foot into the mud and rocks of the bank.

"Curse all the Montgomery women for being short," she said when she couldn't reach the bank.

Suddenly, she stopped as she thought she heard a sound above her.

"Tynan," she yelled with all her might. "Tynan. Tynan. Tynan."

She hadn't finished her last scream before he was there beside her, his back sunk into the mud of the bank, his long arms reaching for her and pulling her to him.

She clung to him like a monkey to a tree, wrapping her body around his, her arms around his neck, her legs around his waist.

He began to go down the side of the bank, scooting along, pushing debris out of the way as he moved. Chris held to him, her face buried in his neck. Even when he started walking, she didn't let go.

"Here," he said at last, peeling her off of him.

When he stood her on the ground, she found that her legs were weak. Both their bodies were covered in mud.

"Sit there for a while and rest." He pointed to an outcropping of rock behind her, and, gratefully, she sat down, out of the pelting rain.

As she looked up at Ty, the misty, cold rain coming down behind his head, she knew she'd never seen anything as welcome in her life. Quite naturally, she put up her arms to him.

He came to her, holding her so tightly she could barely breath. "I knew it was going to rain," he said. "I was getting the tents up when you walked off. I thought you'd have sense enough to come back when it started. God, Chris, you're going to be the death of me. It's a wonder I found you."

Chris was so happy that she was safe and that he was here that she began kissing his neck exuberantly. "I knew you'd find me. I knew it from the moment the ground fell away. One minute I was sitting there and the next I was falling. I wasn't even sure it was raining."

Ty forcibly pulled her arms from around his neck—and he looked like a man in great pain. "Chris," he said in a pleading voice, "have you ever seen a grown man cry? I mean really cry? Like a brokenhearted two-year-old?"

"No, I don't believe I have or that I want to." She was reaching for him again. "Ty," she said.

He caught her hands in his, holding them together in front of him. "Then please stop this," he said. "Please leave me alone. Don't follow me, don't touch me, don't mother me, don't put salve on my back, don't cry when I get mad at you. Don't do anything. I'm begging you, please."

Chris leaned toward him. "It doesn't matter to me that you were in prison. You may think that I'm of a different class than you but I'm not. Ty, I think I may be in love—"

He put his hand over her mouth. "Don't say it. Don't ever say it. I couldn't bear to hear it. We've only known each other for a few days and in a few more we'll never see each other again."

"The number of days doesn't matter. Do you know how many men have asked me to marry them? I receive proposals in the mail. I've been to dinner parties and had two proposals by the end of the meal, but I've never even been tempted—not by marriage or by their attempts at seduction. But you, Tynan, you're the man I want."

Ty's face went through one contortion after another and for just a moment, he leaned toward her as if he meant to kiss her. But the next second, he ran from the dry rock cropping, out into the rain.

"Don't you understand that I CAN'T? I *can't* make love to you. Now get up! We're going back to camp and don't come near me again." He grabbed her wrist and pulled her out into the rain with him, then half pushed her up the steep bank. Once on the trail again, he didn't touch her, just pointed the way back to the camp.

Chris knew that some of the water on her face was a deluge of tears but she didn't know how much until she reached the camp. There were three tents set up, one for each of them. Under a tree, its opening facing away from the other two tents, was a tarpaulin that she knew was Tynan's.

Ty stood back, arms folded over his chest while she went into the tent he pointed to.

It took Chris an hour to change into dry clothes, because her tears kept running down her cheeks. She cried all night long. The first man she'd ever loved and this had to happen.

When morning came, her face was red and swollen, her nose half again its usual size and her head was aching. When Tynan came to tell her that they'd stay in the tents until the rain stopped, she couldn't look at him, but just kept her head down and nodded.

By noon, Chris was exhausted from so many hours of crying and thinking, but she'd made some decisions. Slowly, she built a little fire under the dry leaves of the tent and heated some soup left from the day before.

She took her rain gear from the pile of garments in a corner. There was no furniture in the little tent, just a sleeping roll, a few clothes and now the little fire under the flap outside.

With her back rigid, Chris left the tent. The rain was coming down very hard and when it hit the hot kettle, it gave off wisps of steam.

Tynan had rigged himself a piece of canvas supported by two poles in the front. It left the sides and the front open and, as long as the wind didn't blow the rain about, the occupant could stay dry. Ty was stretched out, his head on his saddle, a book in his hand when Chris arrived.

"I brought you some soup," she said above the rain.

Sitting up, he reached out and took the pot from her as she withdrew biscuits from under her slicker. "May I sit down?"

"I don't think that . . . yes, of course," he said at last, looking at her hard. No one could miss the fact that she'd been crying for many hours.

"I've been awake all night and I've been thinking about what you told me and I've come to some decisions." She took a deep breath. There was no use stalling. "First, I'd like to say that I thank you for telling me what you did. I'm sure it's not something that you tell everyone."

She lowered her head and didn't look at him as he stared in open-mouthed astonishment. "I think the best way to say this is just to get it out. I don't know very much about love, never having experienced it before, at least not love between a man and a woman, but I think I have sense enough to recognize it when I see it. I don't know how or why, but I've fallen in love with you and I want to spend the rest of my life with you. I know your secret now and, after much thought—I don't want you to think that I say this lightly—I know it doesn't matter. I've never made love to a man before so I'll never have any idea what it is that I'm missing and, as for children, I have some contacts in New York and if it's all right with you, we can take in an orphan or two."

Chris stopped and looked up at a sound from Tynan. For a moment, she was astonished because he seemed to be having a sort of fit. Was epilepsy what was wrong with him?

"Tynan," she said, moving toward him.

He had his hands on his stomach, his legs drawn up, his mouth open and he didn't seem to be breathing.

She was ready to call for help when she suddenly realized that he was *laughing*.

She sat back on her heels, watching him as he finally

64

caught his breath and began to laugh as she'd never seen anyone laugh before.

"An orphan or two!" he gasped. "I don't know what I'm missing. I'll take you anyway." With each word, he doubled over harder and laughed more deeply—and Chris's backbone grew more rigid.

"I am certainly glad that I am a source of amusement for you, Mr. Tynan. May we pretend that this conversation never took place?" With that she moved out of his shelter and started back to her own tent.

Ty caught her skirt hem. He was still laughing and weak from the effort. "Don't be mad, Chris, it's just that I—" He broke off and went into fresh peals of laughter at a new memory and Chris wondered how she could ever have thought she loved this idiot of a man. At the moment she wished the earth would open and swallow him.

"Come in out of the rain," he said, making a valiant effort to control himself, but his lips were twitching and his eyes watery.

"No thank you. Please release my skirt so I can get back to my own tent. I don't think we have anything to say to one another."

He began to sober somewhat, although he seemed too weak to stand as he reached up, took her by the waist and pulled her into the shelter. It was like trying to manipulate a stone statue.

"Chris," he began and, again, he gave a little laugh.

Chris tried to get away but he pulled her into his lap and held her there, her hands held firmly against her sides.

He took a full minute trying to calm himself. "Chris," he said at last. "As long as I live I will remember this . . . ah, proposition of yours. I have certainly never been offered anything like it nor have I even heard of something like this being offered to anyone else. It is kind and generous of you."

"May I go now?" she asked, making a move to get off his lap.

"Not until you let me explain. When I said that I *couldn't* make love to you, I didn't mean that I—" He stopped for a moment and worked to control his smirking lips. Chris stiffened even more in his lap. "I didn't mean that physically I couldn't, I meant that there were other reasons as to why I can't touch you."

"You seem to have been doing enough of that," she said through tight lips.

"Sometimes I can't help myself. By 'touch' you I mean to make love to you. That I *can't* do."

"It's me, isn't it? If I were like Mr. Lanier's maid with her big bosom and hips you wouldn't have any problem at all, would you?"

"Damn it! It isn't physical! It's—"

Her nose was almost touching his. "I thought that if the woman was willing then the man *always* was. That's what my mother told me. I've been fighting off men all my adult life and now I offer myself to one and he *can't*. If it's not me and it's not you and it's not fat ladies, what is it?"

Tynan ran his hands up her arms. "Oh Chris, you are killing me. I had it easy in prison compared with this. Why did you pick me and not Prescott?"

Chris started to get off his lap but he pulled her back down. "I won't bother you again, I assure you."

He moved so that his face was near her neck and she could feel his soft, warm breath on her skin. "You'll always bother me. Every time you take a breath, you bother me. And I can't stand to see you with Prescott. Chris, I've never wanted anything so badly in my life as I've wanted you since that first night I held you. I have nearly gone insane in the last few days. I think about you all the time. I can't even stay in the camp when you're there because I'm afraid that I'll do something like throw you on my horse and take you away with me."

"But I offer myself to you and you laugh at me. You've done nothing but yell at me to get away from you since I first met you. I don't understand! *Can* you make love? You're not physically impaired?"

"If you weren't so innocent, you'd know the answer to that right now from where you're sitting on my lap." He began to bite her earlobe and Chris just about melted into him. "If I make love to you," he said, moving down her neck, "I . . ."

"Yes," she whispered, her head back so she could enjoy his touch more.

"If I make love to you, your father will send me back to prison."

"Oh," Chris murmured, not really hearing him. Then she sat up and looked at him. "My father will *what?*"

"He'll send me back to jail. Look, Chris, I didn't want to tell you this and I really tried to get around it, but the truth is, you have been declared off limits to me."

She drew back from him, moving off his lap. "I want to hear the whole story."

With a sigh, Ty leaned back on his arm and looked at her. "I was in jail on a life sentence but your father got me out to rescue his daughter. When you said that he had enough money and power to get what he wanted, you were right. He got me out but he holds the papers and he's made the rules: I touch you and I go back to prison."

"Well, we shall see about that," Chris said. "My father has been giving me orders all my life and I've only obeyed half of them—if that. We'll just go back to him and tell him that he can't do that to us."

Ty took her hands in his. "Chris, he's right. He doesn't want his only child to marry somebody like me. I don't even know how to treat a good girl like you. I don't know how to live in a house like that big one of your father's or even how to stay in one place for very long at a time. I'm not husband material and your father knew it. He didn't want me doing anything to his daughter short of marriage and we both knew I wasn't the marrying kind. Do you understand?"

"No," she said softly, looking into his eyes. "I love you and—"

"No you don't. You've just been too busy with your newspaper over the years to notice men and now you're worried that you're getting old and you think you're in love with the first man you see."

"Then why aren't I in love with Mr. Prescott?"

He leaned back, winked and grinned at her. "I'm better looking. There's no competition."

"I think you're right," she said, moving out of the shelter. "I believe I *have* made an error."

He caught her shoulder and pulled her back inside. "Don't get angry, Chris. Under other circumstances, I'd love to climb into bed with you, but I don't want to go back to that hellhole and I don't want to be unfair to you. You deserve a man who's husband material. I'm not. I hope you can understand."

"I think I understand better than you think," she said

coolly. "I want to apologize for my forwardness, for following you, as you've asked me not to do, and for imposing myself on you. I will try to do better in the future and not give you cause to fear that you will have to return to prison because I have put you in an impossible situation. Is that what you wanted to hear? May I go now?"

"I think you're angry with me. I didn't mean—"

"I am angry with myself," she interrupted. "And deeply embarrassed. I've never thrown myself at a man before and I can assure you that I will never do it again. You won't have any more problems from me, Mr. Tynan. Now, I'd like to go back to my tent and take a nap, if that's all right with you."

He frowned. "Yes, of course. Chris, I really do appreciate the offer, I mean when you thought that physically I couldn't—"

"We shall never know, will we?" she said as she left the shelter.

Chapter Seven

By the time they entered the little town at the edge of the rain forest, Chris had cried all the tears she could cry. She had done a marvelous job of staying away from Tynan. No matter what he said to entice her to stop and talk, she'd ignored him.

Nor did she spend much time with Asher. She did what work was required to keep the camp running and nothing else.

Tynan, after a day of attempting to talk to her, began to stay away from the camp more and more often until, at the last, he was the shadowy figure he had been at the beginning of the trip.

"This has not become the joyous trip I'd hoped for," Asher said with sadness and confusion in his voice. Chris didn't say anything. All she wanted was to get away from the place where she'd made such a fool of herself.

It was still morning when they pulled into the little

town at the foot of the rain forest. The place was busy with shoppers, wagons being loaded, cowboys strolling about, and a few women stopping and talking to each other. Most people halted when they saw the strangers come into town.

At least that's what Chris first thought was the cause of their staring. For the first time in days she came out of her dejection and began to take an interest in her surroundings.

As she watched the people, she became aware that they were actually stopping to stare at Tynan.

He was in front of her, his back held as straight as a piece of steel, eyes ahead, looking at no one. As they passed the sheriff's office, a man ran inside and the sheriff came out within seconds.

"I don't want no trouble," the sheriff called, directing his plea in Tynan's direction.

Tynan didn't acknowledge the man's presence but kept riding in a slow, steady pace.

As they passed a saloon, a garishly dressed woman came out, did a double take when she saw Tynan, then began running through the dirty streets. As they neared a place called the Pink Garter, the double doors swung open and out stepped a tall, older woman with hair an extraordinary shade of red—not natural-looking at all, Chris thought.

"Tynan!" the woman shouted.

Ty put his hand up for them to halt while he went to the woman.

Chris had never strained her ears so hard in her life as she did to hear what the woman had to say.

"You shouldn't have come back here," the red-haired woman said. "You're askin' for trouble."

Chris couldn't hear Ty's answer. With his low voice he could make the sound disappear when he wanted to.

After a moment of listening to the woman, he reined his horse away and motioned to the others to follow him as he led them to a hotel.

"You'll stay here tonight and tomorrow we'll ride out early."

"And where will you be staying?" They were the first words Chris had spoken directly to him in days.

He looked at her a long moment. "I have friends here. Go inside and ask them for a bath," he said before turning on his heel and leaving them.

"What do you think that was all about?" Chris asked Asher.

"The bath? I agree, Miss Mathison, that it's been so long since I had one that I'm close to forgetting what they are too, but you'll remember as soon as you see the hot water."

Chris ignored his attempt at humor. "No, I mean out there in the street," she said, following Asher into the hotel. "Why were all the people staring at Tynan? And why did that woman warn him?"

"I have no interest in anything except a hot bath, a hot meal and a cool, soft bed. I am not interested in any mysteries and as far as I can tell, our guide is one long mystery. Chris, will you please sign the register so we can get a room?"

At the moment, Chris couldn't have told anyone why she had been depressed for the last few days. All she could think of now was that there was a good story at her fingertips. Why was this entire town glaring at one man? Of course it had to do with Tynan's having been in jail but what had he done that made the whole town watch him?

"Miss," the desk clerk said, "would you like to register?"

"Yes," she said absently. She started to write Christiana, but suddenly changed her mind and wrote Nola Dallas.

The clerk, bored, turned the big book around and then his eyes bugged. *The* Nola Dallas? The one that went to Mexico?"

"Yes." Chris smiled as sweetly as she could manage.

"But I thought you were really a man."

"Many people do." She kept smiling at the man. Once, she'd persuaded a guard to open a cell for her with just that smile.

Asher looked annoyed. "We're just here for a little rest," he told the clerk. "Please don't tell anyone she's here."

"I wouldn't think of it," the clerk said, his eyes wide. "I wouldn't tell a soul."

Still frowning, Asher took Chris's arm and led her up the stairs as Chris kept looking over her shoulder and smiling at the desk clerk. "I wish you hadn't done that," Asher said when they were at the door of her room. "Your father was worried about some trouble from Lanier. Of course you didn't actually publish anything about him, but just the same . . ."

Chris smiled at him. "I just wondered if people this far west had heard of me, that's all."

"Oh well, I guess that's all right. You'd better rest now, Chris. I'll have a bath sent up."

Once inside the room, she looked in the mirror. Not bad, she thought, a wash and a comb should make her presentable.

"If you tell people who you are," she said aloud to the mirror, "and they feel that they know you, there's a good chance they'll be willing to tell you what you want to know."

It was an hour later that Chris was washed and she hoped the desk clerk had had time to tell the people who'd just arrived. When she walked into the lobby, people stopped and looked at her and she could hear them whispering, "Is that her?"

Smiling to herself, Chris went out into the bright sunlight. She seemed to remember a ladies' dress shop on the main street. If there was anywhere to hear gossip, that would be the place.

"May I help you?" the clerk asked, but before Chris could answer, the shop door opened and in walked three ladies. The door hadn't closed before two more walked in followed by four more. The little shop was packed with people as Chris made her way to a corner to try on a hat or two.

"You'll never believe who came into town," one of the women said loudly, directing her voice toward Chris. "Of course I couldn't believe it when Jimmy told me, but he said that Nola Dallas was in town."

"You know, the lady who got herself put into an insane asylum to report on what it was like."

"And she wrote that it wasn't safe for decent women to walk the streets alone at night."

"And she almost got herself killed in Mexico for what she wrote about the government," said a third woman.

"How very, very much I'd like to meet her," sighed another woman.

There followed a long, expectant pause and Chris knew they were waiting for her to make the next move.

As if she weren't aware of what they'd been saying, she tried on another hat, then removed it and started for the door. She had her hand on the knob before she looked back at the women who were unabashedly staring at her. "I am Nola Dallas," she said softly.

The flood gates burst after that. Chris was bodily hauled back into the store and asked thousands of questions.

"Did you really write that series on divorce?"

"Did you really spend three days in jail?"

"Weren't you frightened when you got that lobbyist and all those politicians arrested?"

Chris tried to answer all of them at once. All the while she was waiting to hear what she'd come to find out.

"I'm sure that it's none of our business but we think you should look more carefully to your traveling companions," said one woman with her nose in the air.

There was a hush on the crowd. "Oh?" Chris said with all the innocence she could muster. "They seem like such nice men."

"Perhaps one of them is but that Tynan . . ." The women looked at each other and were silent.

Chris modestly studied her hands. "I really know so little about him."

The women began to fall all over themselves in their rush to tell her all that they knew about the man—which, unfortunately, wasn't much. Tynan had been arrested for murder, tried the same afternoon and sentenced to hang that night.

"That seems awfully quick," Chris said.

"It was an open and shut case. He was guilty, everyone could see that."

"But he went to jail instead," Chris prompted.

The women exchanged looks. "During the night, some of the men decided not to wait to hang him—not that I believe in that sort of thing—but the way they rescued him, well . . ."

Chris waited patiently.

One of the women leaned forward in conspiracy. "The ah, ah . . ."

"What Ellen's trying to say is that the harlots of this town banded together and, carrying rifles, they protected this Mr. Tynan until the federal marshal could get here."

"They also demanded a new trial and the marshal said there wasn't any proof that he'd actually fired the gun that had killed the man—there were lots of guns being fired that day—so the marshal gave him life imprisonment instead of hanging."

Chris took a deep breath. "Who is the red-haired woman?"

The women stiffened, showing their goodness and virtue. "Just one of *them*. That Tynan stays in her saloon when he's in town."

"He really can be very nice," said a pretty young girl at the back of the group.

A woman who had to be the girl's mother looked shocked. She turned to Chris. "Some of the girls here have no sense. He's a no-good waster, travels around and makes the girls fall in love with him, then leaves them crying. You're best to stay away from the likes of him, Miss Dallas."

Chris moved toward the door. "I can't thank you ladies enough for telling me this, but now I have a story to research." She looked at the women and smiled.

"I've always wanted to know what the inside of a house of prostitution looks like, haven't you?"

For a moment, the women were too stunned to speak, but they considered Chris to be one of them. They'd read her articles for years and they felt as if they knew her.

"Yes," one of the women in the back sighed and the others began to laugh.

"Wish me luck," she called over her shoulder as she left the dress shop and made her way to the red-haired woman's saloon. Behind her, she heard murmurs of how brave she was.

There were only two cowboys in the saloon when she entered, sitting at a table listlessly playing cards. A big, aproned bartender was sweeping the floor.

"I'm looking for someone, a tall woman with red hair," Chris said. "Is she here?"

"Not to ladies, she ain't."

"Joe," came a voice from the head of the stairs and Chris looked up to see the red-haired woman. "This here little lady is Nola Dallas, the one that dressed up as a showgirl, remember?"

The faces of the bartender and the two cowboys changed as they looked at Chris. "Come on up," the woman called and Chris went up the stairs.

The woman led her to a large room that was very pretty if a bit loud in color for Chris's taste.

"I'm Red," the woman said, motioning Chris to a horsehair sofa. "You wanta drink? I ain't got any tea."

"Red?" Chris asked.

"On account of the hair. I gave up trying to have a name because everybody called me Red anyway, so why fight it? Now, what can I do for you?"

Chris withdrew a notebook and a pencil from her handbag and tried to look professional. "I believe you know Mr. Tynan. Do you know where he is now?"

Red laughed. "If I know Ty, right now he's in a bathtub with three of my best girls."

Chris was so shocked that she dropped her notebook and pencil and bent quickly to retrieve them, trying to cover her distress.

Red sat on the other end of the sofa. "Oh, dear, it's like that, is it? How long did you spend with him?"

"Just a few days," Chris said, smoothing her skirt, not lifting her red face.

"And you fell in love with him," Red said flatly.

"More or less," Chris mumbled then lifted her head, started to say something then stood. "The man is driving me crazy!" she said with passion. "I thought you might know something about him. He seemed to talk to you as if he knew you."

"I guess I know him as well as anyone. I helped raise him. Look, honey, women fall in love with Ty on a daily basis. He's so damned good lookin' and that voice of his can talk a woman into anything. But I can tell you that, as far as I know, he never has anything to do with good girls like you."

"That's just what he said. Oh, Miss Red," she said, moving back to the sofa. "I've never been in love in my life and I don't even know if I am now, but there's something intriguing about this man and I want to know all I can find out about him."

Red looked at her a while. "He deserves more than what he got dealt in life. He's a good boy and he ain't never had a chance at nothin' but bad. If I tell you about Ty, will you tell me how come he's out of jail?"

78

"My father got him out. Have you ever heard of Delbert J. Mathison?"

"About as often as I've heard of beer. Tynan ain't got hisself mixed up with the likes of him, has he? That man will eat Ty alive."

"He's my father," Chris said, then waved her hand in protest as Red started to apologize. "I know him better than anyone. For some reason, he got Ty out of jail to kidnap me from where I was visiting and take me home. Tynan said that it was because he knew the rain forest, but I don't think that's all of it. I think my father had another reason and I have no idea what it is."

Chris lowered her head. "I never met anyone like Ty and I like him a great deal. I sense that there is more to him than one can see right away. I . . . I'm afraid I threw myself at him. He told me that if he touched me my father would send him back to jail. Needless to say, I stayed away from him for the last few days of the trip."

"I told you that Ty never touches innocent girls. The last time he did, he got thrown in jail and would be dead now if some of us girls hadn't stepped in."

With an expectant look on her face, Chris waited for the woman to speak. She was older than Chris had originally thought, but her skin was well cared for and soft looking.

Red got up to get another drink of well watered whiskey. "I don't usually drink this time of day but seein' Ty again and havin' him to worry about makes me wanta get drunk and stay that way. You were right when you said that I seemed to know him. I'm one of four women that are the closest thing to a mother that boy ever had."

She sat down across from Chris. "He wouldn't like me tellin' you this but you give me a lot of pleasure in them articles of yours and I wanta do somethin' for you. About twenty-nine years ago when I was just startin' out in this business—and I was little more than a kid myself—a miner brought a newborn baby to the house where I was workin' and left him to us girls to take care of. That old man was as bad as they come, nobody could stand him. He'd cheat cripples if he could. Well, he brought this baby in and he hadn't even cleaned it, it still had the birth filth on it and it was weak from hunger. We ran around real fast and found a woman to feed the baby and we took care of him as best we could for as long as we had him."

"And that was Tynan? How had the miner come by him?"

"He wouldn't tell us until we'd given him free whiskey, but he said he'd found a pregnant woman wandering in the forest, out of her head. She stopped in front of him—I'm sure he didn't volunteer to help her—and delivered the baby herself. She whispered the single word of Tynan, then died. Knowing the miner, it's a wonder he didn't just walk away and leave the dead woman and the baby. But I guess he had plans to get what he could so he wrapped the boy up and brought him to us."

Red stood, her back to Chris. "We did the best we could but a whore house ain't no place to raise a kid. All the girls adored him and I'm sure we spoiled him rotten, but we had problems we couldn't help. When Ty was about two, we dressed him up in a little suit and escorted him to Sunday School. The ladies of the congregation ran us off. They wouldn't believe that Ty wasn't one of our byblows."

Red paused a moment. "He stayed with me until he was six years old. I never loved anybody more than I loved that boy. He was all that I had."

"What happened when he was six?"

Red gave a resigned sigh and looked back at Chris. "The miner that'd found him came back with a lawyer, said Tynan was legally his and took him away. Two towns away, he stood Ty on a table and auctioned him off to the highest bidder."

Chris sat still for a moment as she let this sink in. A little boy stood on a table and auctioned off as if he were an animal. Slavery had been abolished years ago. "Who, ah, bought him?"

"Some farmer on his way east. I didn't see or hear from Ty for twelve years. By then he was the strappin' big, good-lookin' thing that he is now, but he'd changed. I got him to tell me some of what had happened after he left the farmer's." She paused to smile. "I don't think the farmer was too happy with Ty's leavin' 'cause Ty had a couple of scars on his legs and when I asked him where he got 'em, he said it was caused by differin' opinions about whether he should leave the farmer's or not. I think the man worked Ty like a draft horse. After he left, at twelve, he was on his own. He traveled around, took odd jobs, got into a bad crowd a couple of times, learned how to use a gun, all the things a boy does. Then for a while he seemed to be headed for real trouble but something changed him. I don't know what it was or if it was anything special. A friend of his, an outlaw, got hisself hanged and that may have had an effect on Ty, I don't know, but whatever it was, somethin' made him go straight."

Red closed her eyes for a minute. "Goin' straight just about killed him. He took all the jobs nobody wanted

81

or was too afraid to take on. He'd even go into towns run by outlaws and clean them up. But, since he always left dead bodies behind him, one after another, the good townspeople would always ask him to please leave."

"But that's not fair," Chris said.

"Honey, we ain't even come to unfair yet. Like I said, Ty never did fool around with clean girls, he always had sense enough to stay away from 'em. But that didn't keep the girls from swarmin' around him. They like the way he ignores 'em. Well, one of 'em, a real pretty little thing used to twitch her tail around Ty till he was about to break. Then one day she come into the saloon to get him. I saw her cryin' and he was holdin' her. He's always been a sucker for tears, couldn't stand 'em on a woman. Next thing I knew he was saddlin' a horse and takin' rifles out of a cabinet. This girl said that a big rancher around here was attackin' her father and could Ty help."

Red took a drink of her whiskey. "I told him not to go, that it wasn't his fight, but he wouldn't listen. There was a gun battle and when the dust and gunpowder settled, the big rancher's son was dead and Ty was being hauled off to jail."

"And that's when you rescued him."

"Heard about that, did you? Yeah, we rescued him. He didn't kill that man's son, that girl did and he was gonna hang for it rather than turn her in. It seems that she'd been sneakin' out to see the boy and had only been usin' Ty to make him jealous. But, even knowin' that, he wouldn't turn her in. I got to thinkin' that maybe he didn't mind dyin'. Sometimes he acts like he don't think he's worth much."

"He said he wasn't good enough for me," Chris said

softly. "He said I deserved more than somebody like him."

"Don't you believe it, honey, there ain't *nobody* better 'n him."

"That's exactly what I thought too," Chris said with a grin. "Do you think there's any way I can tempt him into giving me what I want?"

"And what you want is Tynan?"

"With all my heart and soul."

For a long while, Red stared at Chris. "You know, you may be just what he needs." She stopped and narrowed her eyes. "I feel like I know you from years of readin' your stories, but I'm warnin' you that if you think Ty's just one of those cases of yours and you get rid of him after a little while I'll—"

Chris burst out laughing. "This is a turn of events, isn't it? Isn't it usually the father who warns the prospective young man?"

Red returned her smile. "I ain't too good at bein' a mother."

"It seems to me that you've done a fine job. At least *I* like what you've done. My problem is that Ty doesn't like me. At least not the way I like him. How can I get past the threat of prison and the memory of how another so called 'good' girl treated him? And, besides, I think he really likes another type of woman better than me." Chris looked down at her own slight curves.

Red didn't get to answer because of the voice at the door.

"Red, you awake?"

There was no question of whose voice that was.

"Just a minute, Ty, baby," Red called. "You come with me," she said, taking Chris's arm in her hand as she opened a closet door. "This is a place for men that can't but like to watch. You stay in here and listen. I'll find out how much Ty does or doesn't like you. You game?"

It was on the tip of Chris's tongue to ask questions about the closet, but she suppressed herself. "Yes," she whispered, then Red half shoved her into a chair and closed the door.

"I'm just comin', Ty honey," she called and went across the room to open the door.

Chapter Eight

Ty's hair was wet and he was just buttoning his shirt.

"Don't even put it back on," Red said, holding the door open for him. "I want to look at that back of yours."

"It's fine," Tynan said but removed his shirt obediently.

Red ran her hands over his skin, turned him toward the light—and the closet—so she could see better. "It's all right but it'll be weeks before it's fully healed. And you're skin and bones. We need to fatten you up."

He put his shirt back on. "You sound like Chris."

"She that little blonde rode in with you? The one everybody's sayin' is Nola Dallas?"

Ty poured himself a whiskey and sat down on the sofa. "God, that's good. The thing you miss most in prison isn't freedom but the small pleasures of life like good food and drink, a clean bed,"—he grinned—"and women. You ought to pay that Leora more. Whatever you're paying her, it's not enough."

"You're not answerin' my question. Is that little blonde Nola Dallas?"

"Yeah," he said, looking at his whiskey. "Tell me what's been going on the last couple of years. Business good? You seem to have more girls than usual."

"I think some of the girls in the tub with you weren't mine," Red said heavily. "Tynan, stop dancin' around me. What are you doin' back here? Are you free from jail permanently or what?"

He smiled at her. "With a few hitches, I am more or less free."

"Hitches? Such as what?"

"One pretty little blonde that's about to send me back, that's what."

"Oh?" Red asked, eyebrows raised.

"Don't play innocent with me. Even in the tub the girls were giggling about this famous Nola Dallas being here. Is she really all that famous? I mean I know what she's done, her father gave me a stack of newspaper articles to read about her or by her, but I thought that out here . . ."

"Honey, she's what every woman dreams of being: brave, courageous, a fighter, and she's made it in a man's profession."

"More than I've done," Tynan muttered.

"Was it really bad in jail?" Red asked, sitting across from him.

"I think old man Dickerson had friends. I guess he figured that if he couldn't kill me with a rope, he'd have it done with whip and chains."

Red reached out, caressed his cheek and Ty kissed her palm. "But you're out now," she said.

"If I keep my hands off that pretty little daughter of Del Mathison's. And I've had easier jobs."

"You like her, huh?"

"Well enough, I guess. Any man would like a woman who put herself in his path the way she does. The first few times I met her she didn't even have her clothes on."

Red leaned back against the sofa. "Really? I can't imagine that someone of Nola Dallas's fame would have to pursue a man."

"Well, she damn well has pursued me. Said she wanted to spend the rest of her life with me."

"Would that be so bad? A home and kids?"

Tynan stood and refilled his glass. "Are you going to start on that again? Look, even if I did marry somebody, it couldn't be her. Her father holds the papers for my release. I take her back to him, leave her and I get a full pardon. I touch her and I go back to jail. And then there's the money, too."

"For taking her back?"

Ty looked at Red. "Did you see that city dude that rode in behind me? He's a fine, upstanding citizen, born with parents and a silver spoon in his mouth, and Mathison wants his daughter to marry him. I get ten thousand dollars if I bring his daughter back in love with Mr. Asher Prescott. Course she had to go and fall for me."

"How inconvenient for you."

Tynan grinned at her. "It wasn't my fault. I told you she followed me everywhere. I tried to stay away from her but there she'd be—usually stark naked. I'm only human, you know."

"More human than the rest of us. Did you ever think that maybe she *liked* you?"

"A girl like her? All she wanted was a fling before going back to her rich daddy. I'd have one night in the hay, then the rest of my life in jail regretting it. No thanks. Deliver me from good girls. I think I'll just stick with Leora and her kind."

"Oh Ty," Red said, standing, putting her arms round the back of him. "What are you going to do with your life?"

"*Not* spend anymore time in jail. I thought I'd take the ten thousand and buy some land with it."

"The money you get for matchmaking Miss Mathison with that man? You're sure you can do that?"

Ty walked to the window and looked out into the street below. "I admit it's not easy, not with what Mathison gave me to work with. That man has no . . . force, I guess you'd call it. He doesn't even know how to win a girl."

"Not like you do?"

He looked back at her. "Are you mad at me about something? You seem awfully short tempered."

Red sat down. "Ty, honey, I'm gettin' old and you're the closest thing to a son I'll ever have. I'd like to see you married and settled down with half a dozen kids. I'd like to think there's an empty room in your house that's for me if I ever wanta retire."

Ty took her in his arms and kissed her forehead. "Wherever I am there'll always be room for you, but I can't see me with a wife and kids."

She pushed away from him. "That's because you've never been in love."

"Why, an hour ago I was so in love with Leora that—"

"Hush! You know what I mean. Have you ever even asked a girl to a church social? Taken a girl out for a buggy ride and a picnic?"

"Sounds mighty boring to me."

"Well, it *ain't*," she said, glaring at him.

He looked out the window again. "You know, one day Chris and Prescott were singing and it looked like it might be an all right way to pass the time."

"You have a beautiful singing voice. Why didn't you join in?"

He shrugged. "I don't know. I just don't fit in with people like them. Hey! You got any pork in this place? I'd love four or five pork chops tonight."

"We got pork. Ty, are you gonna try to match Chris with that man?"

He took a while to answer, turning back and looking at his drink. "It's my job."

"But you're reluctant?"

"She deserves a lot better than him. She's got spunk. She liked the rain forest and wasn't scared to death of the place. She walked around while he huddled beside the fire. And she pulled her weight in work too. He treated me like a servant hired to wait on him but Chris always helped me unpack the mules." He smiled. "Except for that first night."

He put the whiskey down. "Oh, hell, she's not for me."

Red put her hands on his arms. "Why isn't she? Isn't she Mathison's only kid? I bet if he thought she wanted you, he wouldn't put you back in jail."

"It's my neck if you're wrong, isn't it? Besides, she doesn't want me. It was just that she thought I was the leader and the forest can make you feel as if there's nobody else on earth. It was the time and the place. And the fact that there was no competition."

"So now that you're out of the forest, she won't be interested in you, is that it?"

"I'm sure of it."

Red turned away for a moment. "You know something? I have more faith in this young lady. From reading her articles I think she's not at all flighty. If she said she loved you, I think she does."

"For how long?" Ty asked in disgust. "Deliver me from the faithful love of a good woman."

"How about putting her to a test?"

"Such as?"

"Rory Sayers."

Tynan didn't speak for a moment. "Is *he* here?"

"At the hotel. Want to introduce your Chris to him?"

"She's not mine."

Red smiled at him. "You know what your problem is, Tynan? You've never had to work to get any female. Did you know that there are other things to do with a woman besides take her to bed? You've probably never spent five minutes talking to a woman who wasn't a whore. I'll bet that you don't even know what to do with a girl outside the bedroom."

"I talked to Chris one afternoon in the forest." He narrowed his eyes at her. "Red, what are you trying to do?"

"I want you to do something that's not so easy for you. I think you're half in love with this Chris. Why don't you take her out a few times, talk to her, get to know what she's like? It'll be practice for when you're lookin' for a wife."

"And what if she keeps saying she loves me? I'm not going back to jail for her or anybody else. And I'll not be cheated out of the ten grand."

"There, you see, you can organize a few socials yourself. Take Chris and Prescott for a ride in the country. *Help* him court her. You'll learn from him and he'll learn from you."

"And what about Sayers? What has he got to do with all this?"

"Don't you think Rory would be a perfect match for your Chris? He's rich, established, owns all that lovely timberland and Rory certainly doesn't lack force. Maybe you could get Chris to marry him. I'm sure Mathison would approve and you'd get your ten thousand dollars."

Ty didn't say anything but picked up his empty whiskey glass and refilled it. "I can't see Chris and Sayers together."

"Oh, I can. Rory has so much personality and the women all adore him. You could take Chris and Rory and the handsome young man Mathison chose out in the country for the afternoon and just sit back and think about your ten thousand dollars. It'll be the easiest money anyone ever made."

"Chris may not like Sayers. She's got taste. She's a real lady. All her underclothes have her initials on them, not big and gaudy like Susie used to wear, but tiny initials done in white on white cloth. And Chris asks a lot of questions. She finds out about people. If Sayers tries a line on her, she'll see through him."

"But you'll be there to smooth things over and help Rory over the rough spots, won't you?"

"Chris isn't all that easy to fool. You know that she figured out I was in pain? Even guessed that my feet were blistered from the damn new boots. And she put it all together and figured out about my being in jail."

"Not like other women you've known, is she?" Red said softly.

Abruptly, Ty put his half full whiskey glass down. "Look, I got things to do. I'll see you tonight for supper."

"Yes, honey, you do that. Let's eat at the hotel and invite your friends. Maybe I can help you get the money. I'll make your Chris see what a charming gentleman has been chosen for her. And maybe we can invite Rory. He always livens up any gathering."

"Yeah, well, maybe. Chris won't like him, though. He's all hot air." He put his hand on the door. "And she's not *my* Chris."

"She is until you sell her to someone else."

"Why do I feel like I've been run over by a twenty-car train? I'll see you tonight."

"At six at the hotel," she called after him.

As Chris was dressing that evening, she noticed her underwear, looking at the initials on all of it and wondering when in the world Ty had had a chance to see it. He's seen what's under it, so what's the difference in seeing the underwear, she wondered.

As she examined the lovely blue velvet gown Red had loaned her, with its tight waist, the skirt fitting snugly around her slim hips, and a little bustle in back, she thought about what she'd heard from Tynan that afternoon. He seemed such an odd contradiction of confidence and insecurity, she mused as she left the room.

At the foot of the hotel stairs waited Asher and another man who stepped forward instantly and introduced himself as Rory Sayers—and Chris felt that she knew all about him at once. He was the type of man her father had paraded before her for the first eighteen years of her life. He was handsome in a sharp sort of way: sharp nose, sharp chin, eyes a snapping blue. And he had more confidence than any six other men, confidence that Chris knew came from having had money all his life.

There was coolness behind her smile as she took his arm and allowed him to lead her into the dining room.

Dinner was a disaster. Rory dominated the meal, talking about everything that had been happening in the country in the last two years—the years that Ty had been in prison. And Tynan looked like a sulky little boy who was being punished by having to eat with the grownups.

For just a moment, Chris closed her eyes and prayed for strength.

"Of course you wouldn't know about that, would you old man?" Rory said to Tynan who had his head bent over a plate heaped with pork chops. "You were a bit too busy over the last two years to read the papers, weren't you?"

Before Tynan could reply, Chris said, "I beg to differ with you, Mr. Sayers. Mr. Tynan has read all *my* articles. Perhaps he was selective in his reading."

"Not *Mr.* Tynan," Rory said with a smile. "I don't believe he has another name."

Chris could take no more. She couldn't stand the man's smugness or his catty remarks. She stood. "I'm afraid you'll have to excuse me as I have a splitting headache. Mr. Tynan, would you please escort me out into the fresh air? I think a walk will help clear my head."

Rory Sayers rose, presumptuously taking Chris's arm. *"I'll* take you, Miss Mathison."

With all the haughtiness she could muster, she jerked her arm from his grasp. "Sir, I only met you tonight. I do not entrust my safety to men I do not know. Mr. Tynan, would you mind?"

Rory was aghast. "I'm afraid," he said with empha-sized tolerance for her ignorance, "that you don't know this man. He's—"

Chris hadn't traveled all over the United States on her own and not learned how to handle all types of men. "I have just spent a great deal of time alone with this man and I know all I need to know about him. I am especially aware of the fact that he has the manners of a gentleman."

She turned away to see Tynan standing beside her, an enormous grin on his face, his arm extended. "The lady has taste," he said to Rory. "Sit back down and finish your meal. I'll take good care of her."

With that, he led Chris out of the hotel and into the moonlit street. But as soon as they were outside, he released her arm.

"Why did you do that?"

"Because I can't stand that type of man," she said with feeling.

"Type? But I thought all women liked that kind of man. Most all of them I've ever known do."

"But then you've never met a woman who could run away from home at the age of eighteen and become a newspaper reporter either, have you?"

"No," he said with a grin. "I haven't. Do you really have a headache? Do you want me to take you back inside?"

She stopped and looked at him. "If I promise not to be forward, will you take me for a walk?"

"Forward?"

"Such as pursuing you and asking too many ques-tions and, in general, making a nuisance of myself."

He gave her a startled look, then grabbed her arm and pulled her into an alleyway. Before Chris could speak, he had her in his arms, holding her head against his chest. "Chris, you don't understand, do you? Thank you for what you did in there tonight. If four men came up to me aiming guns at my head, I'd know how to handle them, but give me one spoiled rich boy and I'm at a loss. But you made me feel . . ."

"Like a winner?" she supplied and tried to look up at him but he held her head against him. "Deja vu," she whispered.

"What?"

"I have a feeling that I've been here before, in just this situation. Remember our first meeting?"

"No man could ever forget a meeting like that. Chris, you have to go back inside. I can't go walking with you in the dark."

Chris wanted to stay with him always and, had he asked, she would have climbed on a horse and ridden away with him—to live in the rain forest for all she cared. But she knew she had to obey him. He didn't know how he felt about her and she wasn't about to pursue him.

"All right," she whispered with great reluctance in her voice. "Let's go."

He moved away from her slowly, not looking at her, and allowed her to go first back onto the street. Chris took one step around the corner and saw Rory with Asher coming toward them, and they had the look of a vigilante committee out to rid the world of whatever they considered vermin. She turned back to Tynan. "Kiss me," she whispered urgently.

Ty looked astonished for a split second then he lost no time obeying her, taking her in his arms and kissing her with a passion Chris had never before known existed. She completely forgot about the reason she'd asked Ty to kiss her but returned his passion, her arms going around his neck and pulling him closer—not that he could get closer as he wedged his thigh between hers.

"Unhand her!" came Rory's voice as he pulled Tynan away from Chris.

For a moment, Chris was too stunned to even open her eyes, much less try to speak.

"I should call you out for this," Rory was saying.

Chris was leaning against a building wall and was in such a state of euphoria that someone could have told her a bomb was about to explode under her feet and she wouldn't have been able to move.

"I'm ready when you are, Sayers," she heard Tynan say in a voice deep with threat.

Reluctantly, Chris began to surface because she sensed that this was an argument that she had to stop. But as she moved away from the wall, her eyes opened wide for a moment. The entire back of her dress was unbuttoned.

Standing as straight as she could, not allowing the loose dress to fall forward, she confronted Rory Sayers with his backup of Mr. Prescott.

"Mr. Sayers," she said angrily. "I do not know you and, after tonight, I don't believe I want to. You have no right to interfere in my life and I kindly wish you'd stay out of it."

"Chris," Tynan said. "Stay out of this. This has been coming for a long time."

"I most certainly will *not* stay out of this," she said with so much feeling that the front of her dress fell forward, but she caught it and hoped the men hadn't noticed. If she ever got out of this, she was going to give Tynan a piece of her mind. Of all the audacious things any man had ever done to her, this was one of the worst. She was tempted to let Mr. Sayers have him.

"Miss Mathison, I have to take offense at this. I have met your father several times and I cannot believe that he'd want his daughter pawed by a man of this sort in an alleyway."

Tynan took a step forward, and Chris put herself between the two men. "My father hired this man to protect me and he is doing just that. You, Mr. Sayers, are the unwanted person. As it happens, Mr. Tynan has just asked me to marry him and I have, quite happily, accepted. Now, I do believe that a man has a right to kiss his intended without being molested by the local bully."

Rory Sayers stepped back at that. "Bully? Pardon me, Miss, I had thought you were a lady of higher ideals than to take up with this . . . this criminal. I can only think that you know nothing about him."

"I know that he was put into jail for two years without any evidence." Holding her dress, her back to Tynan, she advanced on Rory. "I know that he's never known who his parents are and that he's never had the advantages of money that you have had. And even though he's not had a formal education, he speaks like a gentleman, reads Voltaire in his spare time, and he constantly puts his life on the line to help other people. Can you say the same thing, Mr. Sayers?"

Rory straightened his back. "You are not the lady I took you for," he said and after one look at Tynan, turned, Asher on his heels, and went down the street.

"He can't say those things about you," Tynan said and started after the men.

Chris planted herself in front of him. "Don't you *dare,*" she said through her teeth. "Don't you dare even think of going after him." She began backing him into the dark alley. "Especially don't you think of avenging my 'honor'. What do you know of a ladies' honor?"

"Chris, I—"

"Look at this!" she gasped, turning her back to him and showing him the unbuttoned dress. "How dare you try to remove my clothing!"

"Oh," he said with a slight grin. "I guess it's just habit. I didn't even think about it."

"Habit!" she gasped. "Whenever you kiss a girl you unbutton her dress?"

"Well," he said slowly, still backing up. "Most girls I kiss *want* their dresses off. You seemed to like it well enough."

"Of all the vain—I should have allowed Mr. Sayers to shoot you. You certainly well deserved it." She began to fasten her dress, struggling with the many tiny buttons.

"He can't shoot at all. All he can do is push a pencil around and flap his gums. Here, let me do that. I can button them as fast as I can unbutton them."

"And I guess you've had practice at that often enough," she said as he turned her around and began to fasten her dress.

"Sometimes you need to get into clothes real fast. There now, all done. I'll pick you up tomorrow."

"Not on your life. Frankly, Mr. Tynan, this has gone far enough. You don't want to go to jail and I'd like to get home to my father. I think that tomorrow we should start south toward my home."

"We can wait one more day. Look, Chris, you're not going to make a fool of me in front of this town—and especially not in front of Sayers. You told him we were engaged and I want at least a day of acting like we're engaged. I'd like to show these people that I can . . ."

"Can get a 'good' girl like me?" she asked softly. She put her hand on his chest. "Tynan, perhaps I've misled you. Perhaps it was the rain forest, the feeling of being isolated, something that made me lose my sense of proportion, but now that we're back to civilization, I think we should stay away from each other. After all, you would have to go back to prison if you touched me."

He took her upper arm in his hand and bent his face close to hers. "Right now Sayers is in a saloon telling half the people in this town that Nola Dallas is going to marry the murderer. And *you're* the one who gave him that idea."

She smiled at him in such a way that he took a step backward. "Tomorrow is Sunday. How about church in the morning and I've been invited to the town picnic later. Shall we appear as an engaged couple? Just for the day, of course, and on Monday we can start the journey home. And then we'll no longer be engaged. Does that suit you?"

"Church?" he asked and even in the darkness, she could see his face turning pale.

"Church," she said firmly and slipped her arm through his. "We'd better get out of this alleyway or my reputation will be ruined, engaged or not. I'll see you the first thing in the morning." They were almost back at the hotel. "Cheer up, Mr. Tynan, I'll make sure that you enjoy the day. Goodnight, dear," she said to him as she smiled at a passerby. "You may kiss my cheek," she whispered, "and don't unbutton so much as a cuff, if you don't mind."

Still too stunned to speak, Ty bent and kissed her

cheek, then looked up to see three women standing in the hotel lobby looking at him with disapproving eyes. On impulse, he grabbed Chris about the waist and kissed her quite thoroughly.

When he released her, Chris had to catch a chair back to keep from falling.

"See you in the morning, sweetheart," Ty said with a wink, replaced his hat and left the hotel.

Chris tried to regain her composure. "Oh, my, but he does get carried away," she said, smoothing her dress front. "Goodnight," she said to the women who were watching her with their mouths hanging open.

Chris whistled all the way up the stairs.

Chapter Nine

Asher Prescott was waiting for her outside her room. His face was grim. "I feel I must talk to you."

"I am rather tired and I . . ." she began then stopped. When a man got it into his head that a woman needed lecturing, it was just better to let him get it out of his system. Chris had learned years ago that "teaching" a woman seemed to make a man feel much better. "Yes, what is it?" She stood there patiently and waited.

"I don't think you're conducting yourself properly and I believe you're losing your sense of proportion. I know you like to champion the underdog but sometimes the underdog isn't deserving of a champion. I believe, Chris, you should know something about the man whose cause you are fighting.

"When he was sixteen he was already known as a gunslinger. He killed not one but two men in a street shootout. By the time he was twenty, he had more enemies than most people have in a lifetime. Did you know that for a while he rode with the Chanry Gang? Once, he was caught and sentenced to hang but the gang blew up the jail and got him out. He's taken on jobs that were suicidal, walking alone into towns against twenty outlaws."

Asher began to warm to his subject. "And the women, Chris! Hundreds of women! To somebody like him, a woman isn't someone to love, she's someone to bed, then leave. You talk of love for this man, well, he doesn't even know the meaning of the word. He's a no-good wastrel and he'll never be anything else."

Chris didn't say a word, just stood there and looked at him.

"You're talking of marrying him but I don't think you understand what marriage is. It's the day in day out of living together. This Tynan can be charming when he wants to but tonight he was morose and sullen. He can't talk, he knows nothing about civilized society, and that woman who everyone says is probably his mother. . . . Well, Chris, I can't believe you even agreed to eat at the same table with her. I for one—"

He stopped himself then smiled at her fondly. "You know what I think? I think this Tynan is interesting because he's a mystery. You solve the mystery and you'll find he's just another run-of-the-mill, cheap gunslinger. What you need, Chris," he said softly, taking a step toward her, "is a husband from your own background. A husband and children."

She gave him a wide-eyed look. "Someone like you, Mr. Prescott?"

"I find you a *very* attractive woman, Chris."

As he leaned forward, his eyelids closing as if to kiss her, Chris opened the bedroom door and slipped inside, closing it firmly behind her. "Kiss *that,* Mr. Paid-to-Marry-Me Prescott."

She went to bed thinking of the coming picnic.

The next morning, Tynan was waiting for her in the hotel lobby wearing a clean suit, leaning against a window frame reading a newspaper.

"Good morning," she said, smiling up at him.

He smiled too when he looked at her, but he looked as if he were smiling through adversity.

Chris pulled on her gloves. "Are you ready to go?"

Ty only nodded, offered his arm to her, and led her out of the hotel onto the street.

There were several other couples also on their way to church and each one of them stopped to stare openly at Tynan and Chris.

In church, Chris pulled Tynan to the third pew, away from the back row where he started to sit. Throughout the service, he was silent, listening to the preacher with attention. During the singing, he seemed familiar with the songs and, as Red had said, he did indeed have an excellent voice.

As they left the church, he seemed relieved that it was over and had gone well. Standing at the door, the minister made an effort to shake his hand and tell him he was welcome.

As they went down the stairs, they saw Red waiting for them in a beautiful big-wheeled carriage, holding the reins to a sleek black gelding.

"I brought you baskets of food for the picnic," she said. "I didn't want you to go empty-handed. Here, Ty, help me down."

"You aren't going with us?" Chris asked.

"A church picnic ain't no place for the likes of me.

You two go and have a good time. And, Tynan, you start to look happier or I'll take a switch to you."

That made Ty laugh as he kissed her cheek. "Maybe I need *both* of you to protect me."

Chris slipped her arm in his. "One can handle you. We shall miss you, Red, but we'll see you tonight. Pray it doesn't rain."

"Honey, I ain't stopped prayin' since you came to town. Now get out of here."

Ty lifted Chris into the carriage and soon they were speeding down the dirt road with the other couples. Chris moved close to him on the seat and held his arm. "Who are the Chanrys?"

"Been snooping again?"

"Of course. Who are they?"

"A bunch of two-bit crooks. Most of them are either dead now or locked away."

"Were you part of them?"

"They wanted me to be. Even told people I was."

"But I thought they broke you out of jail. Tynan, how many times have you been in jail?"

"Total?" he asked seriously. "Even for being drunk?"

"Never mind, don't answer. How did your name get linked with those criminals?"

"I told you. They wanted me to join and when I wouldn't, they got angry. They didn't break me out of jail, a U.S. marshal did."

"Explain, please," she said over the sound of the carriage.

"The Chanrys didn't like the way I told them I wouldn't join their gang no matter what they offered me. You see, they needed a fast gun since their best man had been killed. As revenge, they robbed a bank and kept calling one of the men Tynan. The local sheriff came after me. Only problem was that I was laid up with a broken leg, but he didn't seem to think that was proof that I was innocent. One of the women where I was staying got in touch with a marshal and he came up to investigate. When he couldn't persuade the sheriff not to hang me, the marshal blew up the jail. The sheriff told everybody it was the Chanrys—proof that he should have hanged me."

"Tynan, you are full of the most awful stories."

"When a man lives by the gun, he should expect to be faced with other guns. Here we are. Why don't you take the baskets over there and I'll—"

"No, you have to carry the big one and I have to introduce you to everyone."

"But I already know most of these people. They're the ones—"

"They are the ones who know nothing about you. Now come along."

"Yes, ma'am," he said, grinning. "You do tie them apron strings to a man, don't you?"

"Sometimes, apron strings give a man purpose in life. And they're a lot less violent than guns."

"Hmph! Strangulation is a slow way to die."

She ignored his remark as they walked toward the others. The men and women were separating, the women spreading food on bleached and ironed table-cloths, the men walking together toward the river.

Chris set down a basket of food. "I believe you've met my fiancé, Mr. Tynan, haven't you?" she said. "I'd introduce you by name but I'm afraid I've been in town so short a time that I haven't met you all."

Looking as if they'd just been introduced to a coiled rattlesnake, most of the women nodded tentatively in Tynan's direction.

"Ty, dear, would you please put the other basket there? Thank you so much." She gave him a little signal with her eyes, motioning him toward the men.

He removed his hat. "It's very pleasant to meet you ladies again after all these years." He picked up a roll from the table, winked at Chris and left.

"Miss Dallas!" the women started as soon as he was out of earshot. "You don't know what you're doing. You couldn't know anything about him or you wouldn't—"

"You should talk to Betty Mitchell, after what he did to her, and poor Mr. Dickerson—"

"Mitchell?" Chris said, unpacking one of the baskets. "Wasn't she the girl who was in love with the boy who was killed?"

"Well, she *had* been," one woman said. "Thank heaven it was all over when he was killed."

"Oh, yes," Chris said. "By then she was visiting Tynan in the saloon and seeking him out wherever she could. Why did she and the Dickerson boy end their involvement?"

The women fell all over themselves answering.

"Betty didn't exactly pursue Tynan. . . . Maybe she did go to the saloon but I'm sure he enticed her."

"Billy started seeing a girl who was visiting from Seattle, but I'm sure it would have blown over if that Tynan hadn't interfered."

"Tynan killed Billy, we know that," one woman insisted.

Chris put an apple pie in place. "Billy Dickerson started seeing another girl. Betty started pursuing

Tynan, then Mr. Dickerson went after Betty's father and—"

"No!" one of the women said, then stopped.

Another woman leaned forward. "Betty was in the family way and Billy wouldn't marry her."

"Ah," Chris said. "So Tynan stepped in to help a young girl get the man who was refusing to marry her. And he *killed* this young man? Tynan must have loved Betty to do something like that for her."

The women began shifting the food on the table.

"Betty only loved Billy and after his death she went back east somewhere."

"But I thought she and Tynan were so in love that he killed a man for her," Chris asked, wide-eyed.

The women didn't say anything for a while.

"I do believe my son is pestering your young man," a woman said, looking toward the river.

Four young boys were encircling Tynan, looking up at him with eager faces.

"He won't . . . do anything, will he?" a woman asked hesitantly.

"No," Chris said with confidence. "He is a very good man. Now, shall we call all our good men to the table?"

The men were more tolerant than the women and they didn't seem to care one way or another that Tynan had been in and out of jail. They were more interested in corn on the cob and fried chicken.

Rory Sayers tried his best to make Tynan feel out of place.

"Better than prison food, isn't it, old man?" Rory asked, sitting across from Ty. "But then, over the years you must've gotten used to it."

As Rory reached for a piece of chicken, a woman, the one whose son had been talking to Ty, smacked

Rory's hand sharply with a wooden spoon. Everyone at that end of the table looked up at her as the woman's face turned red.

"I can't teach the children not to reach if the adults do," she said at last, then looked up at Chris who was smiling broadly at her. The woman also smiled. "More beans, Mr. Tynan?" she asked sweetly.

"Why, yes, please," Tynan said, looking at the woman in surprise.

"Tell us what it's like to take a man's life," Rory said as the woman was heaping beans on Tynan's plate.

At that moment, one of the other women overturned a cup of coffee into Rory's lap. As Rory jumped up, one of the men began to laugh.

"Boy, you get married and you'll learn that women have ways of fightin' that cause you to lose the war before you even know it's been declared."

Another man began to laugh and before long, they'd all joined in. Tynan sat there grinning.

"Sit down, boy," someone called to Rory. "You'll dry. Martha, give Sayers some of that cherry cake of yours. That'll make him forget everything else, even pretty little blondes."

Chris became very interested in the inside of a pitcher of milk but she could feel her ears growing warm.

An hour later the food was packed away, the younger children were being put to sleep under shade trees, the adults were gathering in groups and the young ones with the energy were laughing and planning ways to be on their own.

"Will you come with us?" a pretty, dark-eyed girl asked Chris. "We're going canoeing on the river. It'll be a lot of fun."

"We'd love to," she said, holding onto Tynan's arm.

"They're kids. I don't want to—" Tynan began but Chris didn't look at him.

"They want to talk to us. Don't you realize we're almost celebrities to them? You, the notorious gunslinger and me . . ."

"The lady who gets herself into trouble on purpose." He held her back as the others got into the three canoes. They were out of sight of the picnic area. Just as Chris was about to step into a canoe, Tynan gave her a little push, causing her to stumble back against him.

"Chris," he said and there was great concern in his voice. "You've hurt your ankle. Is it sprained? Here, don't walk on it, let me help you."

Before Chris could say a word, he had her in his arms and was carrying her toward the trees.

"She'll be all right," he called over his shoulder to the others. "I'll take care of her."

Chris could hear giggling behind her and knew he hadn't fooled anyone.

"Now that you have me, what do you plan to do with me?" He smiled at her in such a way that Chris said, "You most certainly will *not*. And if you put me down and so much as one button is unfastened, I'll never speak to you again."

"No one has to say a word."

"Tynan!" she gasped.

"Chris, enough is enough. I don't mind adults but spending the afternoon with adolescents looking at me as if I might do something deadly at any moment is more than I can take. I thought maybe we'd go in the woods and . . ."

"And what?" she asked, eyebrows raised.

"I don't know," he said quite honestly. "What does a

109

couple do if they don't—" Again, a look from Chris stopped him.

"Talk, get to know each other. You may put me down now."

Tynan kept walking with her. "Who are the Montgomerys? Your father mentioned them."

"And what did he say? No, you can tell me the truth."

He stood her on an overturned log so that her face was about even with his. "Let me see if I get this correct. He said you were related to them and a more headstrong, stubborn, stupidly fearless lot of people had never been born. Does that sound right?"

"Perfect. They're my mother's relatives, a very old family that came to America during Henry the Eighth's reign."

"Sixteenth century?"

"Yes," she said, smiling at him and holding out her hand. He took it and Chris began walking along the narrow top of the log. "Tell me more about your meeting with my father. What else did he say? What did they say when they released you from jail?"

"Nothing much. They don't do much explaining in jail, they just pull your chains and you follow."

"Whenever I ask you about how you got into prison, whichever time you've been in, you were always falsely accused. Have you ever done anything illegal?" She turned on the log and started back in the other direction.

"Why do you have to know a man's secrets? As a matter of fact I have done my share of outlawing, but I was never caught at it, which is why I keep getting accused when I'm innocent. I guess they figure they can hang me for one crime as well as another."

"And when did you quit and start earning your way in a proper manner?"

Tynan snorted. "I think Red's been opening her big mouth. I've been straight since I was twenty-two."

"Seven years," she said.

"Red *has* been talking. Get down, you're making me dizzy. I know some things about you, too, Mary Christiana," he said as he lifted her down from the log.

"Not as much as you think," she said with eyes twinkling. "It's not Mary Christiana. At birth, I was given the name of Mary Ellen after my paternal grandmother, but my name was changed when I was six."

"All right, it's your turn to tell a story. Sit down here, away from me and don't come too close."

Still smiling, and feeling like the most desirable woman in the world, she sat on the grass and leaned against the log. "I have second sight," she said simply. "I've only had two visions but even one was enough to get my name changed. It seems that it's a tradition with the Montgomerys to name all the women with second sight Christiana."

"So what happened when you were six?"

"My parents and I were in church and I don't really remember how I felt beforehand, but one moment I was standing beside my mother and the next I was in the aisle screaming that everybody had to go outside. My mother said the congregation was too stunned to move, but she knew the traditions of her family and knew that every third or so generation a girl was born with second sight. So my mother yelled the single word that was guaranteed to clear the building."

"Fire," Ty said.

"Yes, except that after the people ran out of the

building in a state of panic, and one of them broke a stained glass window with a chair, they saw that there was no fire. I will always remember the looks on the faces of the people as they advanced on my mother and me. I thought they were going to kill us and I tried to hide in my mother's skirts.''

She took a breath. "They had just about reached us when the sky opened up and a bolt of lightning hit the church and the back half of it collapsed. When the dust cleared, the people looked at my mother and me as if we were witches. I'll never forget my mother's look that day. One of the men said, 'How did Mary Ellen know?' My mother put her nose in the air, took my hand and said, 'My daughter's name is Christiana.' And it has been ever since. Of course my father wasn't exactly delighted since I'd been named after his mother, but Mother promised him more children and he could name them what he wanted.''

"But there weren't any more.''

"No, just me. Some branches of the Montgomerys are very fertile and some are almost barren. There doesn't seem to be any middle ground.''

Tynan leaned back on the grass, stretching full length, his feet toward Chris. "She sounds like a wonderful mother. Do you miss her?''

Chris looked away. "Every day of my life. She was strong and soft, sensible and intelligent, wise and. . . . She was all anyone could hope to be.''

"I think you may be like her, what I've seen, that is.''

Chris grinned broadly at him. "For that, you may turn around here and put your head in my lap.''

"That is an honor," he said as he did as she offered. "This is nice," he said as Chris smoothed his hair back from his forehead. "You're not like any other women I've met."

"Good. Ty, what are you going to do now that you're free?"

"I'm not yet. I have to get you back to your father."

"Yes, but what can you do besides shoot a gun and sit a horse well? Or get drunk and land in jail?"

With his eyes closed, he smiled. "Doesn't sound like much, does it? Well, let's see, what can I do? I guess women don't count, do they?"

"Most definitely not."

"I know," he said, opening his eyes. "I can run four whore houses at once."

Chris let out a gasp. "Somehow I don't think that is a good—"

"No, not the women. I let Red handle that, except if there's a fight, then I separate the women, but one time Red's bookkeeper got killed in the crossfire of a shootout—one I wasn't involved in, I might add—and she asked me to look into the accounts because the bank was about to foreclose on one of the houses."

"Did the bank foreclose?"

"Hell, no. Oh, excuse me. It turned out that little weasel had been embezzling her money. I found it buried under the front porch of his house. And I had to learn to do bookkeeping and straighten the whole mess out. Now, every time I see Red I go over her accounts."

"What a marvelous ability. My father says that half his empire is nothing but book work. You could be of great use to him."

"I'm sure that your father would entrust his accounts to a gunslinger."

"He entrusted his daughter to one," she said softly.

"I guess he did at that," he said, smiling at her and beginning to run his hand up her arm. "Chris, do you really think he meant that about not touching you? Do you think he had any idea what he was asking?" His hand was at her neck.

"Maybe he'd heard about your reputation with women and he wanted to protect his daughter's chastity."

"Of course if neither of us told anyone what had happened, there'd be no way he'd know." He was pulling her head down to his.

"But my husband would know on my wedding night."

"What husband?" His lips were a breath away from hers.

"The man I marry. The man I plan to spend all my nights with."

He was pulling her closer but she was resisting. "But just the other day you were offering yourself to me."

"But then I thought you couldn't and that I was safe. I think we'd better go back to the others."

"In a minute," he said, pulling her to him.

Chris's lips parted for him and again she was amazed at the feeling that passed through her at Tynan's touch. It was as if her bones were disintegrating and she fell down across him.

He was expert at maneuvering her body so that soon she was stretched full out beside him and it was what she wanted when he moved one of his heavy legs on top of hers. Her body arched upwards toward his.

Later, she wondered what would have happened if he hadn't heard voices and moved away from her. Chris just lay there, eyes closed, too stunned to move.

"They're coming back," Ty whispered, lifting her off the ground into his arms. "Get dressed." As if she were a doll, he leaned her against his shoulder and began to button the back of her dress.

"What happens if I wear a dress that buttons down the front?" she murmured huskily.

"Don't. Save my sanity and your virginity and don't tempt me more than you have already. There, stand up and get that dopey look off your face. They're coming."

"Yes, Tynan," she said, allowing him to pull her upright.

Chapter Ten

Chris and Ty were swept away together with the crowd of returning young people. People were getting restless and wanting to eat again and play games. The women took Chris with them so they could ask her questions about some of the stories she'd written and they left Tynan with the men and the boys—who constantly begged Ty for stories of the gunfights he'd been in.

Chris and the women were on very friendly terms. They believed in her so much that they were willing to look differently at a man they'd been so sure was wrong. One of the women bravely asked Chris what a house of ill repute looked like inside and she had a good time entertaining them with stories of red wallpaper and highly polished brass lamps and women who looked very bored. They were all laughing when the shot rang out.

Chris hoped she was wrong, but somehow, she knew that Tynan was involved with that single gunshot.

Grabbing her skirts, she started running, the women

116

behind her. On the ground, surrounded by men, lay Rory Sayers, a derringer in his hand, blood spreading over his shoulder—and standing over him was Tynan. Chris looked at Ty with disbelief on her face.

"I'm afraid I'm going to have to take you in," said a young man who Chris had seen wearing a deputy's badge. "The sheriff will have to deal with this."

Chris's eyes were still locked with Tynan's and it was only after a long moment that she turned away. The face of every woman around her had a look of "I told you so" on it.

Chris lifted her skirt and began walking back to the tables.

"Chris," Tynan called softly from behind her but she didn't look back.

At the tables she began packing food away, trying to stay calm while the others put the injured Rory on a wagon bed and started back toward town. Since Rory was yelling that they were going to kill him and also he was raging that he was going to kill Tynan, Chris assumed that he was going to live.

Minutes later, Tynan walked past her, stopping within a few feet of her, but she didn't turn around, instead, busying herself in putting the food away.

The women came to help her, working in total silence as they gave her looks from under their lashes. After a few minutes, Chris could stand no more. She put down the food, turned toward the road and began walking back to town. She didn't care about Red's buggy that she left behind or about anything else for that matter.

It was miles back to town but Chris walked all the way, shaking her head no at the people who stopped their carriages and offered her a ride.

In the hotel, people were watching her in such a way that she ran up the stairs and into her room, slamming the door behind her. She was so ashamed of herself that she wanted to climb into bed, pull the covers over her head and never come out again. For the last two days, she'd strutted around this town and, in essence, told them they were all fools, that they didn't know a man who'd lived among them most of his life. She'd used the love she'd earned as Nola Dallas to tell them that they knew much less than she did after spending only a few days with the man.

Slowly, Chris began to undress, taking off the dress that Red had loaned her.

How vain I was, she thought, to think that I knew more than they did. And how conceited I was to think that I could reform a man who has chosen a life of crime and violence. How right my father was when he introduced me to men from my own background, men I could understand, not men who went to picnics and shot people who disagreed with them.

She packed her small bundle, put her riding habit back on and took the two dresses downstairs to the clerk. His eyes were different now. No longer was he looking at her with interest, wanting to know more about the young woman who worked for a big city newspaper. Now she was just one of many women who'd fallen for a cheap drifter.

She didn't look at the others in the hotel lobby who were watching her with interest, waiting until she'd gone upstairs again so they could tell others what had happened at the picnic.

"Miss," said a young man behind her, "I have a message for you."

With her eyes downcast, Chris took the piece of

paper, crumbled it in her hand and went up the stairs. Chris sat on the bed and thought for some time. She felt that she owed him this one last visit, to say goodbye, to tell him that she was returning to her father and that she would see that he was given his pardon.

She wrote a note to Asher telling him that she planned to start the journey home tomorrow.

With her shoulders squared, she went downstairs, leaving the note to Asher with the desk clerk, and went outside. As soon as she started toward the jail, she had a following of curious people, some of them snickering. So, the big city girl thought she could come to this town and tell us about someone we already knew, she could almost hear them saying.

Once, a man blocked her passage, and she had to look up at him, giving him her most withering look to make him step aside. He spit a big wad of tobacco juice at her feet, barely missing her.

One thing about people who made a fuss about someone they thought was better than they were, when their idol came to earth, they were very angry about it.

"May I see your prisoner?" she said to the deputy sitting at the desk.

"Oh sure, Miss Dallas," he said, getting the ring of keys from a nail on the wall. "I'm real sorry about what happened. The sheriff should be here tomorrow and this thing will be cleared up. There's someone to see you," the boy said to Tynan as he let Chris into the cell.

Tynan turned around quickly, looking at her with eyes that examined and searched. He didn't seem to like what he saw because he turned away again.

"I got your message," she said, looking down at her hands.

"I've seen what I wanted to, you can go now."

119

The coldness in his voice made her head come up—and her anger surface. "Tell me, are you innocent again? Like with the Chanry Gang? Were you perhaps protecting children from Rory? What was it this time that got you involved in a shooting?"

"Get out of here, Chris," he said softly. "I don't want to fight with you."

"Because I don't have a gun? Oh yes, I know the code of the West. You'd never draw on an unarmed man—or woman. How could you do that to me? Those people *trusted* me! They told me their secrets and I asked them to trust me more. I asked them to give you another chance, to let you start fresh. And they *did!* But what did you do but show them just what you really are, what I was too stupid to see?"

He just stood there with his back to her, his arm up, pressing against the stone wall, looking out the cell window.

"Look at me when I talk to you. If you have no conscience, at least you can pretend to have manners."

Slowly, he turned toward her and he seemed to be a man Chris had never seen before, one of coolness, as if he were far away and not there at all.

"I never lied to you about what I was. I always told you I wasn't for you. But you never listened to anything I said. You were so busy showing the world that you could reform the criminal that you never thought about who I really was."

"I guess I've learned now." She walked toward the cell door. "I won't bother you again. I just came to tell you that I, and probably Mr. Prescott, will be leaving early in the morning. I'll make sure, though, that you will be given your pardon by my father. Deputy," she called.

Tynan was across the room in seconds, barring her exit. "You will not leave without me. I swore to your father that I'd deliver you and I plan to."

"Of course, the Western man always keeps his word. He may kill people on a daily basis, prison may be a way of life to him but he *always* keeps his word. Deputy, you may let me out now."

Tynan slammed the door shut, startling the boy against the wall. "You can't leave tomorrow morning. You can't go across this country with just that man, he doesn't know anything about surviving."

"I have to agree that he doesn't know how to shoot innocent men at church picnics."

"He didn't shoot Sayers," the deputy said. "Sayers attacked him from behind."

"I knew you were innocent," Chris said. "A man like you doesn't get caught when he does something illegal. Deputy, please open this door."

Ty held it shut. "Chris, you can't leave until I get out of here. You need—"

"Mr. Tynan, if I waited for you to get out of one jail after another, I'd never get home. Let me make myself clear. I am going to leave tomorrow morning and start home to my father. You will have your precious pardon and you will get rid of me in the bargain." She grabbed the door and jerked, stepping outside quickly. "When you make your way to my father's, via the jails of Washington, however falsely accused you are, he may even have the ten thousand dollars you've worked so hard for. Good-bye, sir, and I hope we never meet again."

Chapter Eleven

Asher led the way out of town the next morning before the sun was up. She'd mumbled answers to his many questions on the night before, saying her engagement to Tynan had been a farce, something to save him from Rory's barbs. Asher seemed satisfied that she was properly contrite.

As they passed the jail, Chris saw the dark shadowy outline of Tynan standing in his cell watching them. She kept her head up high and didn't return his stare. By the time he got out of prison, she'd be far away.

Neither she nor Asher had much to say as they rode, not really running, but not giving themselves time to enjoy the scenery either. At noon they stopped to rest the horses and eat the stale biscuits they'd brought.

As the sound of thundering hooves came down the narrow little road, Chris's heart nearly stopped beating. But it wasn't Tynan or anyone else interested in them. Three big men on scraggy horses went tearing past them, their heads down, their faces hidden under their hat brims.

"I'm glad they aren't looking for us," Asher said when they'd passed.

Asher didn't talk to Chris much and she remembered how she'd sometimes been rude to him. As he helped her onto her horse, she took every opportunity to smile at him. Now that Tynan was gone, and Chris was no longer blinded by that man's light, she could look at Asher with new eyes. This was a man her father *wanted* her to marry. This man wasn't likely to pull a gun and kill for the smallest offense.

It was nearly sundown before they saw the over-turned wagon, and even then they wouldn't have seen it except for Chris having noticed the way the ground had been torn up. There were deep, fresh gouges in the earth, leading off into the underbrush.

"Let's stop here for a moment," she called, dismounting and running down into the bushes. She hadn't gone but a few feet when she saw the big old wagon on its side, and what looked to be a woman's hand protruding from under it.

She ran back up the bank, shouting for Asher to come and help her. "Under there," she pointed. "We have to get the wagon up and get her out."

He only hesitated for a second, then ran forward.

When they got to the far side of the wagon, they could see only part of the woman's arm. Her head and the rest of her body were buried under the wagon.

"Can you lift that?" Chris asked, pointing to a broken part of the wagon. "I'll try to pull the woman out."

Asher used most of the strength he had as he

123

propped himself against the side of the wagon then squatted until his legs could work to lift the weight.

"Now!" he shouted and the wagon moved.

Chris lost not a second pulling the woman out to safety.

Asher, kneeling, lit a match because the evening was growing very dim, and studied the woman. She seemed to be covered in blood. "She's been shot at least three times," he said quietly.

"But she's still breathing." Chris took the woman's bloodied head into her lap. "We'll get you to a doctor," she whispered to the woman as she began to thrash about.

"My husband," she gasped. "Where is my husband?"

Chris looked up at Asher but he was already searching the surrounding area. Chris could see where he stopped. Turning, he shook his head.

"Your husband is fine. He's sleeping now."

"Can you tell us who did this to you?" Asher asked when he came back.

The woman was having great difficulty talking, and blood was seeping steadily from her wounds. "Three men," she whispered at last. "They wanted us dead because we know about Lionel. We were going to save Lionel."

Suddenly the woman looked at Chris with eyes as red as the blood that was washing from her body. "Help him. Help Lionel. Promise me that."

"Yes, of course I will. As soon as you're better we'll both—" She stopped because the woman's head had fallen to one side and she was dead.

Asher sat back on his heels. "We have to get the

sheriff out here. We'll leave the bodies here for now while I bring the sheriff back."

"Chris," he said sharply because she'd begun to look through the packages that had fallen from the wagon. "What in the world are you doing?"

"Looking for something that will tell who Lionel is."

He caught her shoulders and turned her toward him. "I don't think we should look for the trouble that got that woman killed. We're going home and we're stopping for no one or nothing. This Lionel will have to take care of himself. Now, we're going to a town."

"We can't leave them here like this," Chris said.

He seemed to want to protest, but he stopped, then went to the man's body, and carried it up the bank.

Chris went to the woman, smoothed her hair, crossed her hands over her breast. Even in the darkness, she could see how young the woman was, that her hair, under the blood that stained it, was the color of wheat. She was much too young to have died, especially to have been murdered.

Standing, Chris looked at the bundles around her, a meager lot of women's clothing in a carpet bag, another little sewing bag, one bag of the man's clothes. These had scattered across the ground when the wagon had tumbled down the side of the hill. Something shining in the moonlight caught Chris's eye. When she went to it, she saw that it was a little leather bound book with a brass clasp.

Quickly searching the man's bag, she found a box of matches, lit one and scanned a page of the book. As she hoped, it was a diary and, before Asher saw her, she made out the words, "We must help him" and "Lionel's life may be in danger. He's only a child and he has no one but us."

When she heard Asher behind her, she slammed the book shut and slipped it into the pocket of her habit.

They left the wagon and the bundles where they were for the sheriff to examine, mounted their horses and rode south.

They got to the inn, and, vaguely she heard Asher murmuring complaints and apologies about the food and the dirt of the place, but Chris wasn't really listening. Over a dinner of burned beans, all she could think of was the diary.

When Chris was finally alone in her room, she sat in the bed and began to read the diary. It started three years ago when Diana Hamilton had married the man she'd thought was the wisest, cleverest man on earth, Whitman Eskridge. It hadn't taken her but a few months to find out that he'd married her for her money. Within six months he'd spent everything she brought to the marriage and wanted more.

Chris read how this man had wheedled his way into the Hamilton business—and it wasn't until after Diana's father's suicide that she found out that Whitman had been embezzling funds.

The company went bankrupt, but Diana stood by her husband through all the scandal and the public auction of their belongings. When he said he wanted to go live with her rich relatives in Washington Territory, Diana had reluctantly agreed. She wrote her cousin, Owen Hamilton, a man she'd never met, and begged him for mercy and kindness—and for a roof over their heads.

There were several days when Diana didn't write in the diary, then she took it up again with the news that Whitman had told her that Owen was stealing from Lionel. Chris found this confusing until she'd read a few pages more. As far as she could tell, Lionel was

126

really the owner of the Hamilton holdings in Washington. He was a boy of about eleven, and everything had been left to him in care of his uncle, the man who was Diana's cousin. And Whitman Eskridge had produced some type of proof that Owen Hamilton was cheating his nephew out of his inheritance. Unfortunately, the diary didn't tell what that proof was.

It was hours later when she finished reading and fell asleep, the book across her lap. She had a dream that she was Diana Eskridge.

"Chris, wake up," Asher was saying, shaking her awake. "I pounded on the door but no one answered. Did you stay awake all night reading that book?"

Yawning, Chris nodded.

"Well, whatever it is, I hope it was worth it. I just rode in and I wanted to tell you that the sheriff has the bodies. I'm going to sleep now. I'll see you at dinner."

Chris was tired but she could sleep only fitfully. She kept thinking and dreaming about what she'd read. It was so unfair that the pretty young woman had had such a terrible life. And what would happen now to that poor little boy whose inheritance she was trying to save? Lionel now had no other relatives except his dishonest uncle.

By evening, she was convinced that she should do something about this young woman who had died. She couldn't let her die in vain, couldn't let her agony and pain be for nothing.

At dinner, she asked Asher many questions about the looks of the young woman who'd died.

"Chris, how can you be so morbid?"

"Do you think she was built like me? Was she anything like me at all?"

When he saw she wasn't going to cease, he began to

answer her. "Why don't you tell me what you have on your mind," he said softly.

Chris nearly choked from trying to tell too much too quickly. When she'd calmed herself, she began again. First, she told him about the diary and Diana Eskridge's miserable marriage. "She never had a chance for happiness. And she was on her way to do something very good. She was going to save her cousin whose estate was being stolen from him by a wicked uncle when she was killed."

Asher looked at his plate of food. "Did it ever occur to you that the wicked uncle might have been the one who killed her?"

"Of course it did. But her dying request was that I help by protecting Lionel."

"And just how do you propose to do that? Walk up to this uncle and say, 'Excuse me, but are you stealing from your nephew? If so, would you please turn yourself in and go to jail for the rest of your life?' Really, Chris! This is too absurd."

Chris took a deep breath. "I thought that since this man has never seen his cousin, I might be able to pose as her."

Asher's jaw dropped as he gaped at her. "But if he's the one who has had her killed, don't you think he'll be a little suspicious when you walk in the door?"

"I don't guess he can say that he thought I was dead, can he?"

"Not *you*, Chris, Diana Eskridge. You couldn't possibly get away with this. There's too much that you don't know about her. How are the two of them related? Maybe this Diana has a birthmark that's a family trait. There are a thousand things that you don't know. Why has she never met this man before? No, you couldn't possibly do it."

Chris looked down at her plate and she tried to control herself but she felt the tears coming.

"What's the matter, Chris?" Asher asked, reaching for her hand.

"Tynan," was all Chris could sob. She heard Asher's sharp intake of breath and she realized it was the first time she'd admitted that there was actually anything between her and the guide. But right now, secrecy didn't matter to her. All she thought about was Tynan.

Asher kept holding her hand. "If you went to visit Diana Eskridge's cousin, what about her husband? Surely Owen Hamilton would be expecting the two of them? You can't exactly say that you lost him on the way out west."

"I hadn't thought about him," Chris said, wiping her eyes with her hand. "Maybe I could appear as a widow. Smallpox got him or a rabid dog or maybe Indians on the plains or—"

"What if you appeared *with* him?" Asher interrupted. "What if you came with your husband?"

"You mean get Tynan to pretend to be my husband? After the things he said to me about marriage? He'd probably take after Owen with a gun the first day. He'd no doubt—"

"Could you get that man out of your mind for a moment?" Asher asked angrily. "I was thinking about myself."

"You as my husband?" Chris asked, her mouth open in disbelief.

Asher gave her a look of disgust for a moment. "Do you *really* want to help Lionel or not?"

"I do but . . . besides, Mr. Prescott, you can't do this. I'm sure you have somewhere else you have to be and the last place you want to be is risking your life to save someone you don't even know. No, I'll just have to do this by myself. I'll say that my husband was killed under a stampede of horses when the train stopped for water. Or maybe the water pipe fell on him, knocked him unconscious and he drowned in the middle of the desert. I'd like something awful to have happened to Mr. Whitman Eskridge. He deserves it for the way he treated Diana."

"Chris, if I don't go along on this to take care of you, I'll tell your father where you are and what you're up to this time."

"You wouldn't," Chris gasped.

"Try me," he answered, narrowing his eyes at her.

Chris leaned away from him and suddenly felt his intensity. He'd made several attempts at showing how much he liked her, but now she felt that he sincerely wanted to help her.

Asher smiled at her. "Of course I'll have to read the diary before we go to see just what kind of a son of a—oh, excuse me." He grinned. "Think you can play the dutiful little wife who agrees with her husband no matter what he does?"

Chris's lips tightened into a line. "I can play whatever role is needed. How would Owen Hamilton know what I was like?"

"I'm sure that if he's a man like you think he is, to take away a child's inheritance, to have his relatives killed, then he's the type who would investigate a person. Surely he knows about Diana's father's suicide and he must have heard about the funds I"—he winked at her—"was embezzling."

"You're willing to risk your life for something that's none of your business?" She still couldn't believe he *wanted* to do this. Did he like her that much? Or was it her father's money?

"If you hadn't risked your life so many times as Nola Dallas, there would be fewer reforms in our laws. Chris, I'd be honored to be your husband whether for a night or forever."

"Oh," Chris said, blinking.

"Now, shall we start making plans?" Asher asked. "I think we should stay here today and maybe tomorrow, and read that diary aloud and find out everything we can about Diana Eskridge and her husband. You'll walk into this as prepared as you can be. Agreed?"

Chris looked up from under her lashes at Asher who was smiling as if he were extremely pleased about something. This time tomorrow this man would be her husband—sort of.

When he turned and looked at her, she noticed for the first time how thick his lashes were and now he was looking at her in a way that was decidedly making her uncomfortable. She shifted in her chair while listening to him make plans.

Chapter Twelve

Owen Hamilton's house was a three-story mansion not far from the sea on Washington's west coast. It had taken them three days of preparing for the trip, before Chris and Asher had climbed into a buggy that had to be fifteen years old and ridden west.

Asher and she hadn't spoken a great deal on the way to the Hamilton house, both of them going over what they needed to know to carry off this escapade. They spent the night at an inn, taking separate rooms, and started in the early morning.

They were within a few miles of the house when Asher turned to her. "This is your last chance, Chris," he said. "If you want to back out, now's the time."

"Not unless you do."

Ash chuckled. "This is a man's dream. I get to spend nights and days with a beautiful young lady, I get to do something constructive with my time besides beg banks for loans they won't give and I might get some of the satisfaction you get from helping people. What more can I ask?" He looked at her out of the corner of his eye. "By the way, Chris, I mean to use this time to win you over. By the time we leave here, I plan to have you in love with me."

"Me or my money?" she asked, one eyebrow cocked.

"Did your gunslinger tell you that?"

"No," she said honestly. "But isn't it true that my father sent you on the rescue mission in the hopes that I'd fall in love with you? My father badly wants me to marry, stay home and have babies."

He smiled at her, snapping the reins to make the horse go faster. "It started out that way. I think I was to the point that I would have married a three-headed ostrich if I thought I could have a chance at getting my self-respect back. But the truth is, Chris, it's come to mean more to me. You're the most courageous woman I've ever met. You're the most . . . most interesting woman I've ever met. If we lived together for ninety years, I don't think I'd get bored with you."

Chris had to laugh. "I think that may be one of the nicest compliments I've ever received."

"And now that that strutting criminal is out of the way, I think I'll have a chance. I'll never understand why you ladies fall for that type."

As Chris watched, he shrugged. Was Tynan just a type? she wondered. Was that all he was and nothing more? He had seemed so special, so unique. Maybe she'd been blinded by his extraordinary exterior beauty. A horse pounding along the road beside them made her heart nearly skip a beat, but it was just a cowboy. She relaxed against the back of the seat—relaxed as much as she could in the springless carriage. "You have my permission to try, Mr. Prescott," she said. "You may try."

Two hours later, they arrived at the Hamilton house.

"Now remember that you are Diana Eskridge, a meek, mild-mannered woman and not the notorious Nola Dallas. If you step out of place, I may have to reprimand you."

Chris, with eyes wide, looked up at him and started to speak, but the front door was opened by a fat, aproned woman and Chris put her head down. She'd chosen clothes she thought Diana would wear, simple little calicos, all insipid colors, all hint of stylishness gone. They were the clothes of a woman who'd allow her husband to make her life miserable.

"You must be the Eskridges," the heavy woman with the broad face said. "We've been expecting you for days. Was beginnin' to worry about you. Just set those bags down and I'll get Mr. Owen." She went straight ahead, up some stairs. "By the way, I'm Unity," she called over her shoulder.

Chris stepped farther into the room. They were standing in an entryway, with a music room to the right, a parlor to the left, and to the right, farther down the hall a dining room. She looked up as a man came down the stairs. He was tall, broad-shouldered, with a small mustache over full lips. The last thing in the world that he looked like was anyone's idea of a villain. He was smiling in such a pleasant way that Chris wanted to tell him the truth of who she was.

"You must be Diana," he said and he had a deep voice that instantly made a person relax. "We meet at last."

She offered him her hand. "Yes, finally," she murmured. "May I introduce my husband, Whitman? We can't thank you enough for inviting us to your lovely home."

He smiled at both of them with genuine warmth. "Think nothing of it. I'll be glad for the company and Unity will be pleased to have someone to fuss over. Now, you must be tired. Let me take you to your room. We'll eat in about an hour and until then I'm afraid you'll have to excuse me as I have mountains of paperwork to do. Quite unexpectedly, I have a buyer coming in from the East day after tomorrow and I have to be ready for him. Make yourself at home. There's a garden in back that you might like. Here we are." He opened the door to a large, spacious room with a big, double, four-postered bed, a closet and a little bay-window seat in the corner. Chris was grateful to see a fainting couch along one wall. Ash followed her eyes and winked at her, making her face turn pink.

"This is more than adequate," Ash said. "Thank you very much."

"If you need anything, just let out a holler. We're not formal here. Unity is usually in the kitchen below or sometimes you can find me upstairs. I have a billiards table up there and a complete bar. One of my great luxuries in life. I'll see you in the dining room at twelve-thirty." He closed the door behind him and was gone.

Asher sat on the bed, bouncing a bit to test the springs. "I wouldn't want this to squeak. More marriages are ruined by loud mattresses than any other—"

"He didn't say a word about Lionel," Chris said, cutting Ash off. "Do you think he's here? You don't think he's already done something to him, do you?"

"Buried him in the rosebushes? Owen doesn't look like a man who'd do anyone a bad turn. I never met anyone who welcomed his destitute relatives with such open arms before. How about a nap before dinner?"

"I sincerely hope that you aren't going to persist in talking of the . . . the intimacies of married couples. I think I'll see this garden Owen mentioned. An eleven-year-old boy might be there playing."

Chris went down the stairs to the kitchen. Unity wasn't in the room but the smells of the food cooking were delicious. She felt as if it had been years since she'd had a decent meal.

The garden outside was beautiful, full of azaleas, wildflowers from the mountains, bulb plants. It was obviously the great love of someone and she guessed it was Owen Hamilton. There was a curved stone bench under a big Douglas fir and she sat on it, leaning back against the tree and closing her eyes. At the moment she'd never been so homesick in her life. Her mother used to have a garden like this but since she'd died, her father had not taken care of it. Now, when she visited, she almost cried to see the weeds overtaking it. "You should stay home and see to it yourself," her father kept saying to her.

"You will not be allowed to sit there. That is *my* bench."

Chris opened her eyes to see a boy standing in front of her. He looked a little like Owen except where Owen's face was pleasant, this boy's was scowling.

"You must be Lionel," she said, smiling. "I'm—"

"I know who you are. You're the poor relatives who've come to live off me. Now get up and go away."

Chris just sat there looking at him.

Lionel's face began to turn red. "I told you to get up. That is *my* seat. This is *my* garden. This is *my* house. Do I have to call my uncle to get rid of you?"

"Why, yes, I do believe you'll have to do just that," she said, wondering what Owen would do if he were summoned away from his paperwork to tell a guest to give her seat to a rude little boy.

Lionel's face began to lose its redness but she could see that his anger was just beneath the surface. "You have to obey me."

"Why is that?"

"Because I own everything here and you are at my mercy."

Chris smiled at him, repressing a laugh. "It doesn't look like you own this seat at the moment. Nor do you seem to own any manners. Shall we begin again? I'm your cousin, Diana Eskridge."

Lionel took a step back from her, then, in a split second, he grabbed a handful of mud from a flower bed and threw it onto the front of her clean dress. Before Chris could speak, he ran out of sight.

Standing, Chris looked down at the front of her dress, then started back to the house.

Unity, taking a pan of cornbread from the oven, looked up. "I take it you met Lionel. Here, honey, sit down and we'll get you cleaned up. That boy is gonna be the death of us all."

"I'm sure it's none of my business, but does anyone ever discipline that child?" She took the wet cloth Unity gave her.

"Till their hands near fell off. When you get as old as I am, you learn that kids are as different as night and day. Some of 'em you can discipline with a look, most of 'em you can discipline with a birch rod—and then there's Lionel. *Nothin'* has any effect on him. Believe me, his uncle's tried ever'thing."

"How about gentleness?" Chris asked, wiping at the mud on her dress. "I mean he is an orphan."

"You ain't been here long, but you'll see. Mr. Owen

is the gentlest man alive. It breaks his heart when he has to take a rod to that boy. For years, he wouldn't do it. He kept sayin' he wanted the boy to feel at home here but I've known him since he was a baby."

Chris wasn't sure how much Diana was supposed to know, but she had to chance it. "You were with Lionel before his uncle was?"

"I keep forgettin' that you don't know about us."

"If you'll hand me that bowl of peas I'll shell them for you," Chris said.

"Now this ain't to be usual. You're family, but for today I'll let you help. Now, where was I? Oh yes. I worked for Mr. Owen's brother and sister-in-law; I was there the night Mrs. Laura had little Lionel. That was a happy night. But it wasn't but a few months later that they was killed in that fire. Lionel was only six months old. Of course everything was left to him, with Mr. Owen to take care of the property until Lionel reached twenty-one. He's done the best he could, but that boy . . ." She trailed off, leaving the rest to the imagination.

Chris couldn't get anymore from the woman and Unity spent the rest of their time together talking about what a wonderful man Owen was and how she was fortunate to be able to work for him. Chris thought that this was every homeowner's dream, to find a dedicated servant.

At dinner, Lionel came to the table late, his mouth set into a sulky pout. Owen greeted him and introduced him to his cousins, Diana and Whitman, but Lionel just gave them a sullen look and began to push the food about on his plate. Twice, Chris caught him looking at her with especially hostile looks. Both times she smiled at him.

"What a brat of a kid," Ash said when they were alone in their room. "Has anyone taken a switch to him? And why was he eating with adults anyway?"

"Probably because he owns the place," Chris said as she hung up her meager wardrobe.

Asher ran his hand along the edge of the wardrobe. "I never thought I could come to love a piece of furniture. Remember the first time I saw you? I told Tynan we shouldn't be hiding in a lady's bedroom but he said we had to get to you without your making any noise. We thought you'd be asleep but the bed was empty and we jumped into the wardrobe when we heard you coming back into the room."

"I don't want to talk about him."

"Him? Who? You don't mean that two-bit gunslinger, do you? I thought you were over him. After what he did at that picnic, I'd think you'd never want to see him again."

"I don't. Could we talk about something else? Such as how we're going to find out what's going on in this house? What is making that child so miserable?"

"Being spoiled rotten is all that's wrong with him and if you had any children of your own, you'd know that."

"And you do have children? So many that you're an authority on the subject?"

"I know enough to be sure of what I see. He's been given everything and he expects more. Chris, let's not argue. Let's enjoy this time together." He reached out his arms to her, his hands almost catching her, but she sidestepped him.

"I'm going outside to the garden. I'll see you later. See if you can make yourself useful to Owen and find out something. We're here for a story and that's what I plan to look into." ·

Chris left the room with a sigh of relief. She hadn't given much thought to actually living with a man, of being in the same room with him night after night. But already, she could see the problems that it was going to involve.

Downstairs, she found Owen and Unity looking perplexed. "I'll take care of it," Unity was saying. "You just go back to work where you belong."

Chris bit her tongue to keep from asking what Lionel had done now, but, instead, she politely murmured that she would like to help with whatever was the problem.

"It's merely one of those household complications that can't be helped," Owen said. "But today I do need to get work done before the buyer arrives and I don't have time to—"

"May I be of help?" Chris asked. "I've run my father's house for years."

"We can't ask you . . ." Owen began, then halted. "Diana, I'd be eternally grateful if you'd help. Unity has her hands full and doesn't have the time. Five minutes ago, my gardener said he has to go to San Francisco to take care of a sick sister and he's hired his cousin to run my gardens, only I don't know this man and it'll take me days to tell him how I want things kept."

"Leave it to me," Chris said. "I'll take care of everything. Where are the gardeners? The old one and the new one? I'll get instructions from the old one and give them to the cousin—and I'll ask for references."

Owen was looking at her with his head cocked to one side and Chris thought maybe she'd made a mistake. Diana Eskridge was supposed to be a mouse of a woman, not one who took over someone else's household. But then, men rarely thought anything about housework. A woman could run an army of servants yet a man'd think she didn't have sense enough to handle a twenty-dollar bill.

"Diana, I'd appreciate it very much if you'd help me with this. Domestic responsibilities are my downfall."

Chris gave him a demure smile. "I'd like to help all that I can."

"Al is waiting in the garden for me with his cousin. I give it all to you."

Chris was glad for something to do and she went to the garden with a smile. Maybe she'd be able to find out something if she had access to some of Owen's time. He'd be more likely to tell her something if she were helping him in whatever way she could.

She was walking around a corner when she came face to face with the one man she did not want to see. "You!" she gasped. "Get out of here!" She turned on her heel and started back toward the house.

Tynan caught her arm. "Is that how you treat the new gardener? Will you tell Hamilton that you can't hire me?"

She stopped and glared at him. "I told you that I never wanted to see you again."

"And I told you that you were my responsibility until I returned you to your father. I'm not leaving you alone until you're in his care."

"You were also to bring me back in love with Asher. I can do that on my own. I'm staying here with Ash and I plan to fall in love with him."

"Good. Great. Glad to hear it. I wish you both the best in the world, but you're staying near me too until I personally hand you over to your father."

"That may be what you think but I'm going right now and tell Owen that you are unsuitable as a gardener. I'll

141

tell him that you are untrustworthy, that you may use a gun to do the weeding."

"I hope you do," he said, starting to walk beside her. "I never wanted to be a gardener anyway. I'll just tell Hamilton the truth about who you are and we can go back to your father and we never have to see each other again. And I can get my pardon and you can have your wedding to the illustrious Mr. Prescott and I can get my money for playing Cupid. This suits me fine."

She stopped. "I want to stay here and find out about Lionel. I made a promise to a dying woman."

"Ah, I see, your promise to someone you don't know is sacred but my promise to your father isn't worth anything, is that it?"

"No, you're twisting my words. You have self-interest in this, I don't."

"Enhancing the reputation of Nola Dallas with a story that will break the readers' hearts isn't self-interest?"

"Get away from me," she said but she didn't walk toward the house any longer. "I am perfectly safe and I don't plan to get into any trouble. I'll write a letter to my father saying that you've fulfilled your obligations and he's to give you your pardon and the money. I'll even pay the money from my mother's estate. Now, will you go?"

"And leave you here to take care of yourself? If Hamilton is doing something illegal, do you think he'll stop at violence when he's been discovered? Someone has to protect you from yourself."

"Asher can protect me."

Tynan gave a sound that bordered on a laugh. "And who'll take care of him? You have a choice: either I stay here as the gardener and keep an eye on you, or we both leave now."

Chris hid her fists in the folds of her skirt. "How did you find out where I was?"

He moved his face closer to hers. "Through wearing out three horses and two saddles. Lady, I have done nothing for the last few days but follow you and try to find out where you were. I finally got the sheriff to tell me something about it."

"And what could he know?" Chris asked, glaring at him.

"More than you could guess. He's heard of Owen Hamilton. The man does some big business dealings, controls a lot of money. You're not dealing with a simpleton like Prescott who you can wrap around your little finger."

"I can't wrap Asher—" She stopped because, walking through the trees, was an utterly beautiful woman with dark hair and eyes, a perfect figure, and a graceful walk that emanated sexuality. "Who is that?"

"My bodyguard. I thought since you could make up a new identity, I could too. Pilar has agreed to be my wife for the duration of this fiasco. I figured with your living with the brave Mr. Prescott, and me with Pilar, there wouldn't be anymore of what happened in the rain forest. I don't plan to go back to jail."

"Wife," Chris whispered. "Wife?"

Tynan narrowed his eyes at her. "Yeah, the gardener has a wife. Pilar will be helping out in the house and I'll be out here. Between the two of us, we should be able to watch out for you."

"Where will you live?"

"In the gardener's house, of course. Look, Chris, if

we're going to play this until you get your story, we'd better get started. Are you supposed to tell me what to do?"

"I would love to tell you what to do, Mr. Tynan," she said with a false smile, turning away from him and starting back to the house.

"Don't you want to meet Pilar?" he called after her, laughter in his voice.

Chris kept walking.

Chapter Thirteen

"Diana!" Asher said sharply. "Your cousin was speaking to you."

Chris looked up from her plate of food to gaze blankly at Owen Hamilton, for a moment not knowing who he was.

"You can see what a time I have with her," Asher was saying. "She can be most exasperating at times."

"Yes, well . . ." Owen said hesitantly. "How did you get on with the new gardener, Diana?"

Unity set a large bowl of carrots on the table. "Anybody that looks like him can get along with any woman. I'm not sure I ever wanta see Al's ugly ol' face again."

Owen gave his housekeeper a look of reproach.

"He seems to know what he's doing," Chris murmured. "I think he's worked on a farm."

"*I* don't think he's a farmer," Lionel said. "I think he's a robber. I think he robs banks and kills people."

"There are worse ways to go," Unity muttered before leaving the room.

Asher was watching Chris intently, while she just looked at her food. Thirty minutes later, as everyone was leaving the table, he grabbed her arm. "Come outside with me, I want to talk to you."

Asher practically dragged her into the garden, out of hearing distance of the house. "All right, who is this robber–farmer? Is it who I think it is?"

"Yes," she said, "but I had no idea he was coming here. He says I am his responsibility until he turns me over to my father."

"So now I have to deal with him again. Chris, I hope you aren't going to make a fool of yourself over him this time. I don't think it would fit meek little Diana's image to be seen following the gardener about."

She was glad for the darkness to hide her red face. "No, I am not going to make a fool of myself again. Besides, he brought a woman with him. He doesn't want to have any more to do with me than I with him. Now, does that soothe your jealousy? Could we go in now? I'm awfully tired."

Asher looked at something over her head and then he quite suddenly grabbed her and pressed his mouth to hers. Chris thought it was meant to be a kiss, but it didn't feel like one. Her eyes were open and his were staring at something behind her. She began to push away from him, but just then she heard someone whistling from behind her and she knew who it was. She grabbed Asher closer to her, trying to put some passion into the kiss. It seemed to work for Ash because his eyes closed and he began to pull her to him, but Chris was only aware of where Tynan was.

"Ah, newlyweds," Tynan said as he passed them. "It's so good to see people in love."

Chris pushed Asher away with some force, put her chin in the air and walked past Ty without a backward glance.

When Asher got to their room, she was slinging sheets onto the narrow fainting couch. "I *hate* that man! Absolutely, totally, completely hate that man. I wish he'd go back to jail and stay there forever. I'd like to think of him rotting away somewhere."

"It didn't look to me as if you hated him," Asher said stiffly. "It seemed to me that you were trying to use me to make him jealous."

"Jealous! He said he couldn't stand to see me with other men, but he didn't really care. All he cares about is getting that money."

"Maybe he was jealous after he'd just gotten out of prison and before he'd visited a . . . a place like Red's."

Chris's eyes widened. "And before he'd moved in with the luscious Pilar." She pounded a pillow with her fist. "I truly, sincerely hate that man. I wish I'd never seen him before in my life. I wish I never had to see him again. I wish—"

Asher caught her by the shoulders and turned her to face him. "Chris, you're protesting too much. I know a way to put him out of your mind." He began to lower his head to hers. "You're obsessed with him because you have nothing else to replace him." He touched her neck with his lips. "Spend the night with me. I'll make you forget him. I'll make you forget everything except us. We'll be a real married couple and when we leave here, we can go to your father and have a legal ceremony."

Chris tried to enjoy the lovely way he was kissing her neck. He was a handsome man, he smelled good, there was absolutely nothing at all wrong with him—except that there was no spark. She could have fallen asleep standing up while he was kissing her. As it was, she suppressed a yawn.

"Please, Ash, don't rush things. I . . . I'm not sure of myself yet. I've just been through something awful with one man and I don't feel as if I can trust myself with anyone else. Please understand."

He pulled away from her with a hurt look that made a thread of guilt run through her. She so hated lying for any reason whatever, and she especially hated lying to Ash who'd been so nice to her.

He stepped back. "All right, but I won't give up trying."

"I hope you don't," she said with a smile. There was no screen in the room, so she opened the wardrobe door and undressed behind it, all too aware that Asher was lying in the bed watching her. It made her nervous and a little frightened—but it did not make her want to climb into bed with him. She began to imagine how she'd feel if Tynan were lying in that bed, his shirt off, his hands behind his head, waiting for her. Even the thought seemed to make her skin glow.

She took a few deep breaths before she walked out from behind the door. Ash had on a long nightgown and he was watching her like a cat with a mouse. Chris said a soft good-night, blew out the lantern, and climbed onto the little couch. It was hard and uncomfortable, but it was better than the alternative.

She woke the next morning to Asher kissing her face and neck. For a moment, she enjoyed it until she remembered who he was. "For heaven's sake!" she said, pushing him away. "Really, Mr. Prescott, you must control yourself. I won't be able to stand this sort of thing every minute of the day."

"I told you I planned to make you fall in love with me."

"And you think this is the way? By mauling me at every opportunity?"

Asher stood. He was wearing a robe over his gown and his hair was tousled from sleep. "That's just what your gunslinger called it: mauling." He turned away. "Well, today you won't have to stand my company because your cousin has asked me to drive twenty miles into town to pick up some supplies. You know, Chris, I think the man plans to get all the work he can out of us."

"And what's wrong with that?" she asked, putting on her robe before removing the covers from her body. "We are asking him to support us. The least we can do is help."

"You help in the garden with your outlaw and I get out of the picture. That should suit you just fine."

"He's not mine. I didn't ask him here and I volunteered to help in the garden before I knew he was the gardener. You can't blame me for any of it. Can't we have an ordinary conversation? One minute you're asking me to marry you and the next you're accusing me of carrying on with another man."

Asher didn't answer her but started dressing—behind the wardrobe door. Chris wasn't sure if he was modest or he was saving her delicate sensibilities. She chastised herself for criticizing every move he made. When he was dressed, he left the room.

Downstairs at breakfast, she began to see another Owen. Until now, he'd been the epitome of cordiality, but now he was giving instructions to Chris and Asher with the authority of a general.

"I want the north acre reseeded," Owen was saying. "And I want all two hundred of those bulbs I ordered set by the end of the day. And, Whit, I'll give you a list of what I want from town. You're to take the wagon directly to the saw mill. You can do it all in a day if you don't dawdle. Lionel, eat those eggs. Unity, have you shown the new housemaid what to do? I want the ceilings upstairs washed."

No one else at the table said much. Later, Asher escorted Chris outside. "You don't have to do this. Remember who you are and that we can go home any time you want. I don't want you working as a field hand."

"How kind of you, but I don't mind working at all."

Suddenly, Ash moved away from her. "Diana, even you aren't too stupid to do a little work. Now get over there and act like the woman you aren't."

Chris turned to see Owen approaching with Tynan, both men seemingly unaware of what Asher was saying but she knew that, just as Asher had planned, they'd heard.

Owen said a few more words to Tynan, which she couldn't hear, then gave Ash an appraising look. "Come with me," he said and Asher followed, leaving Chris with Tynan.

"I don't guess you could have volunteered to help with the washing, could you?" Ty said. "Or the horses? It had to be with the garden."

She turned on her heel to glare at him. "If I'd known you were to be in charge of the garden, I would have shoveled coal first. Shall we get started and stop wasting time? I have more to do with my life than spend it listening to you insult me."

"It seems to me that the man you claim as your husband was insulting you worse than I ever could."

"It's part of the charade. Diana Eskridge was a woman who allowed her husband to bully her, so Ash and I are acting out a part."

"You'd better work on it then, because you don't look like the type to take bullying from anybody. Every time he speaks to you in that tone, you look like you're about to set his hair on fire. Here, take this," he said, handing her a box of bulbs. "You know how to plant?"

"You'd think he'd hire more than one gardener to do this. My father's garden isn't half this size and, when it was kept, he had four men taking care of it."

"Ah, but he paid them a salary, they lived on his ranch and he fed them. Hamilton only has to give his poor grateful relatives a roof and food."

"But he seems like such a nice man."

"People aren't what they seem," Ty said with a cold voice.

"Is that supposed to refer to anyone I know?" she asked, setting down the box of bulbs.

"Not unless you claim it. I thought I'd met a good girl who was different, but she wasn't. You're just like all the rest of them. You're excited by the reputation of a man with a gun, and you'll use him however you want, but in the end, when the chips are down, you'll side against him. No more good girls for me. You and Prescott were made for each other."

"I didn't side with anyone else against you. You betrayed me! I trusted you and then at the picnic you shot a man. Do you know how I felt with all those people against me? They were looking at me as if I were a piece of vermin. A man on the street spit at my feet."

Tynan looked at her for a long moment. "Yeah, I know how it feels. I've known all my life. Wait until a man spits in your face and then draws a gun on you."

"Is that what Rory Sayers did?" Chris whispered.

"I twisted his arm to keep him from shooting me and the gun went off."

"But why did the deputy take you to jail if it was all Rory's fault?"

He narrowed his eyes at her. "For the same reason you condemned me without any facts. By reputation. Because I'm not one of the 'good' people like they are—like you are."

Chris took a bulb planter from a tool box by Tynan's feet and began to dig in the soft earth to set the first bulb. "I think I was wrong."

"No you weren't," he said, kneeling beside her. "You were right. People like you and me don't mix. You deserve somebody like Prescott, not a nameless nobody like me."

"I don't think I deserve anyone at all after betraying a friend," she whispered, mostly to herself. "Tynan, do you think you could ever forgive me for not trusting you?"

He looked at her. "No," he said simply. "It may take me a while to learn a lesson, but I do eventually learn it. I think that from now on I'll stay even farther away from girls like you."

He moved away from her, leaving her to do the planting on that side of the plowed field by herself. The sun came out, making her perspire and the soil that was getting on her made her itch, but she didn't notice as she went over the events of the past few weeks. Since Tynan had popped out of the cabinet and held her nude body in his arms, she'd not been the same. She'd changed from a sensible young woman interested only in a story to an Amazon who pursued a man without shame. She'd thrown herself at him in the rain forest; she'd sworn to a woman who trusted her, Red, that she'd not betray him—yet at the first opportunity, that's what she'd done. She was acting like a spoiled little girl: one minute she hated him and the next minute she loved him.

Sitting back on her heels for a moment, she wiped her forehead and looked across at Tynan as he used a scythe to clear some underbrush. His shirt was drenched with sweat and she could see his muscles working under the thin cloth. He looked as if he'd gained some weight in the last few weeks. Against her will, she remembered the raw stripes on his back where he'd been whipped.

She thought of the way the townspeople had turned against her after she'd made one error of trying to help a man who looked as if he were guilty. How people everywhere must have treated a man who was always being accused of wrongdoing! How impossible all the "good" people made it for a man to stop doing wrong.

She turned back to the planting with a vengeance. And she'd been just like them. One time she'd been doing a story on women who worked under the hideous conditions of the sweatshops and she was being very sympathetic when one woman said, "But you can afford to give sympathy because you've never had to be where we are." It hadn't made much of an impression on her at the time, but now she was beginning to understand what the woman meant. It was easy to judge, to say what you'd do in a situation if you weren't faced with that situation.

She had wanted to be Tynan's friend, even his lover, when the only person she had to stand up against was a man who admitted he'd wanted to marry her even before he'd met her. But when she had to face the ridicule of an entire town and risk the reputation of Nola Dallas, she didn't stand up so well. She'd walked away from him at the first sign of trouble.

Chris was sure that she'd never felt so rotten in her life. She had almost earned the trust of a man who didn't give his trust very often and then she'd betrayed him. She was no better than that girl who'd been willing to see Ty hang rather than tell the truth.

And now she'd lost him. He was gone from her as if the few days they'd spent together had never been. The fragile beginnings were broken forever.

Standing, easing her back against her hand, she went to the pump and filled the water bucket. She took a drink from the dipper, shaded her eyes against the sun and looked for Tynan. He was still chopping weeds, clearing the brush away for a new area of garden.

She put the dipper into the bucket and carried it to him. "Thirsty?" she asked.

He turned, smiling at her before he caught himself and the smile disappeared. He didn't speak as he took the dipper from her.

"You look awfully hot. Why don't you sit a while?"

"No thanks, and this is nothing compared to what I've been doing the last few years of my life."

"In prison?"

"Where they put all bad men like me. Move back so I don't hit you."

Chris stepped back and as she did so, she could see

the sweat rolling off his face and dripping into his soaked shirt collar. On impulse, she picked up the bucket of water, cold from the underground well, and threw the contents on the back of his head.

Tynan gasped at the shock of the water, then turned on her in anger.

Chris backed away from him with a little giggle. "I thought you needed cooling off."

"Not from you I don't. I don't need anything from you." He began to advance on her.

Chris put her hands behind her back, a big smile on her face and started moving away from him into the trees. "I didn't mean anything, Ty. Truly I didn't."

"You never mean anything, do you? You didn't mean anything in the forest either, did you, when you nearly drove me crazy?"

"Did I?" she asked innocently. "But last night you didn't seem too upset when you saw me with another man."

"That weakling? I'll worry when I see you with a *man.*" There was a hint of a smile on his lips as he moved toward her, deeper into the shadowy forest.

Chris found herself up against a tree and she made no effort to move as Tynan came nearer her, but she had a look of mock fearfulness.

He caught her about the waist and began to rub his sweaty face against hers. He hadn't shaved that morning and the sharp whiskers were scratching her skin. She squealed for him to stop, tried to get away from him, but he held her tight. Still struggling, she managed to get out from between him and the tree and start running. She took only a few steps before he caught her, pushing her down on the ground and continuing to rub his face about her neck and cheeks.

Chris was squealing with delight when he suddenly stopped.

She looked up at him, smiling, as he got off of her, his face solemn. "Get up," he said.

She held up her hand for him to help her and, reluctantly, he did so. She tried to stand close to him for a moment but he didn't allow that. Silently, she turned her back to him so he could button her dress.

"Stay away from me, Chris," he said. "You're playing with my life and I don't like it."

She turned to face him so that his hands were on her shoulders. "I was wrong to go off and leave you. I should have stayed by you at the picnic. I was wrong and I want you to please forgive me."

He stepped back from her. "It's better that we stay apart. In fact, I think it's better that we call off this entire masquerade. I thought it might be all right since you've done this sort of thing before, but I don't like it. Tomorrow I want to take you back to your father. After I deliver you to him, you can come back if you want. It won't matter to me because you'll no longer be my responsibility, but I can see right now that this won't work. Go back to the house now and get cleaned up and pack. I'll do what has to be done here." With that he turned and went back into the sun to slash at the weeds.

Silently, Chris started walking back to the house.

Chapter Fourteen

As Chris neared the house, she saw Owen getting into a carriage and driving away. Lionel was attacking a young tree with a dull axe, Unity and the luscious Pilar were hanging clothes on the line and, with Asher away for the day, Chris was alone in the house.

She washed and changed her dirty dress and began to think about the fact that tomorrow she'd be going home. She wasn't even going to argue with Tynan about staying at the Hamilton house. Perhaps it wasn't any of her business to try to find out what Owen was doing to his nephew—if he was doing anything at all.

As she struggled with the buttons on her dress, she remembered that she was alone in the house and it occurred to her that now she had the chance to look into Owen's office.

She went up the stairs outside her bedroom and opened three doors before she found Owen's office. It was packed with papers, and there was a big oak filing cabinet in the corner. She had no idea what she was looking for but perhaps she could find it in there, or maybe she could at least find out what Owen knew about the Eskridges.

She had just opened the filing cabinet and seen a fat folder with the name of Diana Eskridge on it when she heard voices on the stairs—and one of them was the voice of Owen Hamilton.

Chris's heart began pounding as she looked for an escape route. There was only one window in the office and it was open. Without even looking outside, she stuck her leg over the casement and climbed out. The door to the office opened just as she pulled her skirt out of view.

She was standing on the smallest of ledges, about the width of a drain pipe, and below her was nothing for three stories.

She flattened her back against the wall of the dormer that contained the window to Owen's study and held on with her hands behind her.

"That trip was particularly foul," a voice Chris didn't recognize, coming from inside the office, was saying. "Are you sure you have all the information? It's him?"

"Without a doubt. When I tell you all the trouble I had getting this, you'll believe me. Samuel Dysan is the name, isn't it?"

Chris leaned toward the window. There was something about the way they were talking that made her want to hear what they were saying.

"What about Lionel?" the stranger asked. "Did you get the little bastard's name on the papers?"

"Wait a minute, let me close this window. There are too many people living in this house for me to keep up with the whereabouts of all of them."

Chris pulled back as he shut the window and locked it. Now she was stuck on the roof, with no way to get back inside.

The men stayed in the room an hour—the longest hour of her life. Behind her, she could hear the muffled voices of Owen and the stranger but she couldn't make out what they were saying. She heard drawers slammed, doors creaking open, then shut again, and all the while she could do nothing but stand there and try to keep her skirt from blowing across the window.

When at last the men left the room, Chris immediately tried to open the window but it was firmly locked.

"Now I've done it," she murmured. Whatever excuse could she give for being outside this window? If Owen was stealing from his nephew, it could be quite dangerous to let him know that she was interested in what he was doing in his office.

With a big sigh, she turned back around, and as she did so, she slipped. She managed to catch herself before she actually fell, but she could feel her hand being scraped. Wincing at the pain, she grabbed for the casement ledge and pulled herself up. She was breathing quite hard by the time she reached her perch again, and she stood there, clutching the wood behind her, and was glad for her safety.

She stood there for quite some time, too fearful to move, when, below her, she began to hear sounds. Within minutes, she saw the top poles of a ladder appear, leaning against the roof line. Holding her breath, she watched to see who was coming to her rescue—or to her trial.

The relief she felt when she saw Tynan was great. "How did you know?" she asked.

He put a finger to his lips to silence her, then

motioned for her to give him her hand. He led her down the roof of the second story, then guided her feet onto the ladder, his arms always surrounding her as he backed down first.

When they were at last on the ground, she clung to him for a moment. "I was so frightened."

"You'll be more frightened if Hamilton finds out you were spying on him," he said, peeling her arms away from him. "Let's get out of here before he sees us."

Chris turned away just in time to see a shadow disappear around the edge of the house. "Ty! Someone was there."

"It's only Lionel. He told me where you were. Come on!"

She ran behind him, down a path she'd not seen before, to a small cottage hidden amid the trees. As Ty hooked the ladder beneath the eaves of the house, she saw blood on the back of his shirt.

"Ty! You're bleeding."

"No, you are," he said, taking her wrist and turning her palm upward, looking at where the skin was scraped away. "Come inside and I'll clean it and I want you to explain what you were doing on that roof."

"Listening," she said as he pulled her inside. The cottage had only one room, half of it kitchen, the other half holding a big double bed. "Is this where you live with Pilar?" she asked quietly.

"Yes," he said as he held her hand over a basin of water and began to clean it.

"Have you known her long?"

"Years."

"And she doesn't ever betray you?"

"I've never found out. We're on the same side. Hold still so I can see this."

"On the same side?" Chris's eyes widened. "You mean she's a lady outlaw?"

"Sure. She can outdraw anybody."

"Oh. You're teasing me, aren't you?"

He looked at her as his head was bowed over her hand. "Climbing out the window was pretty stupid of you. If Hamilton had found you—"

"It was worth it. I heard Owen's visitor asking about Lionel. He said—pardon me, but this is a quote—'Has the little bastard signed the papers yet?' Doesn't that sound as if they're into something dreadful?"

Ty opened a tin box on a shelf by the fireplace and withdrew clean bandages. "No, it sounds like he's met Lionel. The kid *is* a little bastard."

"Then why was he helping you? Ouch!"

"If you'd hold still, I wouldn't hurt you. Lionel and I have an understanding."

"He says he thinks you're a bank robber."

"Now and then. Shrewd kid. Sit down and I'll get you some milk and cookies. I need a drink."

"Did I scare you? Why didn't Lionel give me away and why did he come to you? Who made the cookies?"

"Pilar made the cookies," he said, sitting down across from her at the rough table. "And Lionel has been the soul of helpfulness ever since I cracked a whip around his neck."

Chris took a cookie but put it back on the plate. She realized that her hands were shaking and reached for Tynan's glass of whiskey. In exchange, he took her milk and began eating the cookies.

"We're going home tomorrow," Ty said, not looking at her.

"And leaving Lionel to his own fate, I guess."

"He's not your problem."

"Have you ever heard of Samuel Dysan?"

"No and don't change the subject. Tomorrow we leave."

"What if Asher doesn't agree? That'll be two against one."

"Prescott can stay here for all I care, but tomorrow you and I leave for your father's house."

"Just the two of us?" she asked, running her finger along the whiskey glass.

He took the glass from her and drained it. "It's time for you to go back to the house. You can say you hurt your hand on a sharp rock and couldn't work anymore."

Chris made no effort to move but picked up a cookie. When she was with him, she never wanted to leave. "How is your back?"

"Healing quite well thanks to Pilar's gentle attentions. Chris, go away."

She looked up at him with sad eyes. "I was wrong when I left you alone. I should have gone with you to the jail."

"The world is full of should haves." He stood. "I'm going back to work and I want you to go back to the house and stay out of trouble."

"Maybe I should lock myself inside the bedroom with Asher."

"If you can stand the boredom," he said, slamming his hat on his head and leaving her alone in the cottage.

Reluctantly, Chris left the little cottage and started back to the main house. The sun was gone and the air was beginning to feel like rain.

"It's gonna come a storm," Unity was saying as Chris entered the kitchen. "What'd you do to your hand?"

Chris looked up—and into the dark, pretty eyes of Pilar.

"I cut it," Chris managed to say after a while. No wonder Ty liked her; she was utterly lovely.

"Would you like a cool drink?" Pilar asked in a soft voice. "We've just made an herb tea. It's quite good."

"No," Chris said, wishing the woman wouldn't be nice to her.

"You look a little pale," Unity said. "I told Mr. Owen you shouldn't work outside. You're too little to be able to stand the outdoors."

Chris had no idea what being small had to do with sunshine, but it was the type of comment she'd heard all her life. "Yes, I would like something to drink."

"Pilar made cookies. Have some."

"No, thank you, I already did," Chris said without thinking, then looked at Pilar. There was understanding in her eyes. "On second thought, I think I'll lie down a while. Maybe the loss of blood is making me weak."

Chris left the kitchen and was on her way upstairs when Owen called to her.

"Diana, could you come in here? There's someone I'd like you to meet," Owen called from the parlor.

Chris knew it was the visitor she'd heard earlier and she wanted to meet this man, but as soon as she saw him, she stood still, unable to move. It wasn't that the man was ugly nor was there anything outwardly repulsive about him, but she knew he was a bad person. He was tall, dark, and his face had probably once been quite handsome, but somewhere along the way his nose had been broken and there was a scar that parted one eyebrow. In spite of the slight disfigurements, he was

163

still good-looking—but Chris didn't want to walk inside the same room with him.

"Diana, don't be shy," Owen was saying. "This is a friend of mine, Mr. Beynard Dysan. He's come to stay a while."

"How . . . how do you do?" she managed to whisper, holding out her hand to him, although she very much didn't want him to touch her.

"It's a pleasure to meet you. Owen told me of your father's unfortunate death. I'm sorry."

She backed away from him. "Yes," she murmured. "I cut my hand this morning," she said, showing her bandaged hand, "and I'm feeling a little weak. If you'll excuse me, I must go upstairs." She fled before either of the men could protest.

Upstairs, she stood with her back to the door for a few minutes. Until now she'd not been sure there was anything wrong going on in this house. But after meeting Beynard Dysan, she knew he was involved in something evil.

She almost jumped when she heard the men on the stairs outside her room. Listening, she heard them walking up toward Owen's office. She opened the door a bit.

"I'll be ready to ride in about half an hour," she heard Dysan say. "That way we'll be sure of privacy."

Chris closed the door. They were going to go somewhere to talk and if she wanted to find out what was going on, now was her only chance, because tomorrow Tynan planned to take her home.

She quickly dressed in her riding habit, then tiptoed down the stairs and left the house through the narrow door in the music room. She didn't want anyone to see her. In the stables, she saw that the boy was busy saddling two horses and she slipped inside, chose a sleek black mare, saddled it and managed to get out the side door without encountering anyone.

It was easy to hide in the trees until she saw Owen and Dysan come out and mount, and it wasn't difficult to follow them at a distance. They were traveling slowly, talking, Owen pointing at things now and then.

She followed them for about four miles, across a bridge over a deep stream, down a narrow road, when they turned right onto a path and disappeared. Chris waited several minutes at the crossroad then cautiously went after them. The trees were too dense for her to see very far ahead and her heart began pounding. It would be too easy to ride into them.

With her head bent forward, she listened as intently as she could over the mare's noisy steps. Suddenly, she stopped because close ahead, she heard a loud laugh. Dismounting quickly, she tied her horse and began to move through the underbrush toward the sound of the laughter.

She'd only gone a few feet when she crouched low. Ahead of her, standing on a ridge, were Owen and Beynard Dysan.

"When do I meet Sam?" Beynard was saying.

"Soon now. I don't want any trouble near my place."

Beynard gave Owen a smirk. "So you can save your trouble for your nephew? I never met a more repulsive kid."

Owen smiled. "Isn't he? No one will mind when he meets his fate. See that timberland? This time next year it'll all be mine."

"How do you plan to do it?"

"That cousin of his will. Eskridge has already embezzled, driven a man to suicide, and he beats that little wife of his. It should be easy to prove he'd murder too."

"What about the wife?"

Owen and Beynard exchanged looks. "She's served her purpose. Shall we get on with this? I'd like to get out of here before this storm breaks."

To Chris's utter disbelief, the men turned in unison and started toward her. It was almost as if they knew where she was. Of course that couldn't be but she crouched lower—and the men kept coming.

Then suddenly came the sound of a man whistling and both of them stopped—the men less than a yard from Chris's hiding place.

"Hello!" came Tynan's voice and Chris could have cried in relief. "I guess those horses belong to you, Mr. Hamilton."

"What are you doing here?" Owen snapped.

Chris put her head up enough to see Ty. Over his shoulder was slung a couple of rabbits.

"Unity sent me out for rabbits."

Chris wiped away the first drops of rain that fell on her face.

"And I wanted you in the garden," Owen said.

Chris saw that Dysan, who'd been looking across the valley while Ty and Owen talked, turned to look at Tynan.

"And I expect you back there as soon as possible."

"And withstand Unity's wrath?" Tynan said cheerfully, blinking against the rain that was coming down steadily. "No thanks, I'll stay here and get all three rabbits, just as I was ordered." He paused as lightning lit the valley below them. "You gentlemen are sure gettin' your fine clothes wet," he said in a drawl.

For a moment, Chris held her breath, for the three of them looked for all the world as if they were going to shoot each other. Why? she wondered.

Dysan backed down first. "Let's go," he said, and, quietly, Owen followed him.

Chris crouched low in the bushes, trying to keep the rain out of her face and to keep Tynan from finding her.

There was no hiding to be done. Two minutes after the men left, he grabbed her arm and hauled her up before him. "I ought to take you over my knees. Do you know you could have been killed?"

Water was running off his hat onto her face. "How did you know where I was?"

"Pilar saw you going off and told me." He had a nasty grip on her upper arm. "Now come with me."

"But my horse, it's—"

"You think they just left it?" He started down the hill the opposite way she'd come, pulling her behind him.

She kept her head down against the pelting rain, tripping along behind him. "Where are we going?"

"Home! To your father. You've taken twenty years off my life already and I don't have many more left."

"But what about Asher? They're going to kill Lionel and blame it on Asher."

"That's his worry. You're mine." He stopped at a saddled horse and helped her up, then mounted behind her.

"Can we get back this way?"

"We can get to your father's this way."

"Tynan," she said, turning in the saddle and putting her arms around his chest. "We can't leave Asher there. We have to go back and warn him. Please." She looked up at him with pleading eyes.

He studied her for a moment. "All right, damn it. We'll warn him but then you go."

"Yes, Tynan," she said, still holding onto him as they rode. His muscles under her cheek completely blotted out the thrashing of the rain and the slash of the lightning.

He was traveling as fast as the laden horse would go when its front hooves suddenly came off the ground and Ty fought to control the horse and hold Chris in the saddle.

"Damn!" he said in a way that made Chris twist around to look. Lightning had struck the bridge, and the swollen stream was far too violent to cross.

"We'll have to go back the other way," Chris said, looking up at him.

"There is no bridge on the other side."

He was holding the reins of the horse tightly, both of them drenched with rain, lightning all around them—yet Tynan made no effort to move.

"Hadn't we better go?" Chris asked, wiping water out of her eyes. "This storm is getting worse."

"There's nowhere to go," Tynan said. "We're cut off from the main road and there's only virgin forest north of us."

"Ty! It's getting dark. We can't stay here all night. Is there any shelter nearby? The water will recede after the storm's over."

Ty didn't answer, just sat there looking at the raging, deep stream.

"Tynan!" Chris yelled up at him. "Let's go back into the trees. Maybe we can find a rock overhanging or something."

"There's a logger's cabin near here."

"Then let's go."

The horse was dancing about nervously and the rain was coming down harder, but Ty didn't move.

"What is *wrong* with you?" she shouted.

"You are what's wrong with me," he yelled back at her, then turned the horse and started north.

Chapter Fifteen

The cabin had originally been for a surveying crew that had worked in the area and, since then, it had been maintained by someone, probably Owen since it was on his land—or Lionel's as Chris insisted. It was one tiny room, completely bare except for a fireplace and a stack of wood. There was no furniture. Shortly after arriving, Ty had the horse stabled in a lean-to in the back and a fire going in the crude stone fireplace and the rabbits skinned, spitted and roasting. There was an abundant supply of dry firewood along one wall. Ty had removed the saddle and the bedroll and flung it into the cabin for Chris to take care of while he saw to the horse.

She removed the blanket from the bedroll and was pleased to see that it was relatively dry. Shaking it out, shivering against the wetness of her clothes, she began to be aware of just why Tynan had been so reluctant to stay in the cabin. With the rain coming down hard outside, the fire crackling warm inside, and with the prospect of removing her clothing and putting on the single, loose blanket, she had an idea of what was going to happen.

With a whoosh of a sigh, she sat down on the saddle, the blanket clutched against her. What would her mother say if she knew what her only child was contemplating? Would she be horrified? Would Judith Montgomery have liked Tynan, this one-name gunfighter who didn't even know what the word "home" meant?

Chris turned the rabbits over the fire and tried to think as calmly and rationally as possible. She'd never even considered the idea of seducing a man before. Sometimes she thought it was ironic that all a girl's life she fought off men, starting when she was a child with her mother warning her against taking candy from strangers, and saying no until the very wedding day. Women were trained to say no, so how did she say yes now? Even more important, how did she say yes to a question that was never going to be asked of her?

She stood for a moment and gazed into the fire. Maybe Tynan didn't want her and that was why he was able to resist all her advances. Maybe the beautiful Pilar was enough for him.

She shivered once against her wet clothes and began to peel them off, still staring into the fire and wondering what she was going to do—and if she should do it—when Tynan came back into the room.

Instinctively, she pulled the blanket up to cover her nude body.

Ty, after one quick glance, looked away from her to hang the bridle on a nail by the door, then removed his hat to pour the water out of the brim. "It looks like it'll keep up all night. Are the rabbits ready?"

Chris wrapped the blanket around her and went to

the fireplace to test the meat. "I think so but I'm not sure."

She looked up to see Tynan staring at her and she realized that the blanket she wore was gaping open at both top and bottom. Ducking her head so he couldn't see her smile, she looked back at the rabbits. At least she had some effect on him, if only to make him look.

"I'll test them," Ty said and that buttermilk voice of his was even richer.

She looked up at him through her lashes.

"Get back," he said with force. "Go stand by the wall. No, not on this side, on the far side. Now stay there while I look."

"Tynan," she said, exasperated, "you act as if I have a contagious disease. I can assure you that I'm quite clean and free from all illness."

"Hmph!" he grunted, tearing off a succulent, hot rabbit leg. His clothes were wet and they clung to his muscular body, outlining every hill and valley of his back. She could see where the whip marks had left some scars. "You are worse than disease, lady, you are poison."

"Was prison that bad?" she asked softly.

"Unfortunately, the memory is fading. Here, take this," he said as he removed the rabbits from the skewers. "On second thought, I'll put it here and you can come and get it."

"For heaven's sake, Tynan! I'm not going to harm you. You act as if I were holding a rifle on you."

He looked her up and down for a brief second. "I'd rather deal with twenty rifles. Eat that and then lay down over there and go to sleep. We'll leave very early in the morning so I can get you back as soon as possible. Then, as soon as you get Prescott, we'll leave again. I don't want you near Hamilton."

Chris stretched out on the hard plank floor, chewing on the meat while trying to get comfortable, but not succeeding. The blanket was small and her legs remained uncovered from the knee down. She tried to put them under her but had no success. If she covered her legs, her shoulders were exposed to the cold, and if she covered her shoulders, her legs got cold.

"Will you hold still!" Tynan suddenly shouted.

She looked up at him in surprise. He was sitting on the saddle, chewing on a piece of rabbit and looking into the fire. "Well, Tynan, I'm just trying to get comfortable and not freeze to death."

"It was your idea to come to this cabin so make the best of it and stop complaining—and go to sleep."

"How am I supposed to sleep when I'm freezing to death? And why are you still wearing your wet clothes?" She sat up. "Look at your skin! It's turning blue with cold. Is there anything that we can use for a coffee pot? I'll make you something to warm you up."

He didn't bother to answer her or even acknowledge her presence, but just sat there glaring into the fire and chewing.

Chris moved to sit in front of him, and when he continued to look over her head, she took his hands in hers. "Is something wrong? Does this cabin remind you of something bad that happened to you? Maybe one of the outlaw gangs you've ridden with? Or the man who was your friend who was hanged?"

Ty looked down at her with an expression that asked if she'd completely lost her mind.

His hands were as cold as a piece of metal left in

snow. She began to rub them between her own, blowing on them, trying to warm him.

"Chris," he said in a husky whisper. "I don't think I can take too much more. Please go over there and leave me alone."

"You'll never get warm if you sit there in your wet clothes. You'd better take them off." She looked up at him and she knew that what she felt for him was in her eyes, yet he didn't seem to react at all. He just sat there looking at her, and if there was anything in his eyes, it was sadness.

She was about to say something else when suddenly he reacted. He grabbed her in his arms and pulled her up to put his lips on hers. If Tynan was good with buttons, he was even better with blankets. Before his face was touching hers, the blanket was off, flung somewhere across the room. Chris gasped when Ty's cold clothes touched her warm, bare skin, but her arms went around his neck and pulled him closer.

"Tynan," she whispered as he began to hungrily kiss her neck, his hands running up and down her back, his fingers curving over her buttocks.

He took her head in his hands and looked at her. "Chris," he murmured, "I've never wanted anything as badly as I want you at this moment. This is your last chance to say no because from now on I won't be able to help myself."

Their noses were touching so she turned slightly so she could give him a quick kiss. "Yes," she said joyously. "Yes and yes and yes." She punctuated each word with a kiss.

He began to smile then, a warm, seductive smile that

made Chris's skin tingle. So, she thought, this was the face of Tynan the lover.

With a broader grin, he ruffled her damp hair, leaned forward and began to use his teeth to nibble at her bottom lip. Chris was taken by surprise. She knew the basics of how humans mate, but this had nothing to do with what she'd heard.

"Come here, you tempting little imp," he said, pulling her up higher. She was between his legs, his wet trousers pressed against her ribs, holding her in place while he kissed and nibbled on her ears, her neck, across her shoulder, down her arm.

Chris's neck began to weaken. "Oh, my, but I do like that," she murmured, eyes closed. Tynan's hands began to rub on her body, warming her. He seemed to be able to reach all of her, from the soles of her feet, up her calves, lingering on her buttocks and then his fingertips massaging up her spine.

After a moment, she no longer felt his cold clothes, felt, instead, only his hot hands on her skin, felt only his lips moving over her body—a body which had never known a man's lips before.

He was as smooth at moving her about as he was at unbuttoning her dresses. She had no idea when he changed her to a prone position—but she was aware when his lips first touched her breasts. Her eyes flew open, startled, and she looked at him.

The dark room with only the firelight from behind Tynan made him better-looking than usual and Chris suddenly thought that perhaps Apollo, the god of the sun, was making love to her. She put her hand in his dark hair, pulling his head up to hers so she could kiss him. "I love you, Tynan," she said, putting her arms around him and kissing him. She wasn't even surprised to find that his shirt was gone. No doubt he was as skillful at removing his own clothing as he was with women's.

His hands kept moving up and down her body in a sensual, caressing way, roaming over her stomach, down her thighs, up to her breasts. He felt so good to her, his big, wide shoulders, the way his muscles moved under her hands as he moved, the way his hips were gently undulating against the side of her hips.

Chris's heart was rising in her throat, pounding, as his hands began to caress the soft inner flesh of her thigh, kneading on the skin, touching soft, quiescent muscle. Of her own accord, her legs began to open.

"Ty," she whispered. "My lovely Tynan."

He didn't say a word, but began to move his lips downward as Chris arched her neck back in anticipation of what was to come. His hot, wet mouth closed on her breast, causing a groan to escape her lips. He continued to make love to her breast as his hands roamed over her legs.

When he moved on top of her, she clutched him to her, wrapping her legs about him instinctively. Gently, he disengaged her legs and moved them so they were bent, knees up, by his side.

When he entered her, Chris gasped, opening her eyes to look at him. He lay still on top of her, smiling at her, seeming to be at ease, but there were great drops of sweat on his forehead.

She had expected pain but there was none, only surprise at how lovemaking actually felt. Blinking a few times, she moved her hips slightly upward, toward his, and she saw Ty's eyes close, his head lean back and he entered her fully.

Chris thought her heart was going to leap from her breast as he began to move inside her, so gently, so slowly at first—and the sensation was absolutely heavenly. Slowly, deeply, rhythmically, he moved, touching her in a way that seemed to consume her, to make her grow bigger, to expand until she felt as if she might explode.

"Tynan?" she said and there was some fear in her voice because she didn't know what was about to happen.

He caught her legs, moved them back around his waist then lifted her hips upward so that half of her body weight was supported by his hips. He began to move more quickly and, if possible, more deeply. Chris put her hands up to touch the heavy muscles of his chest, clutching at him, digging her fingers into the thick muscles, wanting to claw him. Her head began to turn back and forth and there were little sounds coming from her.

Tynan's movements quickened until Chris thought she might explode.

Afterward, she lay still, clinging to him, not wanting to let him go.

"You can, can't you?" she said at last.

With a chuckle, Ty moved off of her, but held her close, one arm under her head, one thigh across hers.

"That was lovely," she said, stretching. "Did I do all right? You weren't disappointed?"

"No," he murmured.

"You aren't falling asleep, are you?"

"Not if you keep jabbering. Chris, we have to get up early tomorrow, this has been one hell of a day, what with you climbing across roofs, so I'd like to get some sleep."

"Sleep?" She moved so she could look at him. "But I'm starving and we have so much to discuss. I want to know how you found out about my following Owen and when we'll be married and what we'll do about Lionel and Pilar has to go and—"

"Wait a minute!" His eyes flew open. "Married? Who said anything about marriage?"

"But I thought . . . I mean, after what we did . . ."

He rolled away from her, pulling on his pants.

She watched, the blanket clutched to her, as he built up the fire then lifted the cooked rabbits and began to reheat them. At long last, he handed her a big chunk of meat before he went to stand by the door.

"I never wanted this to happen," he said, turning to look at her. "I meant to keep my hands off of you, just like your father demanded."

"If you're worried about the pardon," she said, mouth full, "I'll see that you get it. My father won't send you back to jail."

"Don't you have sense enough to understand that it's deeper than that?" he asked angrily. "Somebody like me can't marry somebody like you, and besides, I don't *want* to get married."

Chris paused in eating. "Oh, Tynan, you have such a low opinion of yourself."

"So do you when the chips are down."

Chris tried to keep the meat from choking in her throat. "I made a mistake and I apologize. It won't happen again. Especially if you're my husband."

"Well, I'm not going to be!" he said, moving away from the door. "If I *married* every woman I've—"

"Never mind, thank you!" she said quickly. "But, Tynan, I love you."

"You think you're in love with what you see. Chris,

I'm trying to be kind to you. What happened tonight was just what always happens when a man and a woman spend a night in a cabin alone. It was inevitable."

Chris threw the bone in the fire, then stood, wrapping the blanket around her. "Maybe in your world it's inevitable, but not in mine. When I was investigating the Mexican government, I spent three nights alone with a Mexican guard and he never touched me."

"How many guns were you holding on him?"

"One very small pistol," she said with a smile. "Tynan, I—"

"There's no more to be said. I want you to lay down and sleep. It's best if we forget what happened here tonight."

"Forget, but—"

"What do you want from me? Do you want me to tell you the *truth*? The *truth* is that all you are to me is one hot little morsel and I finally took a bite. You're no more or less to me except a way to get a pardon from prison. You're more trouble than a corral full of sheriffs and half the time you're not even as much fun, what with your do-gooder attitude of wanting to save the world. All I want is to turn you over to your father, get my pardon—if he'll give it to me after violating his pure daughter—and get the hell away from you and your kind. Now, have I made myself clear?"

Chris straightened her spine. "Perfectly," she said through a throat that was swelling shut. "And you'll get your pardon. I'll see to that."

She didn't want him to see how horrible she was feeling. Slowly, she turned her back to him, dropped the blanket and began to dress in her damp under clothing.

"What are you doing?"

"Nothing that will interfere with your pardon."

"Chris, wait . . ."

She didn't look at him. "You've had your say, and, if you don't mind, I'd rather not hear anymore. You may have your blanket back. I wouldn't want to cause you more inconvenience. I shall stay here in this corner until morning."

She didn't look at him again as she sat down with her back to the wall.

Chapter Sixteen

Morning came much too soon. Chris had slept very little and her head and eyes ached. Twice Tynan tried to talk to her but she turned away. The rain had stopped and, without a word between them, they left the cabin. Tynan put out his hand to help her mount but she moved away from him and mounted by herself.

They had to ride quite far to find a fordable place in the stream, and all the while, Chris did her best to keep from touching Tynan, and she never once spoke to him.

When they finally reached the Hamilton house, she was never so glad to see anything in her life.

"We're going to leave in one hour," Tynan said but she refused to look at him. He caught her arm as she started to walk away. "Did you hear me? I'm taking you out of this place and back to your father where you belong."

Chris jerked away from him. "I've heard *every* word that you've had to say," she said as she turned away and started back to the house. She hesitated for a moment on the outskirts of the garden, wondering what her reception would be, if Owen knew where she was or if anyone had been looking for her. Idly, she picked a tall daisy, twirled it in her hands before putting her chin back and moving forward. As she entered the garden at the back of the house, she saw Owen, and Asher with his back to her.

Owen stopped talking, his eyes widened and the next minute, Asher turned, saw her, and was running toward her with his arms outstretched. He caught her in an exuberant hug, lifting her off the ground, twirling her about.

"Chris," he said with his face buried in her neck. "I was worried to death. Are you all right? You aren't hurt?"

She hugged him back with enthusiasm. It was so very, very good to feel wanted. "Yes," she managed to whisper because her throat was overcome with tears.

But the next moment her tears disappeared because a shot rang out. She could feel the hot rush of the bullet as it went tearing past the back of Ash's head. Chris looked down at the suddenly headless flower in her hand then at Tynan standing a few feet away, a smoking gun in his hand. He'd shot the flower, which she'd held as she'd hugged Asher, away.

Unity came running from the house. "What's goin' on? I heard a shot."

Tynan was looking at Chris and she was glaring back at him in return, her arms still around Ash.

"Just doin' some weedin', ma'am," he drawled before turning away.

"What was that all about?" Asher asked.

Chris threw the headless flower down on the ground

as if it were poison. "Nothing. Absolutely nothing." She looked up as Owen came toward them.

"Diana, we were very worried about you. No one knew where you were. We've been out all night looking for you."

For the first time, she looked at the two men, saw the way they were dirty and tired-looking, with unshaved cheeks.

"I saddled my own horse when I left," she mumbled. "We found shelter from the rain. Could I see you for a moment?" she asked, turning to the man who was playing her husband.

"Of course, dear, you must be very tired." Like a concerned husband, Ash escorted her into the house and up the stairs to the room they shared.

"All right," he said as soon as they were alone, "I want to know where you've been and what was going on outside. Has that man done anything to you?"

"Not anymore than I've asked for. Turn your head; I want to change out of this. I followed Owen and that dreadful man, Beynard Dysan, out into the forest."

"What makes him dreadful? He was looking for you as hard as any of us were."

"Keep looking out the window, if you don't mind. I don't know what it was that made me dislike him in the first place, but after what I heard, I know I was right. He and Owen are planning to murder Lionel and blame it on you."

"Me? But what do I have to do with the brat?"

"Not you, but Whitman Eskridge, the one who embezzled and beats his wife and—"

"Beats his wife?" Ash said with a smile in his voice. "I didn't know about that."

"Well, I hope you never find out," she said quickly.

"But that's where I was: hiding in the bushes and listening to Owen talk to that man."

"You rode up there and they never saw or heard you?"

Chris thought about the few moments before Tynan had appeared, then it had seemed that the men had known of her whereabouts and were coming after her. But of course that had been her imagination. "The storm was just beginning and they didn't hear me over the rain and thunder. The only problem now is that that . . . man is insisting that we leave here now. In fact, he wanted us to leave directly from the forest and not even come back here to warn you."

Asher didn't say anything.

"Well?" Chris said. "You see that we can't leave now, don't you? We have to protect Lionel." She was dressed and she went to stand before him.

Ash looked down at her. "How did Tynan find you?"

"I don't know. Followed me, I guess."

Asher put both his hands on her arms. "Chris, I think Ty's right. You should be on your way back to your father's right now. If you hadn't come back, I would have looked for you for another couple of days, then I'd have left and gone back to your father's, too. Then everyone would have been safe. It wasn't very smart of you to come back here knowing that there might be a murderer."

She moved away from him. "But what about Lionel? Doesn't anyone care that he might lose his life?"

"All we have to do is alert the local sheriff. If he questions Hamilton, that'll put Owen on his guard."

"So he'll kill Lionel in a very, very secretive way. I'm sure it'll look like an accident and Owen will be no where in the vicinity."

"That's not my concern. My concern is you. I think we should get out of here as soon as possible. Today." He moved toward the wardrobe and withdrew her carpet bag. "I want you to pack right now. I'll tell Owen that the dangers of this place are too great for a lady like you and that I've decided to take you back East where you belong."

"I won't go," she said, glaring up at him.

"Then I shall tell him who you really are. I don't think we'll be welcome after that. Get packed, rest, and I'll be back in an hour or so. I want to talk to Tynan first."

"Don't talk to him!" Chris said angrily. "He wants to get rid of me as soon as he can."

Asher paused at the door. "On the trail back, I want you to tell me what went on when the two of you were gone all night. But now, to discourage you from trying to do something brave and stupid, I'm going to lock this door. I'll see you in an hour."

Before Chris could say another word, he was out the door and she heard the key turn in the lock. For a moment, she leaned against the door and cursed all men everywhere, but then she looked at the soft bed, spread with clean, fragrant sheets, and she walked toward it as if she were in a trance. She was asleep almost before she landed.

The sunlight was coming into the room and Chris was deeply asleep when she felt the hand on her mouth. Her eyes flew open in alarm—only to see a man with a black cloth hood over his face.

"Be quiet, missy, and you won't get hurt. You're gonna take a little ride with us."

She didn't recognize the voice nor the shape of the body. She tried to struggle but the man held her easily as he tied a tight gag about her mouth and then tied her hands. Even when she tried to kick him, he clamped down on her ankles with big, hamlike hands.

He tied her with what seemed to be yards of fine, flexible rope that cut into her when she tried to make any movement, tied her as if she were a corpse bound for burial at sea. When he was finished, little more than Chris's eyes were visible, even her hair, loose down her back, was fastened to her body.

He easily lifted her body and slung it over one wide shoulder and carried her toward the window. A ladder stood ready and, as if she were a rolled-up carpet, he carried her to the ground.

Chris tried to turn her head to see if there was anyone about, but her bindings made movement impossible. A horse awaited him in the trees and he tossed her across the saddle and mounted behind her, then took off quietly so no one could hear him. Chris thought that everywhere she went she was seen by someone, but now that she needed help, no one was near.

She didn't think any more because her captor had speeded their progress and the saddle was pounding into her soft stomach. For the next few hours, she did nothing but try to keep from being sick.

It was nearly nightfall when she became aware that there was another rider beside them. She didn't know when he'd joined them but, when at last the horse she was on came to a stop, she heard the man who'd taken her speak.

"She give you any trouble?"

"No. Yours?"

"Not in the least. Untie her. They'll not last long like this."

186

The man pulled Chris from the horse and put her on the ground. Out of the corner of her eye, she could see another bundle, completely immobile like she was, being removed from another horse. The other man put the semi-corpse next to her but Chris couldn't turn her head to see who it was. It was only when the man began to unwind her and he freed her head so that she could see, that she looked—and gasped.

Pilar lay beside her and looked as surprised to see Chris.

The man removed her gag. "What are you doing here?" she managed to gasp. "What is this?"

"Cut the noise," the big man said. The other captor was tall and thin. "We don't want to hear you. You want some water or not?"

Greedily, Chris's shaky hands took the dirty tin mug the man offered.

"Who are you?" she asked the man. "What do you want?"

"You want the ropes on you again?"

Chris started to reply but she felt Pilar's hand on her arm. Looking at the dark woman, she saw Pilar shake her head slightly. Chris turned away but she said nothing more. Minutes later, the big man hauled Chris to her feet and tossed her into the saddle.

"I don't like talkative women," he said into her ear. "You keep your mouth shut and we'll get along fine. You open it and I'll have to shut it. You understand?"

She saw him throw the hood on the ground but she didn't twist around to look at him; she was too busy trying to keep her seat on the horse and to avoid the man's hands that were beginning to creep over her body.

* * *

"Chris and I are leaving in less than an hour," Tynan said to Asher, his mouth in a straight line, his eyes angry.

"Wait a minute, I want to talk to you."

"I don't have time," Tynan said, starting to walk away. "You can come with us or not, your choice."

Asher caught his arm. "I want to know what happened last night. Where were you two all night? And what do you mean by shooting so close to my head? I ought to—"

"What, Prescott? You ought to what?"

Asher took a step backward. "Look, I'm in this as much as you are. Mathison hired you to take me to Chris, and you were to help me win her for my wife. So far all you've done is keep her to yourself. And now you spend the night with her doing only God knows what."

"That's right, only God knows because I'm sure as hell not going to tell you. Now I'll tell you again: Chris and I are leaving in one hour and you can go or stay, it's up to you."

"I'll be there," Asher said, "don't you worry about that."

With anger on his face, Asher made his way back up the stairs to the room he shared with Chris. Damn! but that man could be highhanded. He was a good man to have on a trail but there were times when he overstepped himself.

He tried to regain his composure before he went to Chris. He'd hated locking her inside, but he knew it was the only way he could keep her from doing something stupid.

Very quietly, he unlocked the door to the bedroom. She'd damn well *better* marry him after all she'd put him through—and all he'd done in an attempt to please her. Right away, he saw that she wasn't there. His first thought was that she'd climbed out the window, but one glance out there, at the impossibly small ledge, showed him that she couldn't have gone out that way.

He didn't even think about his argument or his anger with Tynan, but he ran down the stairs, out through the garden and to the little cottage where Tynan was staying. The dark man was removing tools from a shed at the back of the cottage.

"She's gone. I was afraid she'd do something stupid so I locked her in the room, but she got out. She was really worried about that kid."

Even as Asher was talking, Tynan was pushing past him and heading for the house, stopping only long enough to strap on his gun. He took the stairs two at a time.

"I wish she wouldn't do things like this," Asher was saying. "It's bad enough that she spends the entire night with a—" He broke off as he realized what he was saying. Tynan was now examining the window ledge. "Do you see anything? How could she have gone out there?"

"Believe me, she could have. There's been a ladder here recently, the paint's scraped." He walked back toward the bed, looking at the covers thoughtfully. The sheets were torn off the bed, the spread was on the floor. "Where's Hamilton?"

"I'm not sure. I think he's upstairs. Do you think he's seen Chris? I would imagine that she's the last person he'd want to see." He was following Ty out the door. "Did she tell you what she overheard, that Hamilton was going to kill his nephew? Not that I believed her, I mean, I just came along on this so I could pretend to be her husband. I think a man should take advantage of what he can."

Tynan stopped on the staircase. "If you keep flapping your gums, I'm going to apply some force to that spot." He turned on his heel and started up again.

Owen Hamilton was sitting in his office looking over papers on his desk. Tynan shut the door behind him, locked it, then very calmly walked to the window and tossed the key to the ground below.

Asher plastered his back to the door and held his breath but Owen just looked up with eyebrows raised. "To what do I owe this little charade? Have the aphids been too much for you?"

"Where is she?" Tynan asked in a low, husky voice.

"I have no idea who you mean," Owen answered, a study in unconcern as he shuffled the papers on his desk. "If you think that wife of yours and I—"

He didn't finish the sentence because Ty grabbed him by the collar and pulled him up across the desk. "I want to know where she is and I don't want to play games. Either you tell me right now or you start losing parts of your body, bit by slow bit."

"I have no idea what you're talking about."

"Chris!" Asher said. "I mean, Diana. Where is she? She isn't in her room where I left her."

"Who's Chris?" Owen asked.

Tynan slapped the man across the face. "I don't know how much you know but I suspect it's a great deal. I've already turned that extra set of books of yours over to an accountant friend of mine. I think he'll find out how much you've stolen from that nephew of yours."

"Books, what books?"

Tynan hit him again, this time making the corner of

his mouth bleed. "I'm tired of your lies. I didn't much care what you did within your own family but that little girl is my responsibility and I want to know where she is."

"Who is she? Diana Eskridge was killed."

Ty's grip on his throat tightened. "By you, no doubt, but I'll leave that up to the law. Where is Chris?"

When Hamilton didn't answer, Ty struck him again, then drew his gun and held it to the man's head. "What do you want to lose first? A hand or a foot? I think I can keep you from bleeding to death long enough for you to answer me. Now, one last time, where is she?"

"Dysan took her."

Tynan was obviously surprised by this, so much so that his grip on Hamilton lessened. "What does Dysan want with her?"

"I don't know. He came here because of a cousin of his"—Owen's eyes shifted to one side—"and he decided he wanted the woman pretending to be Diana." He looked back at Tynan. "He had your wife taken too."

"Pilar?" Ty asked. "Who is this man?"

Ty's grip had relaxed so much that Owen was able to pull away and begin rubbing his bruised throat while applying a handkerchief to his bleeding mouth. "He's somebody you don't want to deal with. I don't know much about him. He's very mysterious about where he lives, who he is or anything else about himself. He comes here once a year and buys lumber and horses from me, then disappears. I've never dared ask him much about himself."

"Yet he took Chris," Asher said. "Do you think he plans to hold her for ransom?"

"Ransom?" Hamilton exploded. "Who *is* she?"

"Del Mathison's daughter," Tynan said under his breath.

"Oh Lord," Owen gasped and sat down heavily in the chair. "I thought she was a two-bit actress trying to get what she could." He looked at Ty. "How did you find my other books?"

Tynan didn't bother answering him. "I want to know all there is to tell about Dysan. I want to know where to find him."

"I told you that I know nothing. He just appears and disappears. He said he wanted the two women and it was all right with me. All of you were trying to play me for a fool anyway, following me, searching my office, pretending to be related to me. What did I care what he did to the women? If he wanted them, it was fine with me. I had no idea she was Mathison's daughter. If that man finds out . . ." He trailed off.

"Open the cash box," Ty said. "We're going after them and we'll need capital."

"I don't intend to be part of a robbery," Asher said.

"No one asked you to be. Hamilton, I wouldn't try my patience if I were you. Get the cash."

Owen hurried to obey him, unlocking a small safe behind a picture behind the desk. "You'll never be able to find him. You aren't in Dysan's league. He chews cheap outlaws like you up for breakfast."

Ty took the thick stack of cash. "Then he'll get the worst case of indigestion he's ever had. Now, take off your belt."

Tynan took the handkerchief from the desk and tied it around Hamilton's mouth, then wrapped the belt about his hands, using the holed end to suspend him from a hook he drove into the ceiling. "That should keep you for a few hours. The accountant will report to the attorneys handling Lionel's affairs. I have a feeling that the books you show to them aren't the same ones that I found. And, too, there's the small matter of the murder of the Eskridges."

Owen struggled against the leather that was holding him, his feet barely touching the floor.

"I'm also having Unity take the boy down to Mathison's until this is cleared up. I thought I was going with her but it doesn't look like I will be. I sure do hope that somebody comes along soon to let you out of there. You could be in real pain in a couple of hours if they don't."

Asher stepped away from the door as Tynan started toward it and, to the blond man's surprise, Tynan took a key from his pocket and unlocked the door, locking it again when they were on the other side.

"But I thought that—"

"Don't always believe what you see or hear," Ty said as he went down the stairs and into the kitchen.

Unity, her face white, her eyes filled with fear, was sitting in the kitchen, Lionel standing beside her.

"I don't want to go," Lionel said. "This is my place and I plan to stay here. You cannot make me leave."

Ty didn't say a word but took the boy about the waist and carried him outside to where a wagon and two horses waited. "You'll go and, what's more, you'll help Unity. Prescott will go with you and see that you're safe on the journey. I'm sorry but I can't go with you."

Asher touched Ty's arm. "I want to go with you."

"Absolutely not. I don't need someone fighting me and, besides," he said with contempt, "I need someone who knows which end of a gun to point."

"May I?" Asher said, nodding toward Ty's gun.

Ty handed it to him.

193

Asher took the weapon and, in the flash of an eye, turned and removed a thin tree branch by half inches, using all the bullets in Ty's gun. He handed the firearm back to Tynan. "There are other reasons I was hired by Mathison to go after his daughter. I've handled every gun made today. I can shoot tail feathers off sparrows with a rifle. I may not have the experience you have but I *do* know how to shoot."

Tynan very calmly reloaded his gun then looked up at Unity. Lionel was sitting on the wagon seat with his mouth hanging open. "Prescott is going with me. Is there anyone else who can travel with you?"

"I . . . I don't know who I can trust anymore," she said, on the verge of tears. "But my brother lives about ten miles from here. Maybe he can—" She stopped as Ty took a wad of bills from his pocket.

"Hire him. When you get to Mathison, tell him all of it. He may want to send someone back here but leave it up to him. Tell him I've gone after his daughter and if I don't return with her it'll be because I'm dead—nothing else will stop me. And tell him to worry about her, to worry plenty." He looked at Lionel. "And if I so much as hear a word of complaint about you, you'll answer to me. When you get to Mathison's you can act up all you want. Mathison will take care of you. Now, get out of here." He slapped a horse on the rump and they were gone.

Ty turned and looked at Asher, shaking his head for a moment. "I hope I haven't made a mistake. If you have a gun, go get it. I'll meet you by the stables with two of Hamilton's best horses."

Chapter Seventeen

For three days, the men dragged Chris and Pilar across the country. They were fed little, given no privacy, and allowed no rest. At night the men tied the women's hands, raised them above their heads and fastened the ropes around trees, making it impossible to sleep. Nor were the women allowed to talk to each other. Each morning, they continued to head northeast, the women still bound and now riding together on a horse one of the men had suddenly appeared with—Chris wondered if he'd stolen it.

In spite of her weariness, she tried to keep the direction they were traveling in her head. But on the second day, the men blindfolded her, leaving Pilar to watch the direction, seeing when the horse was about to step into a hole so she could hold Chris into the saddle. Then they removed Chris's blindfold and covered Pilar's eyes.

Although the women never talked to each other, they began to depend upon one another for protection.

At first Chris was very hostile to Pilar, not wanting her help, resenting her touch, resenting her very presence.

Pilar seemed to understand and left Chris alone—until once Chris nearly fell off the horse and had to grab the other woman to keep steady.

"We'll fare better if we're not enemies," Pilar whispered and was struck across the face by one of the men for daring to speak.

After that, Chris's hostility began to leave her. What did she have to be angry about anyway? Tynan was the only common bond she had with this woman and he'd made it abundantly clear that he wanted nothing to do with Chris. If Tynan wanted Pilar, then he was free to choose.

It was late on the third night when the men finally stopped the horses and pulled the two exhausted women to the ground, grabbing their wrists and leading them inside the doorway of a dark house that Chris couldn't see. The men pulled them upstairs and when Pilar's arm knocked against the bannister, they just jerked her harder.

"We can walk!" Chris said, putting out her hand to steady Pilar.

The man holding her didn't say a word, just shoved her up three flights of stairs to the fourth floor. Pilar's captor grabbed a ring of keys off the wall, opened a door that looked to be constructed of several inches of solid oak and pushed the two women inside.

There wasn't any light in the room, but Chris's eyes adjusted to the darkness fairly soon after she heard the heavy door slam behind them. She began to make out the outlines of a large, soft bed in the middle of the floor.

With a gasp of disbelief and tears in her eyes, she stumbled forward, Pilar close behind her, and fell onto the bed. She was asleep instantly.

The sun was already low in the sky when Chris woke the next day, showing that it was afternoon. For a moment, she lay there, looking out one of the tiny windows, flexing each muscle, trying to ascertain what was sore and what seemed to be damaged beyond repair. Holding her arms up, she saw that they were scratched, some of the wounds scabbing, some covered with dried blood, and there were several fierce mosquito bites on them as well.

She moved her head and looked at Pilar who was still sleeping, on her stomach, and Chris wondered if she looked as bad. Pilar was dirty, there were deep dark circles beneath her eyes, and what could be seen of her body protruding from her filthy clothes was disgustingly scratched and raw-looking.

Pilar opened one eye. "Go away," she muttered and turned over.

Chris lay still, waited and, a moment later, Pilar turned to face her again.

"It can't be true," she said. "I thought it was all a terrible dream." Pilar tried to raise herself on her arms but groaned at the pain and collapsed back on the bed. "Where are we? More important, *why* are we wherever we are? And do you think there's a chamber pot around here?"

Chris sat up on her arms, then moved her head in a circle, trying to relieve the cramped muscles. "There's a screen over there, maybe it's behind that."

"I guess this is something I have to do for myself," she said, moving slowly to get out of bed.

Chris also got out, taking moments to steady herself enough to stand up. "I don't think I'll ever be the same."

It was a round room, with three windows along the wall across from the bed, a door to the right, a screen to the left and no other furniture in the room.

Chris slowly made her way over to one of the windows. Outside, she saw nothing but thick forest, trees that had never been cut. Looking down, she could see that the room was at least four stories above the ground.

"I can tell this is going to be easy to escape," Pilar said with a grimace, coming around the screen and looking at the treetops outside the windows. She stopped at the window next to Chris, then turned her head. "Do I look as bad as you?"

"Much worse," Chris said quite seriously.

Pilar gave a sigh of resignation and went back to bed, pulling a pillow under her head. "Do you have any idea what's going on?"

"None," Chris called from behind the screen. "I was hoping you'd know something. Did anyone say anything when they took you?"

Pilar waited until Chris was back in the center of the room. "I think you know more than I do. Tynan had some reason for being Hamilton's gardener and I was never told what it was."

"Oh? You just moved in with him when he crooked his little finger?"

"I owed him a favor, several favors if it comes to that. Look, are we going to play cat games or are we going to work together on this? I'd like to figure out what's going on but if you want to fight over a man, let me know so I can bow out."

"I have no reason to fight over Mr. Tynan. He is dead to me. He's yours."

Chris ignored the way Pilar lifted one eyebrow and gazed at her archly. "I am a newspaper reporter and I write under the name of Nola Dallas. I went to—"

"*The* Nola Dallas? The one that gets herself in trouble just so she can write about it?"

"I'm afraid so," Chris said.

Pilar put out her hand to shake. "I'm glad to meet you. Are we in one of your escapades and someone's going to show up to rescue us at any minute?"

Chris gave her a weak smile. "I think I better tell you all of it." She told Pilar everything, from finding Diana and Whitman Eskridge's bodies to when Tynan said they were going to leave Hamilton's house.

Pilar sat up, hugging her knees to her chest. "I think Ty found out something. He kept leaving the house in the middle of the night and one night he came back with a big book under his arm. He sat up all night reading it, but in the morning it was gone and I never saw it again."

"What was it a book of?"

"Numbers. You know, like Red has."

"Red?" Chris asked. "You mean the woman Tynan knows, in the . . ."

"Yeah, in the whore house." She narrowed her eyes at Chris. "The place where I worked."

"Oh," was all Chris could say. Of course Tynan would want that kind of woman for his wife, or pretend wife, or whatever she was. She put her mind back on the current subject. "Maybe that's why we were kidnapped, because Tynan stole a ledger from Hamilton or maybe . . . Have you ever heard of Del Mathison?"

Pilar gave a little smile. "He's a little before my time

199

but I've heard stories about him. One house threw a wake on the day of his wedding."

Chris's mouth became a narrow line. "He's my father."

"Sorry," Pilar said, but she didn't look sorry. Her head came up sharply. "If you're Mathison's daughter, then you must be rich. Maybe you're being held for ransom."

"That's what I thought. My father always had a horror of my being kidnapped. One of the ranch hands said it was because he had so many enemies, but, whatever the reason, it's something I've been prepared for."

"So why am I here? You think he brought me along to serve as your handmaiden?" Pilar said archly.

"I don't know, but I hope this kidnapper plans to feed us."

"And give us some hot water. I have three inches of dirt on me now."

As Pilar stopped talking, there was a sound at the door and the next moment, the heavy door was thrown open and the two men who'd taken the women were standing in the doorway. Behind them were two women, who looked to be scared to death, bearing trays of food. The men motioned for Chris and Pilar to stand back while the women set the trays on the floor. Next came big ewers of hot water and basins, then two dresses were tossed on the bed. A sewing box was placed by the bed.

One of the women backed against the doorjamb. "You're to wear the dresses tonight. If they don't fit, you can alter them." With that, they were out the door, the men behind them, and Chris could hear the lock being turned.

"Food first or hot water?" Chris asked Pilar when they were alone.

"Both at the same time," Pilar answered and the women did indeed dive into both at the same time, washing with one hand, eating with the other.

"It is possible that our captor has no idea who I am," Chris said with her mouth full as she washed her left arm. "Maybe he thinks I'm Diana Eskridge and this all has something to do with Owen Hamilton trying to kill Lionel. Maybe Owen wants time alone to do his dirty work."

"That still doesn't explain why I'm here," Pilar said. "I didn't know any of what was going on."

"But whoever took us doesn't know that. If Tynan was stealing things from the house at night, it would look as if you knew everything since you two spent every night together." Chris had a difficult time with the last part of that sentence. It wasn't that she any longer had any feeling for Tynan, he'd killed that the night in the cabin, but she did hate losing.

"If that's true," Pilar said thoughtfully, "then he probably took Tynan too. Do you think he's here with that young man of yours?"

"Asher? I can't imagine what he'd want with Asher. He only came along because I needed a husband."

"Whatever has happened, I don't understand it. I rather think that you've been kidnapped for ransom and the men brought me along because. . . . Truthfully, I don't know why I'm here. I have nothing anyone would want."

Pilar was standing in the light, mostly unclothed, her long black hair down her back, her body firm and well rounded, and Chris thought that she had something that any man would want. "I'm here for money and

201

you're here because our captor probably fell in love with you," Chris said under her breath, trying not to let her envy and hurt show.

Pilar said nothing but continued to wash.

When at last the women were clean and fed, they looked at the dresses on the bed.

"Not exactly my style," Chris said, holding a dress up. There wasn't a whole lot of fabric above the waist.

"Well, don't look at me, I haven't worn anything like this in years. Yours is too long and I think it might be too big in a few places."

Chris sighed because Pilar was right. "Maybe you were brought along because you fit the dress."

"Come on, let's get started altering it."

"The bust alone will take hours," Chris muttered.

They sewed until the sun went down, then dressed in the moonlight coming in through the windows. They had no candle, no combs to free their hair of tangles, no jewelry, and no idea where they were being taken.

When the oak door was thrown open, they were ready as best they could prepare themselves. Chris wasn't aware that she was shaking until Pilar slipped her hand in hers, giving her fingers a tight squeeze of confidence.

One of the men pushed Chris forward, Pilar after her, and the two women headed down the stairs.

"How do you even know which way to go?" Asher was shouting to Tynan as the men rode at full speed.

Tynan didn't bother to answer as he led them southeast, not stopping until they came to a dirty little patch of ground covered with tents. The place didn't deserve the name of "town." The streets were deep in half a foot of mud from the recent rain and, as they rode past a tent with a big sign outside that read simply "women," there were two men fighting, wrestling about in the mud. Asher's horse jumped sideways as the fighting men, locked together, lurched toward him. He had to struggle a moment to control the animal and when he could get away, he saw Tynan disappearing into one of the larger tents. Asher dismounted into the mud and followed.

Tynan was at the bar, leaning against it as if he had all the time in the world. There were several tables set up with men gambling. Ty was watching a man who looked clean compared to the rest of the men in the tent, with his gold embroidered vest and two guns with pearl handles.

Asher ordered a beer and had just taken a long drink when the game broke up. Immediately, the gambling man looked up at Tynan.

"I thought you were in jail for some reason or other."

"I got out for the same reason," Ty said. "And now I'm coming to you to collect a debt."

The man gave a curt nod, then walked to stand by Ty at the bar. "Two whiskeys," he said, then lowered his voice. "What is it you want?"

"Information."

"That comes high."

"I've already paid," Tynan said. "Have you ever heard of a man named Beynard Dysan?"

The gambling man choked on his whiskey. When he'd cleared his throat, he looked at Tynan. "Stay away from him. He's bad, real bad."

"He has something that belongs to me and I mean to have it back. Where can I find him?"

"Let him have it. Whatever it is, it isn't worth it. If

all you had to lose to him was your life, you'd be all right, but that man can take more than your life. Stay away from him."

Tynan didn't say a word for a moment. "Are you going to answer me or pretend to be my mother?"

"It's been real nice knowing you, Tynan. I'll send flowers to your grave. I don't know much about him at all except what I've heard in whispers. He has a place up north of here. There's a town up there called Sequona, if anybody knows anything about him, someone there will. And you might ask a few questions about him on the way, but you risk a bullet in your head—probably in the back of your head. This man likes to stay private. He doesn't like anybody looking into his business."

The man finished his drink. "What's he got of yours?"

"Del Mathison's daughter."

The man gave a low whistle. "Mathison's power against Dysan's. That may be a war to end all wars. Tynan, watch your back. Dysan has his hand in everything and he hires people to kill whoever interferes with what he wants. You ought to let Mathison get his own daughter back."

"He's hired me. Thanks a lot, Frank. Consider your debt to me cleared." With that, Ty turned and left the tent, Asher taking a last swallow of his beer and following him.

Tynan paused a moment outside the tent, not looking at Asher. "You heard what Frank said and you can back out now. If you don't lose your life in this you may not be the same afterward."

"And lose out on Mathison's daughter?" Asher said

204

just before a bullet went whizzing past Tynan's head. Ty fell to the mud, his arm coming out and pulling Asher down with him. Asher, not being prepared for the movement, hit the mud face down. He came up spitting. Another bullet came at them and his face went down again. Behind them was the sound of tables being overturned and men shouting as the two bullets had come into the tent.

Asher looked at Tynan, at the man's clean face as he held it above the mud and at the pistol in his hand. Behind them came a voice.

"I'd be willing to bet it's Dysan."

Asher turned to see the gambler, Frank, crouched in the tent opening, a gun in his hand.

"Hang on and I'll see if I can help."

A minute later, Asher could hear the man shout, "They just brought in a load of whores across the street. All of them virgins."

Tynan shouted at Asher to roll out of the way and Ash was glad he did because within seconds, a stampede of men came charging out of the tent. "Now!" Asher heard Tynan shout and Ash, fighting against the resistance of the mud, moved to the back of the tent. He was a little confused as to what he was to do next when Tynan appeared with the horses. "Let's ride," was all Ty said before mounting and leaving the muddy town and what sounded to be a riot behind them.

Tynan led them north, riding so hard that the drying mud began to flake off and fly about them. Toward afternoon, he pulled into the trees, onto a path that Asher didn't see until they were on it, and led them up a hill. It began to rain and both men pulled their hats low over their faces.

It was almost dark when Tynan stopped and dismounted. "There's a cave of sorts over there. We'll spend the night in it," he shouted over the rain.

A few minutes later, they had a tiny fire going, beans and coffee boiling and their clothes were almost dry on their bodies.

"You think we'll be able to find her?" Ash asked, poking at the fire with a stick.

"I plan to," Tynan said. He was leaning back against his saddle, his hat over his face.

"If Dysan just wants money then he surely won't hurt Chris, will he?"

"Or Pilar."

"Oh yes," Ash said. "I remember seeing her in the kitchen. She cleans, doesn't she?"

Tynan pushed his hat back and after one look at the back of Asher's head, took the beans from the fire and began dividing them onto plates.

Ash took the plates and a cup of coffee from Ty. "I guess you have a plan in mind, don't you? I mean, you *do* have a way to rescue Chris. Her father will be furious if you let anything happen to her."

"And you'll lose her money," Tynan said.

"Chris is a very attractive young lady, perhaps a bit headstrong at times, but attractive nonetheless. And I really don't see what's wrong in my taking over the management of her father's estates. He doesn't have a son and Chris obviously isn't interested in finding someone to take over." He gave Tynan a sharp look. "You aren't thinking of marrying her yourself, are you? Mathison's money would be quite a—"

"We'll get along a lot better if you keep your opinions to yourself. Now, put out that fire and get some sleep. We ride in the morning."

It wasn't morning—far from it—when Tynan woke Asher by putting his hand over his mouth. There was warning in Ty's eyes as he motioned for Asher to follow him out of the shallow cave. They carried their saddles and packs and led the horses, as quietly as possible, down the hill. It was still drizzling rain.

"What time is it?" Asher asked, yawning.

"Our last day on earth if we don't get out of here. There was someone outside the cave."

"I didn't hear anyone."

"All right, then you stay but I'm leaving."

Asher took one look about the dark forest, then mounted his horse and followed Tynan.

They rode all day and into the following night, with Asher half asleep in the saddle. When at last Tynan did stop, Asher didn't even recognize the stable for what it was.

"Unsaddle your horse," Ty ordered. "Or do you plan to stand there all night?"

Slowly, Asher obeyed him, shoveling hay and oats into the stall with the horse, then blindly following Ty out into the night and up the stairs at the back of a house. He didn't even ask any questions when Ty levered himself onto the roof, then, crouching low, ran across the roof and jumped onto the next roof. Asher was glad it was dark so he couldn't see how far it was to the ground. After they'd crossed three roofs, Tynan withdrew a key, opened a trapdoor and went down what was obviously an attic stairs. Once inside the building, he silently walked down a long corridor and opened the third door on the left.

A young woman turned over in the bed and looked up sleepily. "Alice, this is Asher and he needs a place to sleep."

The woman pulled the covers back then turned over on her side and went back to sleep. Tynan pushed Asher into the room and shut the door behind him. Two doors down, Ty opened another door.

Red was just getting out of bed, pulling a robe around her. "I thought I heard someone."

"Why is it so quiet?" Ty asked, pouring himself a whiskey.

"Four men rode in and shot the place up. I closed it down after that. Ty, they were lookin' for you."

He downed the whiskey in one gulp. "They've been on my trail for two days. You have anything to eat?"

Red opened a cabinet and withdrew bread and cheese. "I thought you'd come here, but you can't stay." She sat down on the sofa. "Oh, Ty, what have you done now? I thought you'd go straight for a while."

"They're not after me, except to keep me from finding Chris," he said, mouth full.

"Chris!" Red's head came up. "That two-timing little liar? I trusted her and she went off and left you to rot in jail when you were innocent."

"Yeah, well, that's true love for you. Whatever she's done, it's my responsibility to get her back to her father."

"At the risk of your own life?"

Ty just kept eating and didn't answer her. "You have an extra bed somewhere? I put Prescott in with Alice," he said after a while.

"You can have my bed," Red said heavily. "I've had all the sleep I'm gonna get tonight. Who do you want? Leora and you seemed to hit it off last time."

"Just sleep," Ty said, refilling his glass with whiskey. "No women."

He wasn't aware of the way Red just stood there opening and closing her mouth. "All right," she said after a moment. "Just give me your clothes and I'll have 'em washed."

She stood by silently while he undressed down to his underwear and watched as he slipped into bed. She sat by him, smoothing his hair back while he fell asleep, and when he was asleep, she kissed his forehead and tiptoed from the room.

"Tynan!" Red called urgently as she ran into the bedroom. "They've come for you."

Ty threw back the covers and put his feet on the floor. "Where the hell are my pants?"

"Wet. You've only been asleep three hours, but you've got to get out of here. There're half a dozen men downstairs askin' about you."

Tynan ran his hand through his hair. "Three whole hours, huh? Dysan doesn't leave any stone unturned."

"Dysan?" Red said. "You're after Beynard Dysan?"

"I don't need mothering now but I do need a pair of pants. Get me something to wear."

"I ought to refuse. I ought to get the sheriff to lock you up and save you from yourself."

Before Ty could speak, a woman barged into the room. "He's dead," she said with disgust in her voice. "I told you he couldn't take all three of us at once." She stopped talking, her eyes widening. "Why, Tynan, I didn't know you were here."

"And he isn't gonna be for long," Red said, pushing the woman out the door and closing it. "Now everyone'll know you're here and—" Her eyes brightened. "Sit there. Don't move. I have an idea." She left the room immediately while Ty began to search for something to wear.

Minutes later, Red returned with a pile of white leather and fringe over her arm. "That man that just died was from a wild west show and he won't be needin' this anymore." She held up the gaudiest, flashiest garment anyone had ever seen: white leather with three foot beaded fringe hanging from shoulder to wrist. There were also matching pants with silver medallions down the legs and a hat with a band of fake diamonds as big as pennies.

Tynan barely looked at the outfit. "If you don't get me some pants I'm—"

"Here!" Red said, tossing him the leather pants.

"Not on your life," Ty answered, letting them fall where they landed. "I need—"

"Wait a minute, Ty. There are six of them and one of you, and they have this place surrounded. Rachel said she saw a rifle on a roof so maybe there's more than six of them. You walk out of here and they'll never give you a chance. But they're expectin' what they know you look like. They ain't expectin' some fat, drunken ol' snake oil dealer."

Tynan sat down on the bed. "I won't wear that."

"You'd rather die than wear this?" Red gasped.

"With my boots on and my own pants on. What if I was to get buried in that?"

Red rolled her eyes toward the ceiling. "Of all the fool things I ever heard, that's the worst. Look, Ty honey, how are you gonna save that girl if you're dead? And that's what you'll be if you walk out of here wearin' your own clothes. With this on, you can walk right out the front door. Ever'body will be so blinded

210

by the diamonds and silver they'll never even look at your face. And you ain't even seen all of it yet, there's white boots and silver guns with white handles and even silver bullets. It's a real wingdinger of an outfit."

Ty sat on the bed, his jaw rigid.

"You get yourself killed out there and I'll see to it that you're buried in this," Red said.

Ty shook his head. "I hope Mathison appreciates what I've gone through to get him his daughter back."

"Come on, let's get busy. We gotta pad you to make this fit."

An hour later, Tynan stood surrounded by giggling females. Asher, smoking a one-inch diameter cigar, sat in a chair with Alice on his lap.

"It suits you, Tynan," Asher said. "It really suits you."

Red put her hand over Tynan's, which was on his gun handle, as she checked his hair which was whitened with talcum powder.

The women had sewn pillows in the long johns of the dead showman so that Ty could fill out the voluminous suit. He now had a belly that hung over his silver buckled belt, and they'd adjusted the pants so they hung down low, the crotch half way to his knees.

"Too bad to cover that up," Leora said, running her hand over his buttocks.

"Now," Red said, "you look ready, but you gotta get in the mood. That man come in here with pistols blazin'. You gotta go out the same way."

"*I* like to see you with pistols blazin'," Leora said in Tynan's ear.

"He don't have time for that now," Red said. "You ready, Mr. Prescott?"

211

"Any time."

"Then you can help him out, 'cause Ty, you're too drunk to get out by yourself. You got that?"

Tynan nodded silently.

"The horse ready?" Red asked.

"What horse?" Ty asked.

"You'll know it when you see it," Asher laughed. "Believe me, you'll know it."

Red clasped her arm firmly through Tynan's. "Honey, I wanta see you again and this is the only way. Now, give me a kiss and go."

Ty held her for a minute, kissed her cheek then left the room, long, ornate spurs clinking on the wooden floor. At the top of the stairs, he halted, drew both the silver pistols and fired into the ceiling. The next minute he was down the stairs, women hanging onto him.

"I'm meaner 'n a snake and twice as quick," he bellowed, lurching forward, then he grabbed a woman and kissed her while firing a pistol into the ceiling and one at a table full of men. He hit two glasses of beer and narrowly missed a big cowboy.

The cowboy got up and started toward Tynan, but Asher interposed his own body.

"He's drunk," Asher said. "It was an accident."

"You'd better get him out a here," the man growled, still standing, his gun hand loose.

"I'm strong as a grizzly and as eagle-eyed as a hawk," Ty yelled.

"Come on, hawk, let's get out of here," Asher said, pushing Ty toward the door.

"I can outride, outshoot, out—"

Asher, seeing that Ty again had his pistol aimed toward the table of watching cowboys—probably Dysan's men—knocked Ty's arm upward so the shot hit the painting over the bar, making a hole in the plump buttocks of the nude woman in the painting.

"I'm as tall as a fir tree and as ugly as a mule but the girls love me best 'cause I'm as hard and big as a ship's oar," Ty yelled as Ash pulled him out of the saloon.

"Get on the damn horse," Ash said, "before you get us killed."

Standing before them was a white skinned, pink eyed stallion wearing a white leather saddle. Ty didn't even hesitate before jumping into the saddle, wrapping the reins about the pommel, then withdrawing a rifle from the sheath on the side. While standing in the stirrups, fringe flowing behind him, the horse galloping north out of town, Tynan began firing along the edges of the roofs. Some of the men hiding there stood to see what was going on and Ty shot within inches of them.

Asher, on a horse following Ty, was sure he was as white as Tynan's leather suit, but the men on the roof seemed to think they were being treated to a free show, and a couple even fired their rifles skyward in appreciation.

Asher only began to breathe again when they were miles from the town, and abruptly, Tynan disappeared behind some trees. When Asher got to him, he was frantically searching through the white saddlebags.

"What is it?" Asher asked, dismounting.

"I was hoping there were some other clothes in here. Damn! But Red didn't give me any."

"You seemed to do well enough with those. Did you realize you almost shot one of Dysan's men?"

"I counted eleven in all. How many did you get?"

"How many what?"

"Why did you think I made so much noise? I wanted them all to come see what the ruckus was. There were four inside, five on the roofs and two came around from back. I think there may be a couple more south of town. I give them two hours before they realize it was me wearing this thing. So we got two hours to get me all new duds and to get rid of this." He looked at the pink-eyed horse in disbelief. "It'll be like trying to hide a mountain in a dollhouse. I wish we could get somebody else to wear this. Then Dysan's men could follow him and give us some time."

Asher snorted. "Oh yeah, and where are we going to find such a fool? I don't know anybody who could be paid enough money to wear that and if you try to give it to somebody he'll ask why. They're sure to be suspicious. The best thing is to burn it. We've no hope of finding somebody stupid enough to wear it."

"I don't know," Ty said as he mounted, cursing as he had to pull fringe out from under him, "the world is full of all sorts of people."

Chapter Eighteen

Tynan stood plastered up against the white wall of the building as if he hoped he could disappear. Asher was certainly taking his time in finding clothes to replace the white suit. There'd been a few minutes when Ty thought he was going to have to do something about Asher's mouth—maybe shove it down his throat—but Ty had been able to persuade him that it was in his own best interests to help find new clothes.

Slowly, Ty put his head around the building and looked to see if anyone was near. When he was sure the street was empty, he walked the two feet to the horse trough and put his head under. Asher'd had several comments to make on the smell of the French Lilac talcum powder Red had used to turn his hair white.

Just as he was lifting his head from the water, he felt the unmistakable coldness of a gun barrel on his neck.

"Say your prayers," the man said, "cause this is your last minute alive."

"Lester Chanry," Tynan said, drawing back and

215

looking at him. He was a tall bean pole of a man with red hair that reached his scrawny shoulders. His face was covered with freckles, those being the only color on his face since his eyebrows and lashes were so light as to appear nonexistent. He was wearing a bright red shirt with a four-inch-wide row of Indian beading across the shoulders and in his hair were three silver conchos. "Lester, it's good to see you again. In fact, I was just talking about you."

"I'll bet you were. Were you talking about how you killed my brother?"

"That was an accident."

Lester pushed Tynan against the wall. "You killed him and now you're gonna pay for it."

"It wasn't me and you know it."

"That sheriff was chasin' you and you might as well have killed him. You're the one that's gonna pay for it. Are you ready to die?"

"Just so long as you promise to bury me in my new suit."

For the first time, Lester looked down at the gaudy garment Ty was wearing, and Tynan watched his face. "You'll promise me that you'll bury me in it, won't you, Lester? It's my dying wish and a man should have his last wish honored."

"Where'd you get duds like them?" Lester asked with awe in his voice.

"A man had to give up his life before I could have these," Tynan said. "You'll promise me, won't you?"

"Well. . . . Maybe you'd sell 'em to me. I sure like those things."

"Sell them! What would I do with the money if I'm dead? What if I make you a deal? I'll *give* them to you if you let me go free."

Lester pushed Ty back against the wall. "I'll just shoot you and take 'em."

"I bleed real bad. If I cut myself shaving I get blood all over everything. It'd stain the suit so bad it wouldn't be fit to wear and, besides, you'd miss out on the matching horse."

"Horse?" Lester asked. "Are you lyin' to me, Tynan? If you are, I'll—"

"Lester, I'm fighting for my life. You don't kill me and I'll give you this white suit and a white horse with a white saddle."

"White saddle?" Lester gasped. "I ain't never seen no white saddle. Tynan, if you're havin' me on I'll—"

"Just ease up on that pistol and I'll take you to where the horse is hidden and I'll give it to you, with a bill of sale. It'll all be legal. But if you shoot me you'll get a bloody suit—and you know how blood makes leather so stiff—and you'll never find that horse. Some farmer's kid'll find it and have the one and only white saddle in existence. Did I tell you that it has little silver roundels on the bridle?"

Lester took several minutes to consider what Tynan was saying while Ty lifted one arm to show off the dangling fringe.

"All right, I'll do it, but if you try to trick me I'll—"

"Try to trick one of the Chanrys? Lester, I didn't get this old by being a fool. Come on, let's go. It'll be easier to part with my suit if we don't take too long at this," Ty said with a sigh.

As Chris descended the stairs, she tried to pull the top of the dress higher over her breasts, but there wasn't enough fabric to cover what needed to be covered. With one glance at Pilar, she saw that the other woman was hanging out more than Chris ever hoped to be able to expose.

At the bottom of the stairs, the two men stopped, abruptly leaving the women alone in a large room with brick floors and heavy furniture that was covered with silk scarves. It was a rich room with a few chairs, a small table against one wall and little else.

There was a door to the left with a window next to it. Immediately, Chris went to the door and tried it but it was locked. Just as she was starting toward the window, a voice came from behind her.

"You'll find all the exits are locked, Miss Eskridge."

It was a voice she recognized. "You!" she said, turning on her heel.

"I thought you would have guessed by now," said Beynard Dysan. "After the way you followed me around the house and the forest land, I thought you'd know right away that I was the one who had you taken."

"I was following Owen," she said in a half whisper. "Not you."

"I wasn't to know that, was I? Will you ladies join me for dinner?"

Involuntarily, Chris took a step backward, moving away from him.

"We would be delighted," Pilar said, taking Chris's hand and pulling her forward as she took Dysan's arm in her other hand. "We are starving."

Chris let Pilar talk as Dysan led them into a dining room because she wanted to regather her equilibrium. She had to get over her instinctive dislike of this man if she was to find out anything. By the time Dysan pulled a chair out for her, she was calm enough that she didn't cringe away from him.

When they were all seated and food was set before them, Dysan looked at Chris, at the foot of the long table, across from him, Pilar next to him, and said, "Now, what was that all about at Hamilton's? What were you trying to find out?"

Chris took her time in answering. She didn't want to give away too much to this man without finding out what he knew. "My father . . ." she said, then filled her mouth full of food, taking her time in chewing.

"Yes," Dysan said, "I know your father committed suicide, but then that husband of yours had something to do with that, didn't he?"

Chris was sure now that Dysan didn't know who she really was, that he thought she was actually Diana Eskridge. "Whit and I have . . ." She looked down at her food and managed to squeeze a tear from her eye. "I really do love him, but my father . . ."

She looked up at Dysan through damp eyelashes and saw that he was looking at her with great impatience and a lip curled in distaste. Good, Chris thought, let him think that she was a meek, cowardly little thing. Pilar, after a few looks of disbelief at Chris, kept her eyes on the food.

"What did you hope to find at Hamilton's?" Dysan persisted, sounding as if her timidity repulsed him.

"My cousin, Lionel, was in danger. I only meant to help. Why were we taken? What do you plan to do with us? I was only trying to help Lionel. And Pilar has nothing to do with this."

Dysan began to eat. "Consider yourself my guests. I fear that I cannot allow you the freedom of my house but you will have every comfort while you are here."

"But *why* are we here?" Chris said, leaning forward.

Dysan merely looked at her and said nothing more.

"They will come after us, you know," Pilar said softly into the silence.

"Do you mean that husband of yours? Do you think he'll come and rescue you? Shall he threaten me with a garden rake?"

"With a—" Chris said but cut herself off. "Someone will come to find us."

Dysan put down his fork and leaned back in his chair. "I have sent out over a hundred men to patrol the area between here and Hamilton's. They are to shoot to kill anyone who even asks a question about one of you ladies or about me. I assure you that no one will come for you."

"Then it's ransom you want?" Chris asked without thinking.

"And how can I ransom you?" he asked as if the answer greatly interested him. "Who will pay for either of you?"

"No one will pay money," Pilar said quietly, "but someone might be willing to pay with his life. We will be found."

Dysan took a while to study Pilar, looking her up and down in a hot, insulting way. "Perhaps you're right, but we shall see, won't we? Now, I'm afraid that this is all the time I can spare you. You will be taken back to your room and you will wait there."

"Wait for what?" Chris said.

"For when I decide what's to be done with you," Dysan said, then stood and left the room. Chris quickly wrapped some slices of beef in a napkin, and slipped the small package into her pocket. Seconds later, the two men who'd first kidnapped the women came into the room and escorted them back through the entryway and up the stairs to their room.

"So what did we find out except that if we make him angry we don't get to finish our meal?" Pilar asked when they were alone in the room. "Do you *really* think he sent a hundred men to guard the trail behind us or do you think he was bragging?"

Chris was looking out the window, considering how far it was to the ground. "I think that man is capable of any evil. *Why* are we here?" she half cried. "He doesn't know who my father is so we're not being held for ransom. I thought maybe, with these dresses, he'd decided he wanted one of us—physically, I mean—but that doesn't seem to interest him. So what does he want?"

"Do you know something that he doesn't, something that he might want to know?"

"Sure," Chris said. "He thinks I know where the lost Inca treasure is. If he wanted to know something, why didn't he ask us?"

"But all he asked us was if we thought Tynan was coming after us," Pilar said thoughtfully. "Do you think he's after Ty?"

Chris's mouth set in a line. "It seems that the only people who take a great interest in Tynan are those on the side of law and order. I don't think Dysan wants to arrest Tynan for whatever crime he's committed this week."

Pilar looked at Chris for a while. "You certainly are angry at him, aren't you? What's he done to you?"

"Made a fool of me, that's all." She sat down on the bed. "I don't think Dysan wants Tynan. If he did, he could have had him in a much easier way than in this elaborate scheme. He could have taken him on a picnic and Tynan would have gladly shot it out with him. No, there's something else. I think Dysan *does* know who my father is and we're being held for ransom. Then the hundred guns makes sense because Dysan wouldn't want anyone to interfere with his holding of us."

"Us?" Pilar said. "You've never explained why I'm here."

"Who knows? Pilar, do you think that if we tied those sheets together, they'd reach down to the ground?"

"Are you out of your mind?" Pilar said, moving to look out the window. "Can't you see those men with rifles out there? Do you think they'll just wave at you as you climb down?"

"Not if I do it at night."

"Chris," Pilar said with great patience in her voice. "Let's just wait here until your father pays the ransom and then we'll be free."

Chris looked at the dark woman for a long moment. "Free us so we can identify Dysan as a kidnapper? So we can go to a federal marshal and tell who held us captive? No, I don't think that's going to happen. Dysan may get the ransom, but he can't risk freeing us to tell anyone who took us." She paused a moment, her eyes locked with Pilar's. "I think he'll kill us as soon as he receives the money from my father. He has to keep us alive until then in case my father demands proof that I'm alive."

Pilar went back to sit on the bed. "So how long do you think we have?"

"My father will move heaven and earth to get however much money Dysan demands and . . ." She paused a moment since tears were coming to her eyes. Maybe she'd never see her father again, maybe she'd never see anything again except the inside of this room.

"He'll get the money here as fast as horse and rider can travel. If Dysan sent a ransom note south while we were being taken north, I figure we have about two days before the money's here."

"Two days?" Pilar gasped then her head came up. "So that means that Tynan could be here tonight."

"We can't risk it," Chris said, putting her hand on Pilar's. "Do you want to go with me or wait here and hope I make it back with help?"

"I want us both to remain here," Pilar said, then sighed. "All right, I'll stay here. Maybe I can hide the fact that you're gone for a while."

"If Dysan finds out that I'm gone, tell him that you're Christiana Mathison, then he'll want to keep you safe until my father gets the money to him. Now, will you help me get these sheets torn and tied?"

"If I must," Pilar said and found, to her consternation, that her hands were shaking. "I'll help if I must."

Tynan put his hand up to halt Asher as they entered the little town of Sequona. "I want you to go in first. Go to that big saloon there, about halfway down the street, and take a corner table. Do nothing but order a beer and wait for me. Don't talk to a single person, you understand?"

"Don't you worry about me, I can handle myself."

"Take your gun out, put it under your hat and wait. I want you ready when the shooting starts."

"Shooting?" Asher whispered. "How can you be sure there'll be any shooting?"

"How can you be as old as you are and not be sure? You ready?"

Asher just nodded as he reined his horse forward,

down the long, dusty street and stopped in front of the saloon. As he entered, a body came flying out, barely missing him and landing in the street.

"And stay out!" said a man wearing an apron, his big arms flexed, the muscles outstanding.

Asher waited until the entrance was clear, then went inside. He had to stand at the bar for a moment until the back table had cleared of a group of men playing poker, then he took his beer and sat down. As inconspicuously as he could, he removed his gun from his holster and placed it on the table, hidden under his hat.

He was leaning back in his chair, his eyes half closed when Tynan walked in—and immediately he could feel several eyes turn toward the man. So, Ash thought, Ty was right and there were people waiting for them.

Tynan ordered a double whiskey, and, as he was drinking it, a woman sidled up to him, putting her arm about his waist and running her hand over his back.

"How about buyin' a lady a drink?" she said.

Asher straightened his chair, trying to look as if he were interested in his beer, but he was actually trying to watch the men around him. There was one fat, dirty cowboy to his right whose hand was inching toward his gun belt. Get out of the way, lady, he thought with all of his might.

Tynan moved away from the woman just a bit. "Honey, I'd like to share more than a drink with you. You think that could be arranged?"

The woman's smile made her eyes disappear.

"Why don't you go on upstairs and wait for me? I need to wet my throat a little bit and I'll be right up."

The woman, in her dirty red-and-black dress, gave a look of triumph to the few other women in the saloon then started up the stairs. When she was halfway up, Ty turned to the bartender and said loudly, "What I really want is some information. You know the whereabouts of Beynard Dysan?"

There was a split second pause before the first gun was fired. Tynan, obviously watching the room in the mirror over the bar, spun on his heel, crouched low and fired into the belly of the fat cowboy across from Asher. Jumping up, Ash brought his gun up and shot another man on the balcony overlooking the main room of the saloon. As a bullet whizzed inches past his ear, Ash fell to the floor, knocked the round table over and got behind it.

As he was firing, he tried to see where Tynan was so he could protect him. Ty was backing toward an outside door, dodging bullets as he went.

Just as Ty was about to reach the door, Asher saw a man's head in a window to Ty's left. Standing, Asher bellowed, "Tynan!"

Ty turned and fired, the man at the window fell back, and Ty left the saloon just as Asher felt a searing pain in his leg before he could again reach the safety of the table.

Now Asher was alone in the saloon, all guns blazing at him, pinned down behind a little round table, the front door several feet away. He sat down to reload, watching the blood seep from his wounded leg, when he heard the softer more deadly sound of rifle fire in the saloon.

Looking around the table, he saw Tynan standing in the doorway, a rifle at his shoulder. "The next one that moves gets it. Get over here, Prescott," he commanded.

As Asher moved from the table, Tynan shot at a man in the corner and a gun dropped from his hand.

"I'm looking for Beynard Dysan and I want to know where he is. Watch my back," he said under his breath to Asher.

There were only four men left in the saloon now—and five bodies. The others who had been there had either run when the shooting started or were dead now.

"You!" Ty said to a tall man with a scar over his eye. "You'll be the first. I'll take a few inches off your left foot in about two seconds if you don't tell me what I want to know. Where is Dysan's place?"

Tynan put the rifle deeper into his shoulder.

"He has a big place ten miles due north of here," the man said. "But it's guarded and no man that he don't want in there can get in."

"That's my problem." Ty began to back up, Asher in front of him watching the crowd that was gathering in the street. Their saddled horses were waiting.

"Ride like you never rode before," Tynan called to Asher as they made their way north out of town.

Asher followed Ty as they thundered down the road and headed for the forest. For a while, Asher thought Ty knew where he was going but as they left the road and went into the trees he saw Ty stop several times and look around him. "You don't know this country, do you?" Ash asked.

"If I did, I'd have known where Dysan lived. Get down, I think this is it."

"What's it? Where are we?"

"Someone's to meet us here."

"Who?" Ash asked but received no answer as Ty dismounted, removing his saddle bags from his horse. Wincing with pain, Asher dismounted also.

"Let me look at that leg," Ty said as Ash lowered himself to the ground. After a rough, but thorough examination, Ty took a bottle of whiskey from his saddle bag. "This'll sting but it'll kill any lead poisoning. It's not a bad place, more a burn than a real bullet wound. You'll be fine in no time, even if you are a little sore."

Ash nearly screamed when Ty poured the whiskey on the raw, open cut, but he managed to control himself.

"First gunshot wound?" Ty asked, amused.

"The first this week," Ash answered as he tried to get his breath.

An hour later, both men were stretched beneath trees, when Ash heard a sound coming from behind Tynan. He looked at Ty but there was warning in Ty's eyes, telling Ash to be quiet. Pretending to be asleep, Ash watched in fascination as a woman, not quite young, but not old either, came sneaking up behind Ty, making as little noise as a human can make in a forest.

Just as she reached Tynan, who seemed to be asleep, with his hat pulled down over his eyes, Ty reached out, grabbed her and pulled her into his lap.

"Let me go!" she yelled at him.

"Come on, Belle, you're not still mad at me, are you?"

"I'd take a knife to you if I could."

Tynan held her easily in his arms, struggling only with her hands, with which she meant to claw him. "You know I never meant to hurt you, but that girl was only thirteen years old. I couldn't let you sell her to that old man."

"You didn't have to shoot up my place to save her. I lost everything in that. I had to go back on the streets to get enough money to pay for what you did."

Tynan began nuzzling her neck. "I'll bet you made a fortune."

"I did not!" she yelled at him, then began to relax. "Well, maybe I did make some at that. What are you doing here? And askin' about Dysan! You must wanta stop livin'."

"I just want to find him. You know anything about him?"

"Not enough that I want to lose my life by tellin' you. What's he done to you?"

"Taken Chris Mathison," Asher said. "Allow me to introduce myself. Asher Prescott at your service, ma'am," Ash said, removing his hat.

The woman tried to free her hands from Tynan's grip but he still held her. "All right, what do you want from me?" she said with a sigh. "Tynan, one of these days, you're gonna ask for one too many favors."

"What I like about women is that they always know how to give."

Suddenly, the woman stiffened in Ty's lap. "Chris? Is that a woman? Tynan, if you got me out here to help you find another woman, so help me I'll—"

Ty kissed her to keep her quiet. "It's strictly business. I've been hired by her father to take her to him and Dysan has her."

"Then you'd be better off leaving her where she is. She won't be worth much when Dysan finishes with her."

Tynan frowned. "Are you speaking from first-hand knowledge?"

"I saw a girl after he got through with her. He doesn't like women; he doesn't like anybody for that matter. He has a place not far from here, but I don't think he stays there much, I think he goes back East pretty often, and, for the life of me, I can't figure out

228

why he even comes to this godforsaken hole. He has money enough that he can live anywhere he wants to."

Tynan released her hands but she still stayed in his lap. "I heard he has business around here."

"There are rumors that he's involved in whatever evil trick has been pulled lately, but no one's been able to prove anything yet. The law's terrified of him."

Tynan was quiet for a moment. "You said this place of his was guarded. How well guarded?"

"An army post could learn from him. He has men patrolling his big house night and day—and they have dogs on leashes at night. Anybody even gets close and the dogs are let loose. They say those dogs can really take you apart."

"Has *anyone* ever made it inside?" Asher asked.

"Why would anybody be stupid enough to want to try?" the woman asked, looking from one man to the other.

"Belle, you know anybody who's been in the place? Somebody we could ask questions?"

Belle looked down at her hands. "To tell you the truth, I was in there last year. I went with some other girls and. . . . Tynan, I don't like to think about what happened that night."

Tynan pulled the woman to him, hiding her face in his shoulder. "Dysan has a young woman now and he's holding her captive. Prescott and I plan to get her out so I need all the help I can get. If you could tell me anything that you remember about the place, a way in, the floor plan of the house, whatever you can remember, I'd sure appreciate it."

Belle moved away from his shoulder. "You don't deserve my help, not after the way you tore up my place, but I'll do what I can." She looked at him in a seductive way. "I'll do it in memory of that time down in San Antonio. You remember that?"

"Every day of my life," Ty said, smiling. "I use it to judge everything else by. Prescott, you got any paper? Belle's going to draw us a plan."

Ty pushed her off his lap while Asher managed to move his stiffening leg so he could get to his horse. Minutes later, the three of them were hunched over a map Belle was making, and an hour later, the two men were mounting their horses again.

Belle looked up at Tynan. "By the way, Ty, there was some guy through town yesterday lookin' for you."

"What'd he look like?"

"Tall, skinny, long red hair. His arm was in a sling and he walked with a limp. Seemed real anxious to see you."

Tynan leaned down from the horse and kissed her lingeringly. "You tell him you saw me about forty miles south of here."

She smiled at him. "Maybe. I might consider it if you come back through here and make it up to me about what you did to my saloon."

"I might do that." Ty smiled at her, then was off, heading north toward Dysan's house.

Chapter Nineteen

Pilar was sitting on the floor, leaning against the foot of the bed, and, in spite of her good intentions, she was asleep and didn't hear anyone in the room until a hand covered her mouth, startling her awake.

"Tynan?" she asked in disbelief. "Is that you?"

"Where's Chris?" he asked at once.

Pilar sat up straighter. "I don't know. She's been gone for hours and I heard the dogs and men yelling but I didn't hear anything from her. Ty, I'm worried about her."

Tynan's face showed what he thought of Chris leaving the room. "How did she get out?"

Pilar started to stand. "We tore the bed sheets into strips and she went down through the window. Ty! You're injured. Here, sit down."

"I don't have time. I have to find her and soon. Leave that alone, it's not bad, just a couple of dog bites. Why in the hell did you let her go? I don't expect

231

her to have any sense, but you, Pilar, I expected more from you. I told you to watch her."

"How was I supposed to stop her? Dysan said that he'd sent out over a hundred men to stop anyone from finding us. You could have been dead for all we knew and then Chris said Dysan wasn't going to release us since we could identify him."

"Has he contacted Mathison yet?"

"That's what's strange, Ty, I'm not sure Dysan knows who Chris is. He talked about her father committing suicide and about her husband being an embezzler. If he doesn't know that Chris is wealthy, then why has he taken us?"

"I'll worry about what's on the man's mind later. Right now, I'm more concerned about his guns. Did you see what Chris did when she reached the ground? Did she try leaving the grounds or did she go back into the house? She just loves snooping in people's private papers."

"I didn't see because I was pulling the rope up, but I think she probably had to go into the house because the dogs came around minutes after she touched the ground. She wrapped her shoes in pieces of sheet and rubbed them with some meat fat. She was planning to throw the cloth away when she reached the edge of the forest."

"Well, it doesn't look like it worked because she's nowhere to be seen outside. Now, I want you to listen to me and do exactly what I say. Prescott, the man from Hamilton's place, will be here in a minute and I want you to let him help you get out of here. He'll take you over the roof."

"And where will you be?"

"Searching for Chris." With that statement, he went

to the window and proceeded to climb up a rope toward the roof. Pilar could hear him walking softly overhead and then all was silent.

Tynan gave a signal to Asher who crouched behind a dormer on the tall house, then tied his rope about a far chimney and started down. Thanks to Belle, he knew most of the layout of the house and he was heading now toward Dysan's office. This would be the room that Chris most likely would want to explore.

The room was dark and there wasn't a sign of any activity in it—no papers, only a few books, no ledgers with their revealing account numbers, no pretty little blonde snooping through things.

Cautiously, Tynan made his way out the door and into the dark hallway. Listening carefully, he heard voices downstairs, but they didn't seem particularly upset about anything, as they might be if they'd just found Chris haunting the rooms. With his back to the wall, he began to ease his way down the stairs, stopping constantly to listen to whatever he could hear.

According to Belle, the house was a big one and Ty wasn't sure where he should begin searching, but the library seemed like a good bet—not because he thought Dysan might have something there but because Chris would want to search a place like that.

He stopped twice at the foot of the stairs to listen but he heard nothing, so he went across the empty dining room to the closed door that he knew led to the hallway. Still listening and, as quietly as a cat, he made his way through the door and into the hall. The first door on the right was the library.

Once inside the library, he paused, pressed his back against the door and waited. He wasn't sure what it was, but something was wrong. He stood so still that he became part of the shadows, fading into his surroundings so that he disappeared.

The sound of a match being struck made him turn his head—and he saw Beynard Dysan sitting in a chair before him, bringing the lit match up to his cigar tip.

"Bravo," Dysan said. "You were almost silent." He bent forward to touch the match to a lantern on the table before him.

In the light, Tynan could see Chris in a chair beside Dysan, her hands and feet tied, her mouth gagged. Her eyes were wild and she looked as if she'd seen something awful.

"I wouldn't try it," Dysan said as Ty took a step forward. "I have a gun on her and I wouldn't hesitate to shoot her."

Tynan stood where he was, not moving a muscle but trying to look about the room.

Dysan smiled. "I can assure you that there is no way to escape. You got in because I allowed you to enter." He took the cigar from his mouth and looked at it. "I wondered which one of the women you'd go after first."

Dysan stood and walked to stand behind Chris, putting a gun to her head, running his hand along her throat and pulling her head back. "Why do I get the feeling that she's not what she seems? Hamilton said she was his cousin, a mousey little thing that allowed her husband to beat her, but here she is, having escaped down the side of a four-story building, and I somehow sense that she isn't what she appears."

"What do you want? If it's money, you'll be paid. All you have to do is release her."

"Money?" Dysan sounded genuinely surprised. "And do you have money to pay for her ransom?"

"I can get it."

Dysan walked away from Chris but not far enough that he couldn't have hurt her if Tynan tried anything. "And what do you have that you can sell? Do some of the prostitutes you know have money? Will they sell their diseased bodies to get money for you? Or has that miner of yours finally found gold?"

Tynan just looked at the man, not saying a word.

"Ah, the rescuing hero doesn't want to tell what he knows. What can I do to loosen your tongue? Remove pieces of this little lady?"

Still, Tynan didn't move.

Dysan moved closer to Chris and began to run his hands down her arms. "Do you mind that other men touch her? Do you insist that this one is yours alone?"

"Do what you want with her," Tynan said. "She's just a job to me. I get paid to take her back to her father."

"And who is her father that he would pay for her?"

Tynan took his time in answering. "Del Mathison," he said into the silence.

The only sign Dysan gave that he heard was that his cigar shook just once as he held it in his hand.

There was a long silence in the room as Dysan stared at Tynan. "I think I have underestimated you. I thought you only went in for whores."

"I do. I want nothing to do with girls like her. She's been nothing but trouble so if you have some grudge with me, you can leave her out of it."

Dysan ran his hand along Chris's neck. "Shall I test your words? Shall I see how little you care about her?"

"Mathison won't take kindly to his daughter being mistreated and I don't think you're big enough to buck a man like him."

Dysan seemed to be considering this, but, after a moment, he walked toward the door, his gun aimed at Chris and looked out. Immediately, two men appeared. "Take them to the cellar and lock them in."

Tynan stood back as he watched Chris being untied, and when she was released, she fell forward. One of the men caught her arm roughly and jerked her upright. Ty still stood where he was as she looked up at him as she was being pulled along.

Without any protest, he followed behind her, in front of a man bearing a rifle.

They were led downstairs into a deep basement. There was a door against one wall and one of the men took a key and opened it, throwing Chris into the dark, dank little room. Tynan entered of his own accord, standing by the door until the men closed and locked it behind them.

Instantly, he was across the room to Chris, groping for her in the darkness. "Chris, Chris," he whispered repeatedly while running his hands over her body as if he were inspecting her. "Are you hurt?"

Chris clung to him as if she were drowning. "He's a horrible man," she gasped, then choked over her tears. "He told me about three women who'd been here. He told me about using a riding crop and—"

"Sssh," Ty said, holding her, stroking her back. "It's over now."

Chris hiccupped. "The woman *died*. He killed her. He told me in florid detail what he did and how he made the other women watch. The woman bled to death."

"Chris, stop crying. He won't do anything to you now."

"But how could one human do something like that to another? He told me about it and he wasn't sorry. Why wasn't he punished?"

"I don't know, just so long as he didn't hurt you."

It took Chris several minutes more to control herself. "What does it matter to you?" she asked, pushing away from him and moving back against the wall. "I'm well enough to get back to my father if that's what's worrying you." She sniffed.

Ty's hands moved away from her and there was resignation in his voice. "I'll see if I can find a light."

She leaned against the wall and listened to him rummaging around the room. Her head ached, there were rope burns on her ankles and wrists and along with Dysan's hideous stories, her ears were ringing with Tynan's words that she was nothing to him.

She watched as he struck a match and lit a candle. It was a dreary little room, dirt walls on three sides, the heavy wooden door on the other. There was a crude wooden cabinet against one wall, the door hanging off its leather hinges, exposing a few jars of canned fruit and a couple of half-burned candles on the shelves. Except for a few plants trying to grow out of the walls, the room was bare—and cold.

"Let me look at you," Tynan said, his voice cool, his face set.

Chris jerked away from his approaching hands. "Don't touch me. I am perfectly all right," she said. "You don't need to concern yourself with me."

Ty rocked back on his heels. "We'll get along a lot better if we work together. As long as you fight me, we'll never get anything done."

"So you can get me back to my father and you can

get your money? Maybe Dysan will let you go free now that you've told him who I am. Maybe you two can share the money from my father."

"Of all the ungrateful—I ought to leave you here."

"Go ahead. There's the door."

Tynan opened his mouth to speak but closed it again, then stood and walked to the door and began looking at it.

"You have on new clothes again," Chris said after a while.

Tynan didn't answer her but kept looking at the door.

Chris tried to stand up, using the wall for support. "I guess you got Pilar out safely."

"If you'd stayed in your room, you'd be out now, too."

"He knew when you were inside the house so what makes you think he didn't know when you were in the upstairs room?"

Ty didn't look back at her but kept searching the room, inspecting the ceiling which looked as if it were always wet, and the floor which was nothing but hardened mud.

"Dysan said he'd sent out a hundred men to stop anyone from finding us, so how did you get here?"

"Your father's money was a powerful incentive. It got me through clouds of gunfire."

Chris leaned against the damp wall, flexing her sore ankles. "All right, maybe I was rude and I apologize. I thank you for trying to rescue me and I'm sorry that I'm going to cause your . . . that I'm going to cause whatever will happen to us."

He turned back to her. "I think that finding out that you're Mathison's daughter will curtail whatever Dysan planned. Now, I suggest that you sit down and get what rest you can because, come morning, I think he'll take us out of here."

Chris sat down on the floor and was silent for a moment. "You could have gotten away in there. You could have overtaken those two men. Why didn't you?"

Tynan stretched out with his back against the door, his eyes half closed. "Maybe, maybe not. Why don't you get some sleep now? You might need to do some running in the morning."

Chris couldn't sleep, but she was quiet as she sat and watched Tynan across from her. Since that awful night in the cabin, she'd done her best not to think of him, not to remember what he looked like, how he smelled, how he'd touched her, but now, with him so near, it was impossible not to recall every bit of it.

And with the pleasant memories came his words: he only wanted to get her back to her father, that all she was to him was a possibility of a pardon, that she was just one of hundreds of women he'd bedded, no more, no less. Chris remembered with shame the way she'd tried to talk him into marriage. In the flickering darkness, she could feel her face turning red. How childish she'd been, how immature.

And how childish she was acting now, she thought. She kept thinking that he'd betrayed her when the truth was, he'd been more than honest with her, never had he insinuated that he wanted any more from her than a job and a good time.

As she watched him, he opened his eyes and looked at her, and for a moment, Chris almost threw herself into his arms. Whatever she felt for him was not returned and she'd better get used to that fact. He didn't love her and she was going to stop loving him—even if it killed her.

"Would you like to see what I found?" she asked.

He gave a nod, but said nothing, just sat there looking at her with hot eyes.

Probably thinks that since we've made love once, we will again. Not on your life, cowboy! she thought.

Turning away from him, she unbuttoned her blouse and withdrew a long narrow belt of what looked to be silver links. "It's mine," she said, caressing the belt and taking her time before handing it to him.

"It's worn out and it looks old. Where was it? In your carpet bag?"

"No, of course not," she said, taking it back. "I found it here, when I was looking through Dysan's things. He had several treasures in a little cabinet. I think he found them in the sea—salvage. But I knew right away that this was mine so I took it."

Tynan looked at her in confusion for a moment. "You mean that you've never seen this thing before but you think it's yours?"

She looked up at him with a stubborn expression on her face.

"Is this your second sight again?" he said and there was laughter in his voice.

Chris merely kept her jaw set and put the belt back into her blouse.

"What is the thing anyway?"

"I think I'll get some sleep now," Chris said with her nose in the air.

"I didn't mean—" Ty began but he stopped himself. "You want to hear why I have on new clothes again?" he said after a moment.

Chris tried to control her curiosity but couldn't. She

was a reporter to the tip of her toes and she was not capable of resisting a story. Reluctantly, she nodded.

He started with entering Red's place secretly and then went on to tell of the men waiting outside for him. He told of his reluctance to wear the sideshow man's white leather outfit, and of at last agreeing.

Chris listened with held breath, in awe of what he wasn't telling her: of how difficult it had been to get to her. She didn't laugh until he started telling her about Chanry and how the man had loved the suit.

"But won't the men chase him when he's wearing the white suit, and won't they think they're chasing you?"

Tynan grinned at her. "That's the idea."

"Oh, Ty, that's dreadful of you. That man could get killed."

"Hmph! You'd rather I'd have worn the suit and let myself get killed?"

"That isn't what I meant and you know it."

"Then you'll be happy to know that I've already heard that Chanry escaped, a little dented maybe, but he's alive."

"And looking for you, no doubt."

"I seem to be a popular fellow," Ty said.

"Do you have any idea why Dysan wants you? He seemed to be very interested in you."

"I doubt it. He just wanted to see who could get through that gauntlet he set up. Chris, seeing as this might be our last night alive, would you like to—"

He didn't get to finish. "Of all the audacious, disgusting things I have ever heard, that's the worst. After the things you said to me! How dare you ask me something like this! What kind of woman do you think I am?"

"But in the cabin—"

"In the cabin I thought I was in love with you and I

thought you were going to marry me. That was *before* I found out what kind of low-life scum you really are, that you have no more feelings for a woman than what you can get out of her. But I can tell you that you will never, *ever* get anything out of me again."

"I just thought I'd ask," he said and there was a hint of a smile in his voice. "Let's get some sleep now."

Chris didn't say anymore but she didn't sleep either as she sat there, her blood boiling. How dare he? How dare dare *dare* he?

She was still angry when the door was unlocked and opened.

Chapter Twenty

A man grabbed Chris's arm before she was out the door, roughly pushing her toward the stairs.

"You're ours once he's through with you," the man whispered in her ear as she stumbled up the stairs. "And after he's killed the pretty boy," he added, meaning Tynan who was walking behind them. Another man, holding a rifle, brought up the rear.

At the top of the stairs, they were shoved into the dining room where Dysan waited for them. Dysan didn't say a word as the men tied Tynan to a chair, then left the room.

Dysan lit a cigar, looking at Chris standing at the end of the dining table and at Tynan as he sat immobilized in a chair by the window.

"I have waited a long time for this," he said at last. "I've spent years planning this, what I would do, how I would do it. I had no idea that you'd drop the answer into my hands so easily."

As Dysan was speaking, he was looking at Tynan, it was as if Chris weren't even in the room, but she got the impression that she was the answer to which Dysan was referring. She was what Dysan was going to use to do what he wanted to Tynan.

"Before we . . . die," Chris said, "could you tell us why? What have we done?"

Dysan took a long draw on his cigar. "I have no intention of telling you anything. By tomorrow, this house will be a pile of cinders and in the ashes will be the bodies of two people. No one will even be able to identify the bodies. Your father will never know what happened to his little daughter."

"What about the world? Won't they want to know what happened to Nola Dallas?"

Dysan didn't speak for a moment. "You are certainly full of surprises." He turned to Tynan who was still and silent in the chair. "As well as yourself. She isn't like your usual women."

"What is it you have against Tynan? And if you think he wants me for anything, you're wrong. I'm nothing to him, absolutely nothing."

Dysan gave a little smile of delight. "Of course you're not. Now, come here."

Chris stiffened. "I will not."

"For every order of mine that you disobey, I will take an hour from his life. You obey me and he lives longer."

"I can't . . ." Chris began but she stopped at the look on Dysan's face. She didn't look at Tynan because she was beginning to feel her first anger at him. Why didn't he at least make some form of protest? Did he care so little about her that he'd allow whatever happened to just happen to her?

Chris tried to clear her mind. Tynan wasn't going to help, wasn't going to even say anything that might discourage Dysan so it was up to her. What would she do if she were alone in the room with an aggressive man?

She tried to look about the room without seeming to do so and she saw that on the sideboard were two built-in silverware holders. Inside one of them had to be a table knife. If she could lead Dysan that way . . .

She began moving toward Dysan, and his eyes never left hers. "What makes you think that I care anything about him? He's only a cowboy who was hired by my father to take me through the rain forest. Did you know that he'd been in jail? My father had to get him out of prison to lead the expedition. He's not my type of man at all."

Dysan watched her and Chris was glad to see that his eyes went down to her hips a couple of times, from the way she was swaying them, he could hardly miss them.

"I like a man with power." She was standing close to him now, both of them in front of the sideboard. "Do you have any idea how very wealthy my father is? Can you imagine what an empire you'd have if you were to merge your kingdom with his?"

Dysan looked amused. "Are you trying to seduce me? Do you think you can make me forget what I really want? You are a bystander who got caught in the crossfire."

Chris was inches away from him now, her face just below his. "I'm trying to save my own neck. If you and I merge, so to speak, we can have control of a great deal. If you murder me, my father will pursue you to the ends of the earth. Your life will be hell."

"And what about him?"

"What does he matter? Let him go. We don't need him."

Dysan smiled down at her. "Nice try, princess, but it won't work. The both of you die. Mathison would never let someone who'd once threatened his little girl into his kingdom."

Suddenly, he grabbed Chris about the waist and pulled her to him, grinding her mouth with his, forcing her lips open and thrusting his tongue inside.

When he released her, her revulsion showed on her face.

He thrust her away from him. "And you think you could pretend to *want* me," he said between closed lips. "I don't like to be thought a fool. Now come here."

Chris was really afraid of him now. He wasn't going to fall for anything she'd planned, he was going to torture her in front of Tynan, then kill Tynan in an equally disgusting way—and she wasn't even going to be told why she was dying.

Hesitantly, she walked toward him, and when she was in front of him, she voluntarily put her arms up to go about his neck. She began to kiss his neck, moving over his lips, trying to shift his interest entirely onto her—and while she was kissing him, she was trying to reach the box of silverware behind him.

Feigning passion as he again put his tongue in her mouth, she managed to get the box open, and with one eye open, she saw that there was a set of six table knifes, handles up, in the box. Now, if she could only reach one of them. She was almost there when Dysan suddenly turned and grabbed her hand, her fingertips held an inch above the handle.

"Going to stab me in the back, my dear?" he said before he slapped her across the face.

Chris hit the floor, her hand going to the corner of her bleeding mouth.

Dysan advanced on her, and Chris scooted backward on the floor.

It was just as Dysan reached her and had his hand raised to strike her again that Tynan sprang from his chair and grabbed Dysan about the neck, a small knife held to the evil man's throat. "I think it's time that you pick on someone your own size," Tynan said.

With that, Ty spun the man around and slammed a right fist into his face.

Dysan went down on the nearest chair and hit the floor next to Chris. Tynan didn't give him time to regain his breath before he was on him again. "You coward!" Tynan said under his breath as he grabbed Dysan and began to beat him.

Chris got up and tried to stop Tynan from killing the man, but Tynan was so angry that she couldn't make him hear her. She kept watching the door, fearing that any minute, one of the guards would come in and take them back to the cellar. They had to get out now while they had the chance.

She jumped on Tynan's back, hoping that her weight would have some effect on him.

Tynan shrugged her off and, again, Chris went skidding across the floor. It was a long moment before Tynan realized what he'd done. He dropped Dysan, allowing the man to slide down the wall to the floor in a bloody heap while he went after Chris.

"That was a fool thing to do," he said, lifting her up from the floor.

Chris shook her head to clear it. "We have to get out of here while we can. What took you so long to get loose?"

"Have you ever sawed through half-inch ropes with a pen knife? And you didn't look like you were in any misery. Maybe you want to stay here with Dysan rather than escaping with me? Maybe you two can still merge empires once you get rid of the cowboy."

"Could you go into a jealous rage later? I'd like to get out of here and we still have to get past the guards and the dogs outside."

After helping her to stand, Tynan went to Dysan and hauled him up. "You're going with us and if the dogs get too near, I'll throw you to them. Chris, hand me that piece of rope."

As Tynan tied Dysan, Chris looked out the window. "What do you think our chances are? There are guards everywhere."

"I'm hoping that Pilar and Prescott got away."

"They didn't. They're in the cellar now," Dysan said before Tynan put a dirty handkerchief from his back pocket across Dysan's mouth.

"Then we have to get them out," Chris said, heading toward the door which led to the stairs into the cellar.

Tynan shoved Dysan against the wall and grabbed Chris's arm. "What makes you believe him? If they're locked up, then after I get you out safely, I'll come back for them—alone. You understand me?"

"Because you'll go back to jail if I'm not safe? Pilar and Asher don't matter to you, do they?"

Tynan closed his eyes a moment, then turned back to Dysan and began to search him, removing a small derringer from inside his coat pocket. "All right, let's go. Chris, I'm taking him out the window first, then I want you to follow us when it's safe." He paused a moment, looking at her. "And I want you to swear to me that you won't do anything stupid like try to get back into the house to find the others. You understand?"

Chris nodded, but she was thinking about Pilar and Asher hidden away in the cellar. Wouldn't it be better if the two of them tried to get them out, instead of Tynan coming back alone later?

"Chris!" Tynan hissed at her as he stood outside the window. Dysan was giving him trouble so Tynan cuffed him once on the side of the head.

There was a low brick wall in the back of the house, a place for flowers and kitchen herbs. Ty crouched down behind the wall, forcing Dysan down in front of him. He kept turning to look at Chris, as if he expected her to disappear and he wanted to be able to go after her as quickly as possible.

They were at the end of the wall when Ty stopped and put his head up. The forest was several yards away and Chris could hear men talking nearby on the other side of the wall and the dogs in the distance. It would probably be only minutes before the guards found them.

Tynan leaned back against the wall and checked Dysan's derringer to make sure it was loaded. "Chris, I want you to stay behind us. I'm going to use Dysan as a shield and get us to the forest. You think you can do that? I don't want any more trouble than I already have. No going back for the others."

It was obvious that he hadn't believed her when she'd said that she would obey him.

Tynan looked toward the forest for a moment then back at Dysan. "And you give me any trouble and I'll blow your head off."

"All right, let's go," he said, grabbing Dysan and pulling him upright.

They left the safety of the wall and stepped into the open ground—but they stopped there because no one was even interested in them. They could see about a dozen guards, one with four dogs on a leash, but not one eye was turned in their direction. The guards were frozen where they stood, staring at something around the corner of the house.

Chris could hear bells in the distance.

"Get back!" Tynan said to Chris, shoving Dysan back toward the wall.

"What is it?" Chris asked.

"I think it's a peddler's wagon," Ty said. "Pilar used to work on one. If it is them, then we'll do better to leave with them. The dogs will smell our trail in the forest in no time."

"But how do we get out? We can't just walk to the wagon. And what do we do with him?"

"We leave him here, then we make our way toward the front of the house. We'll figure out a way to make Prescott see us."

Chris watched as Tynan tied one of Dysan's ankles to a spike in the top of the brick wall, allowing the rope to fall only enough so that Dysan wasn't dangling, but he was very uncomfortable. "Something tells me that I ought to kill you now," Ty said under his breath. "I think you're going to be nothing but trouble and there'll come a time when I'll regret having missed my chance." He looked up at Chris. "You ready?"

"Ty, are you sure it's Asher and Pilar? Maybe it's really a peddler's wagon and they're actually locked in the cellar."

Ty didn't answer but grabbed her arm and pushed her back toward the house. Looking inside the window, he made sure no one was about then climbed inside and helped Chris after him.

She followed him as he led her through the house, keeping her back to the walls as he instructed her, while he checked each room they passed for signs of a guard. Once, he slipped inside a room and Chris heard a dull thud, as if a body were hitting the floor, then he returned to the hall and motioned for her to follow him.

Chris didn't question how he came to know the plan of the house so well, but just trusted him. He stopped in a bedroom at the far end of the house.

"It's Pilar, all right," he said after looking out the window. "She's on top of the wagon dancing, and Prescott is driving. I don't know how much longer we have before they get tired of watching her. On second thought, considering what Pilar's wearing, we may have the rest of the week."

He turned back to Chris. "How fast can you run?"

"I . . . I don't know. If someone's chasing me, I guess I can run rather quickly."

"I'm going to create a diversion and I want you to climb out the window and run to the wagon and get in the back. Think you can do that?"

"But what about you? I can't go off and leave you."

"After the way you were kissing Dysan, what do you care about me?"

"Dysan?" she asked, bewildered. "I was trying to get a knife from the box. I had to divert him. Tynan, are you jealous?"

"Definitely not. Now, are you going to get out there or are you going to waste time and maybe get us all killed?"

She nodded at him, but she didn't like it. She hoped he wasn't going to do something that would get him caught again. She didn't think Dysan would be so easy to overpower the second time.

"Good girl," he said and started to turn away, but then abruptly turned back and pulled her into his arms. His kiss was hard and quick, so quick, in fact, he only undid three buttons, but it was a kiss filled with feeling. He released her as abruptly as he'd taken her. "I'll be all right," he said over his shoulder. "You just get yourself out of here when you hear the gunshots."

It seemed to Chris that it was the longest few minutes of her life while she waited for Tynan to begin firing. She crouched below the window and peeped out to see the tall, gaudily painted peddler's wagon surrounded by men with rifles over their shoulders. On top of the wagon was Pilar, dressed in odd, voluminous trousers of pale blue silk and a tiny top of matching silk. It was apparent that the costume hadn't been made for someone of Pilar's dimensions because the fabric strained everywhere, threatening to split apart at any moment. Chris guessed that that was half of the men's fascination with her—the hope that the garment would give way while they were watching.

While Chris was watching Pilar undulate, there suddenly came the sound of gunfire from the back of the house and the guards' reaction was instantaneous. They all took off running toward the sound.

Chris lost no time climbing out the window and running across the lawn to open the back of the wagon and climb inside. She heard Pilar yell down to Asher, on the wagon's seat, "She's in," then the wagon started off at a breakneck speed.

Chris grabbed the side of the wagon and tried to hold her balance. The wagon was full of merchandise, from bolts of cloth to pots and pans to farm tools, nearly all of it fastened down so it couldn't fly about when the wagon moved.

The back door of the wagon flew open just as Chris regained her balance. As she reached forward to close it, she saw that they were traveling away from Dysan's big house.

"No!" she gasped, but there was no one in the back of the wagon to hear her.

If she was to get Asher to turn around, she had to do something and do it fast. Fighting the rocking of the wagon, she began to climb over the boxes that were stacked toward the front, grabbing a small handled axe off the wall as she moved.

It took three swings before the axe went through the front partition and came out uncomfortably close to Asher's right ear.

He turned to look at her in disbelief as she used her feet to kick the rest of the way through the thin wood. "You have to go back," she yelled at Asher. "You can't leave Tynan back there."

Pilar hung down from the top. "She's right," she shouted over the sound of the horses. "We have to get Tynan out."

"Then I'll go back but you two women stay here," Asher said even as he was halting the horses.

"No!" the women screamed at him in unison.

Asher didn't say another word as he flicked the whip over the horses and headed back toward Dysan's house.

Chapter Twenty-one

Chris held on for her life while Asher drove the wagon back over the ground they'd just covered. Their only hope of rescuing Tynan was that Dysan hadn't been discovered yet and his men didn't know that the peddler's wagon was involved in the escape.

Above her head, she could hear Pilar singing and making noise to attract attention.

"Cover this hole," Asher yelled as he whipped the horses harder.

With unsteady feet, falling several times, Chris managed to hang a piece of cloth over the hole she'd made in the front of the wagon. Just as she'd caught the edges of the cloth on a piece of splintered wood, Asher called, "I see him and he's running toward us. Oh Lord. Get down! Both of you women get down," he yelled as the first shots rang out.

Chris, with her heart pounding, flattened herself on the floor of the wagon—or as close to the floor as she could get with all the merchandise scattered about.

Overhead, she heard Pilar hit the roof very hard, almost as if she'd fallen. Immediately the gunfire increased to a torrent.

Inching forward on her belly, she pushed one of the wagon doors open. Tynan was running down the road with men and dogs on his heels, the men firing their rifles as they ran. The bullets were hitting the back of the wagon at a regular rate, some of them whizzing inches over Chris's head.

She moved closer to the door and stretched her hand out toward Tynan. "Come on," she yelled. "Come on."

Ty yelled something back to her but the blood was pounding so hard in her ears that she didn't understand what he was saying.

"You'll never get out of jail," she screamed at him.

It was then that one of the bullets hit Ty in the leg. He faltered and she thought he was going to fall but he kept on coming.

Chris made a dive through the merchandise, one box that was sliding across the space hit her hard in the side, but she continued until she reached the front and stuck her head out to Asher and bellowed for him to slow down, that Tynan had been shot and couldn't run.

Then she went back to the rear of the wagon to put her hand out to Ty. Asher couldn't slow down much or Dysan's men would catch them.

Tynan reached the wagon and Chris's hand just as the dogs reached Ty's heels. She helped to pull him into the wagon as Ty yelled to Asher to get the hell out of there. Ty had to shake one dog off his ankle even as the wagon bounded forward, leaving Dysan's men standing where they were.

Immediately, Chris started examining the gunshot wound on Ty's right thigh.

"Do you know if Prescott has horses ready?" he shouted to her over the noise of the wagon.

"I don't know anything. Ty, you're bleeding a lot."

"There's a place we can go. How is Pilar? Is she still on top?"

"Yes and I haven't heard a sound from her since the first shot."

Tynan frowned. "Have you got something to tie around this to stop the bleeding? It'll take us a good four hours to get where we can rest."

"Yes, of course I can, but, Ty, you need a doctor."

"About three of Dysan's men need an undertaker. Why did you come back? Why didn't you get out of here while you could?"

"We came back to save your ungrateful hide," she said as she tore off a long strip of her petticoat and began to bind his leg.

She'd barely finished tying his wound when Asher brought them to a halt that nearly sent Chris and Ty flying out the back door. Within seconds, Ash was at the back door.

"I have horses waiting. Pilar said there was an old man you knew who had a camp near here and you could lead us to him."

"How is she?" Ty asked.

Asher climbed to the top of the wagon and after a long, long moment of suspense, yelled down that she had been shot.

Ty, his wounded leg stiff in front of him, maneuvered himself out of the wagon. "How bad?" he asked quietly as he stood on the ground.

"She's alive but she's bleeding a great deal."

Chris was already climbing the little ladder that was attached to the side of the wagon and making her way up to Pilar. She gasped when she saw the woman. Pilar looked to be laying in a pool of blood, and her face was completely white.

"Ty," Chris called down, "she's wounded in her shoulder and she's unconscious. Her heartbeat is strong but she's weak. Can you help us get her down?"

"Yes," he said impatiently.

Chris worked as quickly as she could, wadding cloth against the wound and trying to tie it, but the location made a tourniquet impossible. The thud Chris heard on the roof must have been Pilar falling after she'd been shot. The guards had taken aim at the easiest target: the woman on the top of the wagon.

"We'll get her down to Ty," Chris said to Asher when she had Pilar taken care of as best she could. "Help him all you can as he's wounded too," she whispered.

Ty caught Pilar and held her then began walking with her to the waiting horses, the blood seeping from his leg, his forehead covered with sweat.

"Give her to me," Asher said, taking Pilar in his arms. "You lead."

Tynan merely nodded as he handed Pilar's inert body to Asher and started toward the horses. "There's some rough terrain ahead of us, but I don't think they'll be able to follow us. I don't want any heroics, you understand, Chris? If I tell you to go on ahead, I expect you to do it, you understand?"

"I can follow sensible orders. Shall we ride before Dysan's men find us standing here?"

Asher mounted, then Ty put Pilar in the saddle before him, so that he was holding her in place. "You think you can hold her?" Ty asked and there was a sadness in his voice that Chris was sure came from not being able to take care of her himself.

Within seconds, both she and Ty were mounted and they started to ride.

He was right when he'd said that it would be a difficult trip. They went straight up for a while, then across a boggy area that sucked at the horses' feet, then across several of Washington's cold, swift streams. For about a mile, they walked the horses through the water, hiding their trail from their pursuers.

Chris kept looking back at Pilar, whose eyes were still closed as Asher held onto her. She looked even paler.

"Watch where you're going," Tynan said in a tight-lipped way that told how much he was worried.

Once, they heard the dogs on a ridge above them and they moved their horses into the shelter of trees near a sharp rapids in the water. Chris's horse slipped but Tynan caught the reins and pulled her back to safety.

When the men and dogs were gone, they rode down the stream into the forest, going the opposite direction of their hunters.

It was nearly dark when Tynan stopped his horse and stiffly dismounted. "Wait here for me. He won't want any visitors."

"Who won't?" Chris asked but Tynan had already slipped into the trees and didn't answer her.

"The old man." It was a ragged whisper from Pilar. "Could I have some water?"

Quickly, Chris dismounted and removed her canteen from the back of the horse. Asher held it to Pilar's lips while Chris examined Pilar's wound. The bleeding had stopped, but she didn't look as if she had much strength left.

Chris's head came up as she heard the blast of a shotgun from somewhere close.

Pilar leaned back against Asher. "It's the old man," she said. "It's the man that found Tynan when he was born."

"The miner?" Chris asked.

"Whatever he calls himself. Mostly he sells whatever comes his way."

"Like six-year-old little boys," Chris said with disgust as she recapped the canteen.

Pilar didn't answer as she continued leaning against Asher, while Ash gave Chris a look that told her they needed to rest soon.

Tynan came back, moving silently through the trees, appearing almost as if from nowhere. "We have a place for a couple of days but no more," he said as he watched Chris remount and looked at Pilar with concern. He stayed back and let Asher go first, then started out beside Chris. "He's not like other people," he said to her, his eyes on the narrow trail ahead of them. "Don't turn your back on him and don't trust him. Don't tell him who your father is and don't think there's anything good about him. And don't ask him questions."

"You really hate him, don't you?" she whispered.

"Yeah, I really hate him," Ty said as he moved his horse forward to lead them up the steep hillside to the miner's cabin.

It was a nasty little building, filthy beyond belief, clinging to the side of a rock wall that fell down into a ravine below. Chris thought that the rock probably wanted to rid itself of something so dirty. There were half rotted carcasses around the doorway and the flies were so thick that they were like a black, moving curtain. Nearby were piles of animal skins and a pot of rancid meat. A scrawny dog that Chris had at first thought was dead was tied to the front wall.

"We'll leave Pilar out here while we clean this place up," Ty said as he yanked away the rope that held the starving dog in place. The poor animal limped to a pot of water with scum on it and began to lap greedily.

Ty helped Pilar off the horse while Chris stood and stared at the place, brushing away flies, trying to cover her nose at the smell.

"I ain't givin' no charity," came a voice from behind her. "You pay for what you take. I never asked for you to come here. What'd you let that dog loose for? He'll eat ever'thin' in sight."

Chris turned to see a gnarled little man with black, rotten teeth, his face twisted into an agony of misery as he saw that Tynan had begun to throw the rotten meat carcasses into the canyon below.

The old man ran toward Ty. "What are you doin'?" he whined. "That's my *food*. You're tryin' to kill me, just like you done your own mother. You wanta starve me."

Tynan ignored the old man's hands clutching at his arm and looked over his shoulder at Chris who was staring dumbfoundedly. "See to Pilar," he commanded, "and, Prescott, see if you can shoot us some fresh game. Chris, take that pot and scrub it out with sand and go up that hill to the stream and get some fresh water."

"Take, that's all you ever do. Took a woman's life

before you took your first breath. Now you want to take what's mine."

Tynan took a tool that had once been a shovel and began to use it to remove a half foot of debris from in front of the cabin, throwing it into the crevasse far below. At one animal carcass, he stopped to examine it, then tossed it to the dog that was cowering a few feet away, its breath coming quickly against its ribs.

The old miner made a lunge toward the dog to grab the meat from the starving animal, and the dog, reverting to instinct, began to fight for its life. As Chris watched, the old man took an ancient pistol from inside the layers of filthy clothes he wore and shot the dog in the leg. The animal began to whimper.

With a look of triumph, the old man took the half-rotten meat from the dog, put it under his arm, and started back toward the shack.

Tynan, with unhurried steps, walked to the old man, took the meat from him and went back to the dog. "Chris," he said as he examined the dog, "can you look at this? I don't think it's bad. He never could shoot."

It took Chris a moment to react and move from Pilar's side. With eyes wide, she went to where Ty knelt by the dog.

"Put a bandage on its leg and, here." He handed her his gun. "If he bothers the dog again, shoot him. It won't be any great loss to the world."

Chris watched, with her mouth open, as Ty gave the dog the meat and the wounded animal began to eat.

Ty put his hand under her chin and shut her mouth. "With this many flies around here, you can't afford to be astonished. Fix the dog then go get us some water. And then there's the cabin to be cleaned. You think this place is bad, wait till you step inside."

"Does he have a name?" she asked, nodding toward the old man.

"Not any that he ever gave anybody. Of course, I never tried paying him for it."

"You mean, you've been around him since you were born and you don't know his name?"

"That's right."

"You came after my gold, didn't you?" the old man wailed. "You want everything I have."

"All I want is shelter in a place that's hard to find," Ty said as he went back to cleaning the area. "I sure as hell don't want anything else from you."

Chris saw that the dog was indeed only grazed then she went to get the water bucket. It was slippery with slime. "Ty, your leg," she said, looking back at him. The tourniquet was gone and there was dried blood about the wound but now, with this new activity, it was beginning to bleed again.

"I can't stop now," he said. "Go get the water."

As Chris took the bucket and started up the hill, the old man stopped in front of her. The foul smell that rose from him took her breath away. "He don't have a mother. He killed her."

Chris moved away from him as she'd moved away from the piles of rotting meat.

By the time she returned with the newly clean bucket and fresh water, Asher was back with a deer he'd shot and Tynan had cleaned a place under a lean-to for Pilar. Chris saw that his leg was bleeding steadily.

Asher prepared a fire and began to roast the meat while the old man crouched on the outside of the group watching them suspiciously.

Tynan eased himself down onto the ground near

where Pilar rested on a blanket covered pile of hay. For just a moment, Chris saw pain register on his face. It was growing dark now and the only light was from the fire.

"We have to make some plans," Ty said and he sounded very tired. "Prescott, we'll have to take turns keeping watch."

"Watch?" Chris asked. "But surely Dysan's men won't be able to find us here. The dogs won't be able to track us after the number of streams we crossed, and, Ty, you need to rest."

"I thank you for your concern, but it's not Dysan who needs watching. It's him." He nodded his head toward the old miner. "If he thinks there's a reward for us, he'll find whoever wants us and bring them here. We have to stay awake to make sure he doesn't leave."

"Oh," Chris said, taking meat from Asher and moving to lift Pilar. Tomorrow she'd try to make a broth but for now this would have to do. "Then as long as we stay here someone has to stay awake and watch him."

"If we want to stay alive," Ty said.

Asher cut off chunks of the roasted meat. "Pilar needs a doctor and she needs to rest. And you're in worse shape than you let on."

"I'll be all right," Ty said. "But I agree that we have to take care of Pilar, it's just that I don't know anywhere else that's as safe as this—or it would be safe if he weren't here."

Asher threw the old man a piece of meat as if he were a dog, and the man grabbed it, hiding it from the others, eating it with watchful eyes. "What we need is some help," Asher said as he looked at Chris. "If we could get a message to your father, he could send an army of men to escort us back to his place. I don't think even Dysan wants to take on Mathison's men."

Chris drew her knees to her chest and gave a little smile. "Yes, my father could defeat him. But he's there and we're here."

"You have to go get him, Prescott," Tynan said. "You have to leave the women and me here and travel as fast as you can and bring Mathison back."

"And leave you to the mercies of that?" Asher asked, motioning toward the old man. "Do you have any idea how many people are looking for you?"

Tynan looked toward the dark sky for a moment. "About half a dozen Chanrys, a hundred or so of Dysan's men and . . ."

"And Rory Sayers would probably like a piece of your skin," Chris added.

"And what was the name of that man on the far side of the rain forest?"

"Ah, yes," Chris smiled. "Hugh Lanier. I don't imagine he's over his anger at what I wrote." She smiled at Tynan, remembering the way he'd helped her that day.

Tynan leaned back against a post. "So half the world is looking for us, two of us are damaged, and we have a traitor—if he were given the chance to be—in our midst. It doesn't make for a secure, healthful future."

"I'll take him with me," Asher said softly. "I'll take the old man with me and leave the three of you here alone and I'll bring back Mathison with every man he can spare."

"He'll slit your throat the first time you turn your back on him or the first time you sleep."

"I'll not turn my back on him and if I sleep, I'll tie

him up. It's our only chance and you know it. You can't take care of him here and all I have to do is get him fifty miles south of here and then Mathison can have him. It's our only chance. One man might make it out of here, but not two women and a wounded man."

Chris could see the way Tynan was considering Asher's words. She could see how much he hated them, how much he hated being put in such a position. And she also realized that he must be hurt more than he was allowing them to know if he were so much as considering what Asher proposed.

"Ty, it's the only way," Chris whispered. "We can't move Pilar and we can't leave her here. Dysan is out there and someone has to go for help." She arched one eyebrow at him. "Are you afraid you won't get your pardon if someone else brings my father to me?"

Tynan looked at her for a long time before he spoke. "Prescott, you'll leave early in the morning. I'll stay awake tonight and watch the old man and you sleep. I want you rested in the morning. Now, the both of you go to bed."

Chapter Twenty-two

Once Tynan sat down, he didn't seem able to get up again. Chris rebandaged the wound in his leg, finding that the bullet wasn't in it as she'd feared. While she worked on him, he lay still, leaning back against the post, his eyes closed, seemingly unaware of Chris's hands on his thigh. She tried to touch him as little as possible, tried to not show how the sight of his torn flesh upset her.

"I don't think Prescott can handle the old man. Prescott's not mean enough. He's too trusting."

"Ty, how long did you spend with that man? Did you really have to live with him?"

"Off and on until I was six, but kids learn fast. It didn't take me long to learn that I had to take care of myself."

"As independent as you are, why didn't you run away when he . . . when he sold you? Couldn't you have gone back to Red's?"

Tynan opened his eyes and looked at her. "I was

266

drunk, and he kept me that way for two days before the"—Ty grimaced—"sale."

"But you were only six years old."

"I've never met a little kid yet that didn't like beer. You ought to get some sleep now. You'll need rest for tomorrow."

Standing, she took the bucket of bloody water and moved away from him, watching him as he leaned against the pole. He looked as if he were asleep but she could see the dark light of his eyes between his lashes. He planned to stay awake all night to protect them from the old man—but he didn't tie the man or incapacitate him, and she wondered why.

She moved away from Ty to go back to the spring to get fresh water.

"Chris."

She was startled to hear Asher's voice so near.

"May I speak to you?"

"You should be asleep. You have a hard ride ahead of you tomorrow and Ty says—"

"Ty says! That's all I hear, that Tynan says this and Tynan says that."

"He is the leader of this group," Chris said, "and it's been his decisions that have kept us from getting killed." She continued on her way to the spring.

He caught her arm. "I didn't mean to be angry. I guess I'm just jealous. Chris, the real reason I wanted to talk to you is . . ."

"Yes," she said, looking up at him in the moonlight. "What did you want to say to me?"

"I wanted to ask you to marry me."

Chris was taken aback for a moment. All she'd been able to think about for the last few days was getting away from Dysan. "Isn't this rather sudden?"

"You know it isn't. Chris, I've fallen in love with you, with your spirit and your courage. Any woman who'd chop through the back of a wagon to make herself heard is the woman I want to spend my life with, no milksop women for me."

"And it's not my father's money? Or the fact that he's offered you a position in his business? That doesn't make me more attractive to you?"

Asher opened his mouth to speak but nothing came out. Instead, he drew Chris to him and kissed her softly and gently. "At one time, I thought that I'd have married Del Mathison's daughter if she were as ugly as my father's favorite mule, but then I met you and everything changed. Chris, you're like no other woman I've ever met. I wish with all my heart that you'd marry me. And if it's your money you think I'm after, I'll give up all claim to it. I think that with you at my side, I could start over again, and this time I wouldn't fail."

Still holding her in his arms, he smiled down at her. "I don't think you'd allow any failure on my part. I think if there were a setback in my finances, you'd crack a whip over my head, and not allow me to give up."

She smiled back. "No, I don't guess I do give up, not if I want something badly enough." Suddenly, she thought of Tynan. "Unless I have to give up," she murmured.

"I think we'd make a good pair," he said. "We'd have my level-headedness and your spirit. I could keep your feet on the earth and you could prevent me from giving up when the going gets rough."

She laughed. "You make us sound like a merger."

He snuggled her closer. "Some mergers can be quite good. Chris, please say you'll think about it. I'll do

268

whatever you want. If you want me to renounce your father's money, I'll do so. Whatever you say."

"That seems rather drastic and my father does want someone to help him run the place."

"Are you saying you'll marry me?" he asked, his eyes alight.

"Like hell she will," came Tynan's voice from behind them. "Get your hands off her, Prescott. And if you don't, I'll shoot them off."

Chris moved away from Asher. "You're supposed to be asleep."

"Is that what you were hoping? That I was asleep so you could meet him behind my back?"

"Now just one minute, Tynan," Asher said. "I have every right to do whatever Miss Mathison wants. After all, you were hired to help me win her. Oh, Chris," he said as he realized what he'd revealed.

"It's all right, I knew. Tynan, you have no right to interfere in what I do. Now, I want you to go back to—"

She didn't finish the sentence because Tynan grabbed her arm and pulled her to him. He couldn't walk very well as his leg was stiffening, but he could force her closer to him. "Prescott, go back to the camp and see to Pilar and watch the old man. I'll be there in a minute."

Asher started to protest, but one look at Tynan made him decide against it and he turned back toward the cabin.

"Get your hands off of me!" Chris said, trying to jerk away from him, but not succeeding. "You have no right to interfere in this. Besides, I believe my father hired you to *help* him fall in love with me."

"I don't even want to know how you found that out, but that was before . . ."

"Yes? That was before what?" She was looking up at him with anger flashing in her eyes.

He grabbed her to him, burying her face in his shoulder for a moment, then kissing her as if he were starving.

"Please don't, Ty," she said, her voice sounding as if she were in agony. "Please leave me alone." She tried to push away from him, but he wouldn't release her.

"Chris, I can't stand to see him touching you. I just can't stand it." His hands were going up and down her back, caressing her, touching her neck, his thumbs toying with her ears.

She managed to push away far enough to look at him. "*You* can't stand it? What right do you have to prevent me from doing anything? What right do you have to even voice an opinion? I made an absolute fool of myself over you and you threw everything in my face and now you stand here and tell me I can't talk to a man who has the most honorable of intentions."

"My intentions toward you are honorable. I've always been fair and honest with you. And now I'm saying that if Prescott touches you again, I'll shoot him. I can't be more honest than that."

"You!" she gasped and gave a lunge that separated her from him. "What you want from me isn't honorable. All you want is a . . . is for me to . . ." She was glad the darkness covered her red face.

"So what's wrong with that? You didn't seem to mind the last time. Ah, Chris, I don't want to fight. We had a good time that night and, besides, I haven't had any women since then."

Chris was sure that her anger was about to make her explode. "You haven't had any *women*—plural—since then? Am I supposed to feel sympathy for you? Am I supposed to do what you want merely because you've been on the run and haven't had time to—"

"I had time," he said. "I just didn't want any that were offered."

Chris sputtered for a moment. Was he actually asking her for sympathy? "So now you're . . . and I'm supposed to . . . of all the dastardly, disgusting, repulsive things—I want you to know that Asher asked me to *marry* him. He didn't ask for a quick assignation, he wanted to marry me, to live with me forever."

"He wants to live with your father's money forever."

"So what's the difference between you two? He wants my money and you want my body. Neither of you seem to want *me*. Well, let me tell you, Mr. Tynan," she advanced on him, "I'm not sure I want either one of you. I certainly don't want what you offer."

He caught her arm. "Chris, you do want me. I know it. I can see it in your eyes. And I want you, so why not?"

She gave him a serious look, the muscles in her jaw working. "And do you plan to include marriage in your offer?" she asked softly.

He took a step back from her as if she'd just contracted a contagious disease. "Marriage? Chris, you know that's impossible. Your father would send me back to jail on a life sentence and then you'd have no husband. I couldn't do that to you."

"Men!" she gasped. "What convenient memories you have. My father said that you'd return to prison if you *touched* me, yet you were more than willing to risk that because it was something you wanted. But now you hold it up to me when the matter of marriage is mentioned. Listen to me, Tynan, and listen good. I am *not* going to go to bed with you again and you can believe me." She turned on her heel and started up the hill toward the spring, grabbing the bucket in anger.

"You'll give in," Ty said after her, "and you'd better not let Prescott touch you."

"You hardheaded, vain . . . cowboy, I'm never going to let you touch me again!" She dug the bucket into the spring water, then, on impulse, stuck her face under the cold water. She wasn't sure whether she needed cooling off from her temper or from Tynan's kisses, but, whichever it was, her blood was steaming.

She stayed at the stream for a while before returning to the cabin and settling down beside Pilar to sleep. She woke repeatedly during the night, sometimes sitting up with a jolt and looking around her. Each time she woke, she saw that Tynan was still leaning against the post, still watching the old man.

By the time morning came, she felt as if she'd not been asleep at all. She sat up, rubbing her aching back and looked around her. Ty was gone from his post and Asher was in the yard in front of the cabin saddling his horse. She walked toward him.

"The old man's giving Ty trouble," Ash said in the way of a greeting. "We may have to tie him on his horse just to get him out of here."

Chris stifled a yawn. "I hope he ties him face down over the saddle."

Asher caught her arm and pulled her close to him. "This is the last time I'll see you for a while. I hope you'll miss me. I hope you'll think about my proposal. I hope you'll . . ." He began to kiss her neck. "I hope you'll say yes."

The next minute, Asher was on the ground as Tynan

jerked him away from Chris. Ty stood over him, feet apart, fists ready.

"Come on, Prescott, get up. You've been asking for this for a long time. Or aren't you man enough to maul somebody your own size? Do you only pick on women?"

"For heaven's sake!" Chris said, going to Asher to help him up.

Tynan advanced on the man.

"If you touch him again," she said, "so help me, I'll ride out of here with him. What in the world is wrong with you?"

Tynan lowered his fists and there was a bewildered expression on his face. "I don't know," he said in wonder. "Prescott, you better go now so you can use all the daylight. The old man will go with you but you'll have to watch him every minute. I think he understands now that we're hiding out so he'll do what he can to make money off that knowledge."

As Asher stood, Tynan looked a bit sheepish for a moment, then he turned back toward Chris. "You wouldn't go, would you? I mean, I'd have to bring you back and someone needs to stay with Pilar."

Chris looked at him for a long moment. "No," she said at last, "I won't leave. Not if you don't hit Asher again. Now, could you leave us alone? I'd like to say good-bye."

Tynan didn't move a step. "You can say good-bye right now. He has to leave."

"If you think—" Chris began, ready to give him a piece of her mind, but a call from Pilar stopped her. "Yes, I'm coming," she answered, then deliberately turned and put her arms around Asher, meaning to kiss him good-bye, and show Tynan that he had no right to give her orders. But her lips never reached Asher's because Tynan pulled her away from him and held her to him, her back against his front.

"Get on your horse, Prescott," he said in a deadly voice.

Asher hesitated for a moment, but, then, with a sigh, he put his foot in the stirrup. "We'll settle this later," he said, glancing back to the old man who was sitting atop Tynan's horse and ready to leave.

Tynan, still holding Chris, stepped back. "Make sure you watch him night and day. Don't give him a minute or he'll take all you have and maybe your life with it."

"Yeah," Asher muttered and, with one quick look at Chris, reined his horse away. "Come on, old man," he called over his shoulder and then was gone from sight.

Chris pushed away from Tynan. "Release me, you oaf!"

She turned to look at him, anger in her eyes. "What right do you think you have to tell me what to do? Just who do you think you are?"

Tynan looked completely confused, seemed to want to say something but, instead, turned on his heel and went up the hill toward the spring.

Chris stood there for a moment, glaring after him, before she went to Pilar.

"I thought there was going to be a fight there for a moment," Pilar said as Chris handed her a full canteen.

"I'd like to take a club to his head," Chris said. "He doesn't want me but then he hits anyone else who *does* want me."

Pilar leaned back against the hay as Chris began unbandaging her shoulder. "Oh, he wants you all right. He wants you badly."

"And I know exactly how he wants me." Pilar

smiled. "I've never seen him like this. Even that time with that rancher's daughter, he wasn't like this. We all hoped then that he was going to settle down, but it didn't work out."

"Was that when he ended up in prison?"

"Red tell you about it?"

"Most of it. Pilar, how do you know Tynan? Why were you living with him at Owen Hamilton's?"

"He saved my husband's life."

Chris stopped cleaning Pilar's wound. "Your husband?"

"I used to work with Red when I was younger. Tynan was there, the prettiest, sweetest little boy you ever met, and we all adored him. After the old man took him away when he was six, I hardly ever saw him again. And when I did see him, I'd see that he'd grown harder. He'd seen a lot in his short life and it'd made him cynical. But by then I'd married a rancher and we had a couple of kids of our own and I wanted to forget where I'd known Ty."

"Children?" Chris whispered.

Pilar smiled. "Two little boys. They're nine and seven now." She paused a moment. "One day I was in town and I saw Tynan on the street. He grinned at me and started toward me, and all I could think of was that he was going to let the 'good' townspeople know where I came from and they were going to see that I wasn't the respectable rancher's wife they thought I was. I hate to say it, but I ducked into a store and acted as if I didn't know him. Ty was the perfect gentleman and two days later when I ran into him again, he acted as if he'd never seen me before in his life."

"So how did he save your husband's life?"

"I don't like what I did then. I wouldn't speak to Ty

on the street but a week later, when my husband was being threatened by a big rancher trying to drive us off our little place, I didn't hesitate to ask Ty for help—and Tynan didn't hesitate to come to my aid."

"But later, when he asked you to help him get into Hamilton's house, you agreed."

"I didn't even ask what he wanted. I just kissed my family good-bye and went with him. Jimmy didn't ask what he wanted either, because he knew he could trust Ty."

Chris's hands paused in rebandaging Pilar's shoulder. "Why *did* he want you to come and pretend to be his wife?"

Pilar smiled. "He wouldn't say, wouldn't answer me when I asked him. But one day, he muttered something about a curvy little blonde who was trying to tempt him out of his soul."

"Hmph!" Chris said. "Some tempting I've done! I made the fatal error of liking him, just plain liking him. I liked the way he took on responsibility when he was leading us through the rain forest. And he helped me when I needed him."

"And then he also happens to be the most beautiful man alive," Pilar added.

"That had nothing to do with it. He was so quiet. With most men who are silent, I usually find that they just plain don't have anything to say, but I thought that maybe Tynan did have something to say, but he was repressing it. I'm not sure what it was, but I was certainly drawn to him."

"Was?" Pilar asked. "You aren't any longer?"

Chris rocked back on her heels. "He isn't any different from other men. He only wants one thing. I thought he felt the same way about me that I did about him, but he told me he wanted nothing to do with me, that I was wrong about him. He told me to leave him alone—except of course I was free to . . ."

"To go to bed with him?"

Chris nodded, her head down. "I'm not any different from a hundred other women to him."

"I've never seen him act like he did a few minutes ago with another woman. I've never seen even the slightest sign of jealousy before. Are you sure you aren't different?"

Chris stood, taking the bowl of dirty water with her. "I'm quite sure. He's made it clear what he wants from me and he just doesn't want anyone else to have what he's being denied. Tynan doesn't love me any more than he loves . . . than he loves that old dog. Now, I want you to rest and I'm going to cook something, if I can find anything around here that's edible."

"Anything will be all right," Pilar said thoughtfully. "Ty will help you. He is quite capable of handling anything."

"He can't handle love," Chris said softly. "He can't find love at the end of a gun or by using his fists, so he runs away from it. Go to sleep now."

Chapter Twenty-three

Chris spent an hour trying to make a stew with the few ingredients from around the cabin and from the saddle bags. There hadn't been much time to pack when they'd been escaping Dysan and now they were feeling the lack of provisions. She looked at the cabin and decided to see if there was anything inside it. So far, the smell of the place had kept her from getting too close to it.

Holding her breath, she went to the door and looked inside. This looked as if it were the old man's treasure trove. He seemed to have kept everything he'd ever owned. No matter how worn out it was, how deteriorated, how many bugs infested it, the old man had kept it.

Chris glanced over her shoulder toward where Pilar was resting and she felt a renewal of courage. What was a little unpleasant smell or a few crawly things compared to a human's comfort?

She took the shovel that Tynan had leaned against the outside wall of the cabin and began to carve a way into the interior.

Two hours later, she had made a huge pile outside by the edge of the cliff. She wasn't going to push anything over until she'd had a chance to inspect it in the daylight, but, mostly, there seemed to be improperly cured hides and hardened pieces of food that were covered with ants.

In the back corner of the single room, she found a little wooden crate, the kind used to ship fragile items across the sea. Lifting it, she carried it outside into the sunlight.

It had a big lock on it, but, like everything else in the cabin, the lock was rusting away, so, after a few minutes of work, she managed to open it. There were a few dollars inside, with mold growing on the bills, a big rock that looked as if it were solid gold, and in the bottom was a photograph of a young, pretty woman. Chris held it to the light, wiped the mold off a corner, and studied the woman. She looked happy and pleased about something and ready to take on the world. With a smile, Chris put the photo in her pocket and began to close the box.

"Anything interesting?" came Ty's voice from behind her.

"You should be sleeping," she said. "You were awake all night."

"I got enough. What are you doing? I never saw a woman who liked to snoop more than you do."

"I wasn't snooping, I was cleaning."

With an infuriatingly knowing little smile, he sat down beside her. "Cleaning inside locked boxes?" he asked, nodding toward the big, rusty lock on the ground beside her. "Find anything interesting?"

"Only about two pounds of gold," she said smugly, holding out the big rock to him. "This is why your miner doesn't want to leave this place."

Ty took the rock, leaned back on one elbow and looked at it. "Fool's gold," he said. "The old man doesn't know gold when he sees it. Up on the side of the hill, there's a place where he's been digging for years. He was digging it when I was a kid."

Chris took the rock from Tynan. "If there's no gold, why does he stay here? Why does he live like this?"

"He believes there is gold and facts have nothing to do with this man's beliefs. As for why he lives like this, he's just afraid to let anything go. If he can't sell it today, he'll keep it until it's worth something."

"Like babies. They're not worth much as newborns, but strong little boys can work." Tynan didn't reply to her, just gazed at a bird overhead, seeming to be content to lie still for the moment. "How has he lived up here? He must have had money for food from somewhere. Has he always stolen things and sold them?"

Tynan took a while to answer. "He used to steal but now I send him money when I can."

"You? But why? After what he did to you and the way you hate him, I'd have thought you'd do nothing for him."

"That old man is the closest thing to a father I've ever had. Besides, I didn't want him selling any more children."

"I wonder how someone like him got to be the way he is. I wonder what awful things happened to him. I bet he was in love once. Maybe he lost her and never recovered."

Ty was looking at her as if she'd lost her mind. "What makes you think that old man ever loved anybody?"

"I found a picture of the woman he loved."

"Let me see it," Ty said softly and Chris gave him the photograph. He looked at it a long while before handing it back to her. "He said he threw it over the side and I believed him."

"You've seen this?"

"It was my most treasured possession for most of my life."

She hesitated. "Who is this woman?"

"I've been told she's my mother."

"Your mother? But, Ty, don't you realize that if you have this maybe you can find out who she is? Find out who you are?"

"I know who I am," he said with a set jaw.

Chris looked at the picture for a while. "What's her name?"

"I have no idea."

"But didn't you ask?"

He looked at her. "Who was I going to ask? The old man told me she said one word before she died and that was, 'Tynan.' "

"Did you show the photo to the women in . . . to Red and the others?"

"Sure, they saw it, but no one knew who she was. They thought it was all real romantic and they kept buying frames for the picture, then the old man'd come and take the frame and sell it. It was a great source of income to him for years."

Chris turned the picture over. "It says something on the back, but I can't make it out."

"Sa. It has the letters Sa on the back and the rest is faded. I used to imagine that my mother's name was Sarah."

"You've spent a lot of time looking at this, haven't you?"

Tynan didn't answer her, but lay on his back and looked at the sky. "I missed seeing the sky while I was in prison. What you can see is covered by iron bars. And I didn't like the noise either."

Chris wanted to hear more about the photo. "How did the old man get this picture? If she had this, she must have had other things too."

"He sold everything else, even her clothes and her underwear. I imagine he threw her naked body off the side there. Or else it's still around here."

"Tynan! How can you be so crass? The woman was your mother, and she died giving birth to you."

He sat up. "She died from three bullet wounds in her back."

"But who wanted to kill her? Why?"

"Is there anything to eat around here? Maybe I could scout up some game."

"Are you going to answer me? Do you have any idea why someone would shoot a woman who was carrying a child?"

He looked down at her. "Why do men cheat at cards? Why do men get drunk and try to kill each other? I don't know. She wandered in here with three big holes in her back, lay down, gave birth to me, said 'Tynan,' then died. That's the sum of all I know. The miner watched her give birth, planned to leave both her and the kid, but then he thought he could sell what clothes she hadn't bled on and the screaming brat, so he stripped her and carried me down the mountain. That's it, Chris, that's all there is to tell. He sold everything except the picture. Nobody wanted a photo of a woman they didn't know, so I took it one summer when he had me up here working. Now, can I eat?"

Chris sat on the ground and looked at the picture. "She's a very pretty woman."

"Was. She *was* pretty. She's been dead for a long time. Chris, why are you so all-fired interested in my mother?"

"I'm interested in—" She stopped abruptly. She'd almost said that she was interested in him. "I'm a reporter," she said, rising. "I'm curious, that's all. I'm curious about everything."

"Well, I'm curious about what's cooking in that pot." He moved closer to her. "Maybe you could go hunting with me."

"I can't leave Pilar."

"She can go with us. It'll do her good to walk around some."

"I don't think so. I need to clean up around here and . . ."

Ty moved even closer to her, then put his hand to the side of her face. "Chris, please go with me. I promise I'll behave. I won't do anything you don't want me to."

She took a step away from him. He could use that voice of his to make a person's resolve melt. "I shouldn't. I should . . ."

"Should what?" he asked, following her as she backed away.

"Chris!" Pilar called. "I'd love to get some exercise. Could you go with Ty for my sake?"

"I . . . I guess so," she began, looking into Tynan's

smiling eyes. "But don't you try anything," she warned. "I'm not going to give into you."

His eyelids lowered. "Sweetheart, I haven't even *asked* you yet."

After Tynan had eaten most of the stew Chris had cooked, he took his rifle, helped Pilar to stand and started up the little trail behind the cabin. Chris complained twice about his walking on his injured leg, but he just grinned at her.

"Remember the time you and the Chanry boys robbed that bank down in Texas and—" Pilar began.

"Robbed the bank?" Chris gasped. "Robbed a bank!"

Ty winked at Pilar. "She thinks I'm as clean as a new snow, that I'm innocent on all counts."

"I've seen you shoot people. I took him to a picnic and he got into a fight with a man and the man got shot. On a church picnic, mind you."

"Rory Sayers," Ty said to Pilar as if that were answer enough.

"I never met anyone who was asking for it more," Pilar said. "Ty, didn't you have a garden up here when you were a boy?"

Chris trailed along behind the two of them and felt as if she'd just entered a party and she was the only one who didn't know everyone. Pilar and Ty talked easily about things that were meaningless to her. They exchanged names of people and places, fantastic happenings such as repeated brushes with the law, shootouts, the names of outlaws she'd only read about.

At the top of the hill, Tynan moved some underbrush about until they saw a little clearing. "It was here," he said, "and I planted carrots and potatoes and strawberries. The strawberries didn't make it and the rabbits kept eating the tops of the carrots as soon as they grew above the ground. Look at this," he said, holding up a rusty can that had been flattened. "One of my first targets. I used to practice up here for hours."

"Not much else to do," Pilar said. "Is the old man's gold mine near here?"

"Not far, just along that trail."

Pilar turned and started walking but Chris held back. Tynan went to her, and, before she could stop him, he put his arms around her. "Feeling a little lost?"

She pushed at him but he still held her. "Of course not."

"We could tell Pilar to go away and you and I could go into the bushes. I know a place that was made for making love. It's quiet, secluded, near a little stream and flowers grow there all summer long. Would you like to make love on a bed of flowers?"

"No I wouldn't," she said, but there wasn't much conviction in her voice. "I don't want to be any man's woman of no morals."

"Morals? What do morals have to do with making love? Chris, honey, I could make you feel so good. We could make each other feel good."

She twisted away from him. "Leave me alone, Tynan. I'm not going to be one of your women and you'd better get used to the idea. I'm going to go home to my father and I just might stay there and marry some rancher and have a dozen or so children."

"Who do you have in mind?" he asked angrily. "Prescott?"

"I'm sure Asher would make a fine husband and he has asked me and I just might say yes. What does it matter to you, anyway? You don't want to be saddled with a wife and kids. You've made your choice and I've made mine, so what do you have to complain about?"

She could see the anger in his eyes.

"You call yourself a woman of morals, but what's the difference between selling yourself for a few bucks and selling yourself for a piece of paper and a gold ring?"

She glared up at him. "At least *I* get to choose what the price will be—not you." She swept past him and continued up the trail after Pilar.

She found Pilar standing outside a dark hole that seemed to be the mine entrance, holding a rock like the one Chris had found in the chest in the cabin.

"It's full of this stuff. I guess he thinks it's gold and everybody is just too stupid to know that it is." Pilar looked up at Chris. "Uh-oh, it looks like you two have been at it again."

"No, we haven't. He is the most stubborn man. He can't seem to get it through his thick skull that when I say no, I mean no. Hasn't *any* woman ever said no to him before?"

"I doubt it," Pilar said seriously. "But then I've never seen him pursue a woman before you either. He usually just sits down and that face of his does the rest. At worst, he has to open his mouth and speak and if there's one woman who hasn't yet thawed, she will when she hears that voice of his."

"I expect more from a man than just beauty and a nice voice. And Tynan doesn't seem capable of giving that."

In the distance, they heard the sound of a rifle shot. "I think he got us something to eat. Let's go and meet him," Pilar said.

When Chris seemed determined to stay where she

was, Pilar took her arm. "In a few days your father will be here and you'll never have to see Ty again. This is the first rest any of us have had in ages, so let's make the most of it; all right?"

Reluctantly, Chris allowed Pilar to pull her forward. She wasn't about to show anyone how the thought of never seeing Ty again made her heart jump into her throat.

When they found Tynan he was already skinning a small deer and Chris built a fire. Soon the smell of roasting venison filled the air.

"Nice place, isn't it?" Ty asked, handing Chris a piece of meat.

She looked around and realized that this was the place he'd just described—the place where he'd wanted to make love to her. "It's all right," she said coolly. "Pilar, why don't you tell us about the joys of married life? And about your children? How old are they?"

She ignored Tynan's heartfelt groan as she turned her head and began listening to a homesick Pilar as she told about her husband and children. She didn't gloss over the hardship of their lives, or dismiss the constant poverty and struggle, but there was a lovely sense of togetherness that Chris knew she wanted in her life. In turn, Pilar asked Chris about her newspaper stories and said how exciting all that must be.

"It was, but I'm ready to settle down."

"She's been ready ever since a certain party jumped out of a clothes wardrobe," Tynan said from behind her, his voice heavy with sarcasm. "She thinks that if a man touches her, he has to marry her."

"That's not true at all!" Chris said, turning on him. "I don't know why I ever thought I was in love with you. You are insufferably vain and are too used to getting your own way. I doubt if I'd marry you now if you were to beg me."

"Don't hold your breath. A week from now, I'm going to be free. I won't have the responsibility of taking care of some spoiled little rich girl who thinks she can have whatever—or whoever—she wants merely by asking. I'm going to be *free,* you hear me? Not you or anybody else is going to take away my freedom."

"Stop it, both of you," Pilar said. "You sound like my two boys. Look, we have to spend the next few days together so why don't we try to get along? Ty, you're probably angry because you haven't had any sleep and your leg hurts. Why don't you lay your head in Chris's lap and she'll tell us a story? I'd offer my lap but I plan to stretch out here and sleep myself."

Chris didn't look at Tynan and there was a long moment of silence. "All right," she said at last. "Maybe we do need some rest. You may use my lap."

"Only if you swear this won't be taken as a marriage proposal."

"If you were one of my children," Pilar said, "I'd smack you for that. Now lay down there and behave yourself."

Chris leaned back against a tree and Tynan lay his head in her lap. For a moment, they were very stiff, touching as little as possible.

"I read a book in French last year, *Le Comte de Monte Cristo,* I could tell that story," Chris said.

"Only if the people don't get married and live happily ever after," Tynan said, his head turned, his eyes closed.

"It's a story about greed, betrayal, infidelity, murder and revenge. I think it might be your autobiography."

"Sounds all right," he said, snuggling his head in her lap.

"I'm sure the French nation will be pleased that you approve." She started her story, telling of the revenge that began over two men in love with the same woman.

"Figures," Ty grunted, but said nothing else while Chris's voice began to soften as she told the story.

Within minutes, she heard the soft sounds of Pilar's breathing as she slept in the drowsy afternoon. Tynan also seemed to be asleep, and, feeling safe, she began to stroke his hair back from his face. He looked so young with his face relaxed. There was a dirty bandage on his leg, dirty from his constant moving about the forest, showing through the hole in his trousers that the bullet had made.

She kept on with her story, even though she knew that both her listeners were asleep, but she liked stories and she liked to tell them. At the tragic end of the story, she stopped, her hand on the side of Tynan's face, her fingers buried in the curls of his dark hair, and listened to the birds.

"I liked that," he said softly into the stillness.

"I thought you were asleep," she said and started to move her hand away.

He caught it in his own. "No, I wanted to hear the story. A store clerk told me that at about the time I was born, the miner sold him a book. I always wondered if it was a book from my mother and, if it was, what it was. I've always liked stories." Idly, he began to kiss her fingertips, as if it were the most natural thing in the world to do.

"Will you stop that?"

"Chris, if I were going to get married, I swear, you'd

be the first woman I'd consider. In fact, thinking about living with you is the most tempting offer I've ever had. You're pretty, enthusiastic in bed—"

She gave a sharp look at Pilar but she seemed to be sound asleep.

"And you're the most interesting woman I've ever met. I've talked to you and told you things I've never told anybody, but, the truth is, I'm just not marriage material. I don't think I could stay in one place for very long—that is, if I ever get out of jail where your father would throw me if I dared think I was going to marry his precious daughter. Don't you see that it just wouldn't work?"

Chris didn't let the anger she felt show. It seemed that men could rationalize anything. He didn't want to get married—was probably terrified of the idea—so he tried to tell her that he couldn't because he was only thinking of her. "I understand completely," she said with sympathy in her voice. "You don't want to get married and I refuse to sleep with a man who won't marry me. We'll leave it at that."

He turned his head to look up at her. "But, Chris, shouldn't we take what happiness we can find? When we can find it? Before we're separated forever and never see each other again?"

She gave him her sweetest smile. "Not on your life."

For a moment, she thought he was going to start yelling at her again, but there was just the hint of a smile on his full lips. "You can't blame a man for trying." He turned his head again and resumed kissing her fingertips. "By my calculations, we have at least four more days before Prescott returns with your father. Who knows what will happen in that time?"

"I know what will *not* happen," she said smugly, but

290

Tynan didn't seem to believe her as he began applying his teeth to her sensitive palm.

"There you are, old man," Asher Prescott said as he readjusted the smelly man's bindings for the third time. There was a part of Asher that was bothered by what they'd done: they'd taken the man from his home and now he was being bound hand and foot, yet the old man had done nothing to merit such abuse. So, when the old man had complained that the ropes were too tight, Asher had had pity on him and loosened them.

"I'm going to get some sleep now," Asher said, rubbing his eyes. He'd been in the saddle for almost two days and he knew that if he didn't rest, he'd never make it to Del Mathison's house.

With one last look of sympathy at the old man who huddled against a tree, his little dark eyes looking suspicious, Asher settled down to sleep, using his saddle as a pillow.

The old man seemed as if he too slept, until he heard the soft snores from Asher, then he wiggled his hands and the ropes fell away. "Fool," he muttered, looking at Asher's sleeping form with contempt as he untied his feet. "Fool."

He stood, making no noise at all, looked around a bit until he saw a large rock nearby then picked it up and crept toward Asher. He brought the rock crashing down on Asher's head as he slept.

The old man stood over Ash for a moment, looking at the unconscious form before ransacking his pockets. It took him only fifteen minutes before he'd taken everything of value from Asher, leaving him lying there in his underwear only, his saddle and gun gone, no money, no boots. For a moment, the old man contemplated taking his underwear or at least cutting the buttons off, but he heard a horse in the distance and decided to get out of there.

As he mounted one horse, leading the other one, he began to mutter, "You think you're so smart, Mr. Mother-Killer Tynan, but I know somebody that'll pay to know where you are. I know somebody. I'll show you." He cursed and muttered as he traveled north toward the Dysan estate.

Chapter Twenty-four

Chris tried her best to stay away from Tynan for the next two days, but it was almost impossible to do. If she went for water, there he was. If she stopped for a moment to look at the scenery, there he was, his eyes on her in invitation. Once, she jumped when she heard something in the underbrush and Ty was there to put his arms around her and hold her. They heard shots in the distance on the morning of the second day and her heart was in her throat as Tynan, with rifle in hand, crept down the steep path to see who it was. She nearly cried with relief when he came back to tell her that it was only hunters and they were far away.

"Worried about me?" he asked, his eyes hot and showing his desire for her.

Chris picked up her skirts and fled from him.

"Anything wrong?" Pilar asked innocently. She'd taken over the cooking ever since Chris had ruined some of their precious flour trying to make biscuits.

"That man is the worst!" she said, her heart pounding.

"He certainly does like you."

"Well, I don't like him."

Pilar snorted. "Didn't your mother teach you not to lie?"

"I think there were many things my mother didn't teach me," Chris said softly. "Such as how to say no to persuasive gunslingers. Pilar, I think I'm weakening. Two more days of this and I won't be able to say no to anything he asks of me."

"I have an idea Ty knows that."

"Well, I have to be strong. I am *not* going to give into him and that's final. No matter what he says to me, no matter how he looks at me, I'm not going to give into him." She looked at Pilar with great sadness and worry in her eyes. "But if he kisses the back of my neck one more time, I'm lost."

Pilar turned back to her biscuits with a smile on her face.

Chris succeeded in staying away from Ty for the rest of the day but that night he asked her to take a walk with him.

"I didn't ask you to run off with me, Chris, just take a walk," he said when he saw her lips form the word 'no.' "I swear I won't touch you since I know you can't trust yourself with me, but at least—"

"Can't trust myself with you! I most certainly can trust myself with you. I could spend the rest of my life on a tropical island with you and still resist you," she lied.

"That's great," he said with a grin. "Then you can go with me into the moonlight right now."

Chris knew she'd talked herself into a corner and so

she appealed to Pilar for help, but Pilar refused to go with them, saying that her arm hurt too much. Of course it hadn't hurt while she'd pounded dough, but now it was too painful for her to even move.

Reluctantly, Chris started walking up the little trail toward the spring, Tynan behind her.

"Are we competing in a road race or are you afraid to walk beside me?" he asked.

She stopped and turned toward him. "Of course I'm not afraid to walk with you. It's just that you don't realize how slow your sore leg makes you."

"Is that it?" he said, smiling in a knowing way. He took her arm in his. "Then maybe you should help poor little invalid me," he said.

They walked together for a few moments, Chris trying to stay away from him in spite of their locked arms.

"A few weeks ago, I couldn't get rid of you. Every time I turned around, there you were, demanding that I take off my shirt or shoes, and the first few times I saw you, you weren't wearing a stitch of clothing. Now, you'll hardly get near me."

"That was before," she said, looking straight ahead.

"Before the night in the logger's cabin? Before the night we made love and had such a wonderful time?"

"It wasn't such a wonderful time to you. You told me you wanted nothing to do with me, that I was just one of many women to you."

"Maybe I was a little hard on you that night, but you scared me to death with your talk of marriage and kids. Can't you forget that and we could start over? We were getting on so well until you decided you just had to put that noose around my neck."

She pulled her arm away from his. "I don't want to

put a noose around your neck. Marriage is different. It's for two people who love each other and I stupidly thought that's what we did that night—made love. I was in love with you or I wouldn't have done that . . . I wouldn't have let you touch me. But it wasn't love to you. You don't love me, you never have. You got what you wanted, but I didn't."

She turned away to hide her tears.

He pulled her to him, turning her so that her face was buried in his chest. "Chris, I don't think I've ever had a woman in love with me before, and I have no idea what it means to be in love. I'm sorry, I don't mean to hurt you. Maybe you just think you're in love with me because I can handle a gun and I'm not like anyone you ever met before and—"

She looked up at him. "I've met hundreds of gunslingers and hundreds of outlaw criminals and I resent your telling me that I don't know my own mind. I can tell you that—"

She stopped because Tynan kissed her, hungrily drinking from her lips, caressing her back, pushing her hips into his, trying to envelop her with his hard, hot body. Chris knew she wouldn't last long if he continued touching her.

"Please don't," she whispered when his lips moved to her neck. "Please don't touch me. I can't bear it. I can't resist you."

"I don't want you to," he said as his teeth took her earlobe.

It was when his lips touched the corner of her eye and he tasted a salty tear that he stopped. Abruptly, he drew away from her. "Go on then," he said with suppressed anger in his voice. "Go back to your cold bed and stay there alone."

Chris's tears began in earnest then and she fled down the steep, dark path to the cabin. Pilar didn't say a word as Chris fell down onto the pallet beside her.

Chris cried for a long time before she made a decision. She didn't care whether he married her or not, and she didn't care if he loved her or not. Right now all she felt for him was desire and she wanted it to be the way it was that night in the logger's cabin. She wanted to feel his hands on her body, wanted him to make love to her again.

Sniffing, but feeling better now that there was no more indecision, she got up and left the lean-to shelter. She knew that Tynan slept not far from them, a little way into the trees so that, should anyone come to the cabin during the night, he'd not be seen. She went to his sleeping place but he wasn't there.

Slowly, with deliberation, she removed all her clothing, stretched out on his blankets and waited for him. When he didn't come, she went to sleep, smiling at the thought of how he'd waken her.

"Chris," Tynan said, pulling her into his arms. "Oh my beautiful, lovely Chris."

Sleepily, she opened her eyes. It was daylight, the birds were singing, the smell of the early morning forest was all around them—and Tynan's hands were on her body, pushing away the covers and caressing her skin. His hands ran over her hips with the eagerness of a boy's with his first puppy.

"You came to me," he whispered. "You came to me. I didn't sleep last night. I just wandered in the forest. Oh Chris, you're driving me crazy. My beautiful, beautiful Chris, you are making me more miserable than when I was in prison."

Chris could feel her skin glowing with the joy of his

words. She sincerely hoped that she was making him miserable—at least as miserable as he was making her.

He brought her head up to his and kissed her as if he never meant to let her go, his hands in her hair.

Her arms went around his neck to pull him close. This is what she'd wanted for so long, but what she'd been fighting against for what seemed to be forever.

He stretched her out on the blankets and moved to lay beside her, touching her gently, while, at the same time, removing his own shirt.

With his leg between hers, he rubbed his rough clad skin against hers while kissing her.

Abruptly, he pulled away from her and put his head up as if he were listening. "I have to go. Someone's out there."

"It's just Pilar," she said, trying to pull him back down to her. "She won't come here."

Tynan moved away from her and pulled his shirt back on. "Someone's coming up the trail." He gave Chris a look of resignation. "It's my luck that it's your father here all ready." Chris thought he looked on the verge of tears. "You'd better get dressed. If it's not him, we can continue this later and if it is, he might not stop to ask questions if he found his little daughter kissing the hired hand." When she opened her mouth to speak, he stopped her. "Don't give me any argument, and don't make this harder for me, just please get dressed and let me see who this is."

Tynan moved away from her, standing and watching her with eyes that bore an expression of sadness, desire and pain. When she was dressed, he grabbed her arm and pulled her to him. "I've aged twenty years since I met you. I hope with all my might that this is *anybody* except your father." After a quick kiss, he released her, took her hand and led her into the cabin clearing.

Chris could see Pilar's sleeping form under the lean-to.

"Go look in my saddle bags and you'll find a pair of field glasses. Bring them to me."

Chris ran to do what he asked. Pilar raised on one elbow to look at her.

"Happy this morning?" Pilar asked.

"I've been happier," Chris said, searching inside the saddle bags. "I would be extremely happy if Tynan'd bothered to return to his sleeping roll last night."

Pilar groaned, then asked, "What's going on now?"

"Ty says he hears someone coming up the trail. I haven't yet heard anything but he's gone to see. Ah, here they are."

"I'm coming with you," Pilar said and was out of her sleeping pallet in a second and was soon running down the hill behind Chris.

Tynan was stretched out on a rock, as flat and as unnoticeable as a lizard and he had to call to the women before they saw him. "It's them," he said with great sadness in his voice. "I knew it would be." He reached out his hand to Chris for the glasses.

Chris and Pilar climbed on the rock beside him. "You're sure it's my father?" Chris asked, excited.

"Whoever it is, I hope they've brought us some supplies," Pilar said.

"From the size of the group, I think Mathison's brought his entire ranch."

Chris took the glasses from him. Her father was unmistakable, sitting on top of the horse that looked too small for him, riding with his back as straight as a railroad tie—and even at this distance he looked angry. She put the glasses down and saw that Ty was looking at her with a teasing smile on his face.

"Want to borrow my gun to protect yourself?" he asked, one eyebrow raised.

"Who's the man with him?" Pilar asked, looking through the glasses.

"Never saw him before," Ty answered.

Chris heaved herself up from the rock. "I guess I better get this over with. If either of you have delicate sensibilities, you'd better leave now. My father's temper is . . ." She couldn't think of anything that would adequately describe it.

She took a deep breath for courage, then started down the hill toward her father and the men who rode with him. She was hesitant at first, but as he came more clearly into view, she began to pick up speed until he saw her.

Del Mathison spurred his horse forward in a burst of speed that left the others standing.

Chris lifted her skirts and took off running as fast as her legs would carry her—and Del's horse came charging toward her. When he reached her, he didn't slow, but extended his arm and hauled her up to toss her in the saddle behind him. It was a trick he'd taught her when she was a child, and it'd come in handy in her life, such as the time Tynan had run his horse through the freight office.

As Chris held onto her father, she saw that Ty had followed her down the hillside, gun drawn, protecting her as she'd run away from the shelter of the camp. She turned to see the man who'd been riding beside her father stop and help Tynan mount behind him.

Del didn't waste any time when he reached the cabin. Before he even dismounted, he began yelling at Chris.

"Of all the damn fool, stupid things you've ever done, this is the worst. So help me, I'm never going to let you out of my sight again. You and your mother's whole family, none of you ever had a lick of sense."

Chris stood on tiptoe and put her arms around his neck. She was glad to see that he looked as good as he always did: big, handsome, with the head of a lion, thick gray hair spreading out like a mane around his handsome face.

He hugged her back for a moment, then pushed her away. "Do you know what hell you've put me through? Do you have any idea the number of people that've come to me and told me you were within inches of being killed?"

"How many?" she asked solemnly.

"Don't you get smart with me, young lady, I'll do what these men *should* have done with you. Where is that young pup I sent after you? He was supposed to *protect* you."

Tynan stepped forward. The area in front of the cabin was filling with men and their horses. "Are you asking for me?"

Del looked Tynan up and down, took in the dirty bandage on his thigh. "I see she's about done you in, too."

Tynan straightened. "I take full responsibility for everything that's happened. There were several times when I had the opportunity to get her back safely."

"Hmph!" Del snorted. "You couldn't very well control her when you were in jail. And what's this I hear about you two being engaged?"

301

Chris held her breath as she looked from her father to Tynan. It looked as if Ty weren't going to say anything, and Chris suddenly realized the seriousness of this moment. If she said they were engaged, her father could send him back to jail. She thought of Ty's back as it'd been in the rain forest. She thought she could control her father, but she wasn't positive. What if she were wrong? If she were, then Ty would be returned to prison.

"We're not engaged," she said softly. "I just said that to prevent a fight. He's been a perfect gentleman at all times and he did everything he could to protect me. He even saved me from Dysan."

Chris watched her father as he continued to study Tynan and after a moment, he grunted, but made no other comment.

"I'm hoping that Chris will accept my proposal," said someone behind her and she turned to see Asher standing there. There was a bandage across his forehead. With a smile of possession, he put his arm around Chris's shoulders. Her father looked at her as he had when she was a child, and she knew he was trying to figure out if she was telling the truth or making up one of her highly imaginative stories. Chris couldn't meet his eyes, so she looked down at her hands clasped in front of her.

Pilar broke the silence. "Let me introduce myself," she said, moving toward Del, hand outstretched. "I'm Pilar Ellery. We've never met, but I've certainly heard a great deal about you. You wouldn't happen to have some food in those saddle bags, would you? We're all starving."

Del shook her hand, but he didn't smile at her, and

Chris knew that he was upset, deeply upset, if he didn't smile at a pretty woman.

She moved away from Asher's proprietary grasp and slipped her arm through her father's. "I'm sorry I caused you so much trouble. I didn't mean to."

Del looked at her for a long moment and she saw a sadness in his eyes. Was something troubling him besides her being in danger?

"Miss Mathison, may I introduce myself?"

Before her stood the man who'd ridden beside her father. He was about the same age as her father, a tall, slim man with black hair that was graying at the temples. He had the lean, hard look of a man who was used to physical exercise, but at the same time, he had an elegance that could only have come from generations of selective breeding. Even though he looked at home with a gun slung around his hip, she could easily imagine him on a dance floor or holding a wine glass.

"I am Samuel Dysan," he said in a deep, rich voice.

"Samuel Dysan?" She looked behind him toward Tynan, then back at the older man. "You're the one Beynard . . ."

"He is seeking me?" The man looked surprised.

"I heard him saying that he'd searched for years for Samuel Dysan."

Sam and Del exchanged looks. "Oh yes, I see. And when did he tell you this?"

"I, ah . . . he didn't really tell me, he, ah . . ."

Tynan stepped forward. "She hid in the bushes and listened."

"It was for a good cause!" she snapped at him. "Lionel was—"

"Lionel?" Del said. "You mean you did something

for that brat you sent to me? I turned that kid over my knee three times in one day."

"You *beat* Lionel?" she gasped. "He's just a little boy."

"I should have taken my hand to you more often, but, no, I had a soft heart and thought that little girls were different. I'll not make a mistake like that again. I mean to raise this boy right, so he has some sense and doesn't go off to big cities and write stories that get him shot at. Do you have any idea how many people have said to me in the last few days, 'Yeah, she was here, left three dead bodies behind her'?" He looked up at Tynan. "Between the two of you, there're about a hundred fewer people in this world."

"I don't think that's fair," Chris said. "Tynan did what he had to do. He—"

"Except when I shot Rory Sayers," Ty said in all seriousness.

She turned on him. "And what were you supposed to do? Stand there and let him shoot you? You saw the way all those people were egging you on, trying to make you do something exciting. There was nothing else you *could* do. You *had* to protect yourself."

Suddenly, she stopped as she realized what she'd said. She'd told him she was wrong to have left him alone in jail but she'd thought that out logically. This time there was passion in her belief in him.

Tynan stood there looking at her for a moment, an angelic smile on his face, then he turned toward Del. "Sir, she only gets into trouble because she wants to right all the world's wrongs. I think you've done a damn fine job of raising her. Now, would anybody like to eat?'' He held out his arm. "Miss Mathison, may I escort you in to dinner?''

Chris felt a little weak-kneed as she took Ty's arm. She'd never been around a man who didn't cower in the presence of her father. Every other man did just what Asher was doing now: standing back and looking on quietly.

They joined the others—Del had brought about fifty men with him—and ate the first decent meal they'd had in days. Chris kept smiling at her father as he glowered at her as she tried to answer all his questions without telling the truth about the danger she'd been in. She didn't want to upset him more than she had already. She never really lied but then she didn't tell him all of it either.

"You went to Hamilton's knowing that he'd had his cousin killed?''

"I wasn't sure of that. I mean, it was an awful wagon accident. I'm sure the fall could have killed any number of people and all I wanted to do was help a little boy. Besides, I had the two big, strong men you sent to me to help me. What could possibly have gone wrong?'' She didn't dare meet the eyes of Tynan or Asher or Pilar.

Del leaned toward her. "What went wrong was Dysan. Do you have any idea what that man's like?''

"Yes, I do," she said softly. "Papa, do you think you should talk about him like that now?'' She gave a pointed look toward Samuel Dysan.

Mr. Dysan put his plate down. "You can't offend me. I know more than anyone what my grandnephew is like. I have had the misfortune of watching him grow up.''

Chris's curiosity came to the surface. "Then why did

305

he say he'd been searching for you for years? Didn't he know where to find you?"

Del began to tell his daughter to mind her own business, but Chris kept her eyes on Samuel. The man was watching Tynan, looking at him with such interest that Chris began to look from one man to the other. Samuel caught himself.

"I have never understood the workings of the boy's mind," Samuel said. "His mother married my nephew because she thought he was the heir to my holdings, and when she found out he wasn't, she turned her son against me."

"And who is your heir?"

"Christiana!" Del yelled at her. "I will not stand for your lack of manners."

"I apologize, Mr. Dysan. It's just the reporter in me. I thought there might be some doubt about who was your heir if the woman thought her husband was going to be."

Samuel put his hand on Del's arm. "It's all right, I don't mind the questions. I have a son but he disappeared at sea many years ago. Perhaps I'm a fool but I have always had hopes of finding him again. But, even if I never found him, I would never leave a penny to my grandnephew."

"He seems to have enough money as it is."

Samuel's face turned hard. "Whatever he has, he has obtained by stealing, cheating, lying, killing."

"Oh," Chris said and looked down at her plate.

"Mr. Tynan," Samuel said, "I have had some experience with wounds. May I take a look at your leg?"

Tynan looked surprised. "If you'll look at Pilar first."

"Yes, of course," he said, smiling at Tynan.

"You know . . ." Chris began, looking from one man to the other.

"And what was that you wrote about Hugh Lanier? You accused that poor man of some of the worst crimes of this century," Del yelled at her.

Chris gave her attention back to defending herself to her father.

Chapter Twenty-five

Chris couldn't get away from her father for even a minute all that night. She wanted to talk to Tynan alone, but he seemed to always be busy. And then there was Asher. He obviously wanted to prove to Del that he'd done his duty and Chris was planning to marry him, because he was never two feet from Chris's side. He kept saying things like, "Have another biscuit, Chris, I know how much you love them." He made it seem as if they were on intimate terms.

Tynan, on the other hand, kept calling her Miss Mathison and tipping his hat to her in the most formal way.

"He treat you all right?" Del asked her when she was frowning at Ty's back because he'd again acted as if he'd never met her before tonight.

"How'd you get him out of jail?"

Del Mathison gave a little snort. "I don't plan to start telling you all my secrets. I got him out, that's all you need to know. He tell you he was in jail?"

"I guessed it and he answered my questions. Who do you plan to tell your secrets to? The man you picked out for me to marry?"

"You have been asking a lot of questions. You and Prescott get along?"

"Well enough," she answered. "He's asked me to marry him, if that's what you had planned."

Del looked at her for a while. "It's time you settled down and gave me some grandkids."

"Yes," she said softly. "That's just what I want to do."

They didn't speak any more as they prepared for bed. Del went to the foreman of the small army of men he'd brought and set up watches all night. Chris, wrapped in a blanket, watched as her father stood in the moonlight and talked to Tynan for a few minutes.

"He seems like a sensible young man," Samuel said from near her. "Del said he was in prison for murder."

"Yes, but he didn't kill the man—at least not the man he was imprisoned for killing, and, yes, he is the most competent of men."

"You weren't . . . frightened of him, of being alone with him?"

Chris turned to give the man a look of disbelief. "I'd trust Ty with my life, with the life of anyone I loved. He's a good, kind, intelligent man who has never been given a chance in his life. Yet, in spite of that, he's trustworthy and has the highest of ideals." She stopped, feeling a bit embarrassed. "No," she whispered, "I was never afraid of him."

Samuel Dysan smiled at her in the darkness. "I see. Well, good night, Miss Mathison. I'll see you in the morning." He went away from her whistling.

The next day, Del woke the entire camp long before

sun-up. Sleepily, Chris looked out of the covers and saw that Tynan was already loading a couple of the pack horses. She threw back the blanket and went to him.

"Good morning," she said, smiling at him.

He didn't look at her, but moved to the far side of the horse. She followed him.

"Go get the coffee ready," he said under his breath. "We'll need a few gallons of it."

"Ty . . ." she began.

He turned on her. "Look, Chris, it's over. You go back to your world and I go back to mine. You become the little rich girl and I'm the ex-convict. It's over. Now, go get the coffee ready."

Quick tears came to her eyes. "It's not over, Ty. You know how I feel about you."

He put his hands on her shoulders. They were hidden from the others by the horses. "Chris, I told you it wouldn't work. I told you that from the beginning. Right now you think you . . . that you're in love with me, but you're not. You love the adventure and the excitement, but you also love the luxury of your father's house. You wait, you'll see. Two weeks in your father's house, after you give a few parties, after you've had a few baths and bought a couple of new dresses, you won't even remember me. If I walked into the parlor, you'd worry that my clothes were going to get the furniture dirty. And you won't even believe that you once thought you were in love with somebody like me."

She looked at him for a long minute. "I hope you make yourself believe that. I hope you can sleep at night. I hope you . . ." Her anger left her. "I hope that someday you realize that you love me just as much as I love you." She jerked away from him. "I have to make coffee. When you're man enough to tell yourself the truth, let me know, I'll be waiting."

She ran away from him, stumbling over Samuel Dysan, but she didn't look at him either. She kept her head down and helped the camp cook prepare breakfast for the many cowboys who were preparing to ride.

When they mounted, ready to ride, she saw that all around her the men had their guns ready. She was encircled by her father, Sam, Tynan and three of her father's hired men. Asher and Pilar were likewise guarded. "Do you think Dysan's out there?" she asked Samuel beside her.

"I think he's out there," he answered grimly. "We have something he thinks belongs to him."

Her father called for them to ride before she could ask another question.

They rode south for two hours before they encountered Beynard Dysan's men. He approached them with all the confidence in the world, as if he knew the outcome of what was about to happen.

Del called a halt to the group behind him, and Tynan put his horse directly in front of Chris. He, Del and Sam were in the front of the army facing Dysan's hundred or so men.

"You were looking for me?" Samuel said and there was such coldness, such hatred in his voice, that Chris shivered.

"Not you," Dysan answered. "You know what I want. I want what's rightfully mine."

"No," was all Samuel said.

"Then I'll take it," Beynard answered. "And I'll take all of you with me."

Samuel reined his horse forward, snatching the reins

from Del's hand when Del tried to stop him. Sam rode up to Beynard. Behind her, Chris could hear rifles being cocked, barrels of six-guns being rolled to check that all the chambers were loaded.

While Sam and Beynard talked, Ty moved his horse back to stand by Chris. "If I give you the order, I want you to ride like hell toward those trees," he said under his breath. "You understand me? No heroics."

Chris looked up to see her father turned around in his saddle and he was nodding to her that she was to do what Tynan said.

"Pilar?" Ty said over his shoulder. "Be ready to ride."

Chris, a lump of fear in her throat, watched as Tynan moved back into place beside her father. The two men she loved most in the world in front of her, the first ones to be killed if Dysan's men began firing. She was sure her heart was going to break her ribs as she strained to see Samuel talking to Dysan.

It seemed an eternity before Sam turned back toward Del.

"This fight is between the two of us," Samuel said. "Winner takes all."

Del nodded at Sam while Tynan looked on with eyes that were dark.

Chris reined her horse forward. "What's going on?"

"Nothing for you to concern yourself with," Del said, his eyes on Samuel's back.

"The two of them are going to settle it," Tynan said. "Whoever wins gets the spoils of war."

"But Samuel is an old man," Chris said. "He can't possibly have the reflexes of the younger man. And, besides, he has a right to leave his estate to whoever he wants."

Del gave her one of his looks that told her he wanted her to shut up. "I am the executor of his estate. If Sam loses, I'll see that the right person gets his money."

"But then Dysan will be after you and—"

"Chris," Tynan said softly. "Come over here and be quiet."

She ignored her father's look as she obeyed Tynan and moved her horse next to his. Her hands gripped the pommel until they were white as she watched Samuel and Beynard ride down the trail and into the trees. It seemed forever until they heard the first shot.

Chris gasped and held her breath and waited. And waited.

There was a second shot, then nothing.

She looked at Tynan, saw that the muscles in his jaw were working, then he kicked his horse forward and tore past the hundred gun-bearing men who had been hired by Dysan. He galloped into the trees to where Samuel and Beynard had disappeared.

Chris watched his cloud of dust for a moment, then she too kicked her horse and went after Ty. Behind her, she could hear her father shouting at her, then at his men, but she didn't stop, just kept following Tynan into the trees.

She reached the clearing just as Ty was dismounting.

Samuel and Beynard were lying on the ground, both of them bloody. She jumped off her horse while it was still running, skidding to a halt just as Tynan was lifting Samuel.

The older man smiled up at Tynan. "It's just a scratch. I can get up."

Tynan turned to look at Chris. "What the hell are you doing here? Get back to your father."

313

"I came to see if you were all right," she answered angrily. "I thought you might need help."

"Not from a half pint girl, I don't. Now, get back to—"

Sam struggled to sit up, using Tynan's help. He was smiling broadly. "As much as I like hearing the love play between the two of you, I think I'm bleeding to death."

Chris smiled at Tynan with an I-told-you-so look, while he opened and closed his mouth twice, with nothing coming out.

Just then Del Mathison came riding into the clearing amid rocks and dust and a flurry of anger—all of it directed at his daughter.

"What happened here?" Tynan said in a half yell that was obviously meant to stop Del's tirade.

Sam struggled to sit up while Chris ran to get bandages from her saddle bags. "We drew and I won. I thought he was dead but I went to him. He was my brother's child, I knew him since he was a boy. There were times when I thought there was some hope for him, but his mother never allowed him to forget who she thought he was. No matter who he hurt, she was there behind him, telling him he had every right to do whatever he wanted. She hated me."

"And made him hate you," Chris said, handing Tynan the bandages. Ty cut the man's shirt away. The wound was in the fleshy part of his upper arm, not bad, but painful. Chris moved so that Sam could rest against her while Ty bandaged him.

"Yes, he hated me. Said he wanted to show me he could make as much as me." He paused. "It's over now."

"How'd you get shot?" Ty asked.

"I went to him after I'd shot him. He had a derringer up his sleeve. He used his last breath to shoot me with it."

Chris leaned forward and kissed the man's forehead. "It's over now and we can all go home."

Samuel took Chris's hand and, while holding it, he looked up at Del. "This is what I wanted," he said quietly.

Chris started to ask what he meant, but Del interrupted her with orders of what to do to get the place cleared up.

They buried Beynard where he fell, putting up a crude cross to mark the place. The men who'd come with him disappeared into the trees quietly, and, after Samuel had had a few minutes alone at the grave, they began to ride south.

Chris knew she should have been relieved that now they were more or less free, that now it was safe to return home, but the closer they got, the worse she felt. As soon as they reached her father's house, Tynan would leave her life forever.

Asher came forward and began to talk to her about the scenery and recounted all their experiences since they'd first met. He talked abnormally loudly when he recalled the way he'd first seen her—stark naked, and Chris thought that, for some reason, he wanted her father to hear the story. And he'd only ridden toward the front after all the danger was over. It was difficult for her to give her attention to what he was saying.

On the second day, Tynan called a halt to the group, telling Del that they were near Pilar's home and he wanted to return her.

"I'll leave you now that you have your daughter back safely," Ty said, his side turned toward Chris.

"We'll wait for you, or we'll all go to see that the lady is returned safely, and then you can go back with us," Del said.

"No, sir, my job was to get your daughter back and I've done that. I think I'd like to go now."

Del took a while to answer him.

"Del," Samuel said, "doesn't he have a pardon coming?"

"Yes, of course. It's right here in my pocket." It took him some minutes before he could get it out to hand it to Tynan.

"Thank you, sir. I hope I did a satisfactory job for you."

"The money, Del," Samuel prompted.

Chris sat on her horse rigidly. With each passing moment, she expected Ty to say that he couldn't leave her, that she meant more to him than all the money in the world and that he'd risk jail if it meant he could have her. But he never even looked at her. Del took a long time opening his saddle bag and withdrawing a leather pouch.

"There's ten thousand dollars in there. That's what we agreed on, isn't it?"

"Yes, sir." Tynan put out his hand to shake Del's. "If you have anymore need of me, I'll be around. Mr. Dysan." He tipped his hat to the older man.

Chris didn't breathe as he turned toward her—but he didn't look at her, just nodded in her direction, gave one of his infuriating hat tippings, mumbled, "Goodbye, Miss Mathison," then turned away, Pilar beside him.

Chris sat there for a moment, barely aware of Pilar waving to her, then she leaned across her horse and grabbed her father's pistol from his holster and aimed it at the back of Tynan's head.

"What do you think you're doing?" Del shouted as he knocked her hand skyward.

The pistol rang out, the bullet flying a foot over Tynan's head, but he still didn't turn around.

Del took his pistol from his daughter. "Of all the fool things—"

He stopped because Chris had buried her face in her hands and began to cry. She *had* been only a job to him, a job to make money and, in the end, he hadn't cared anything at all about her.

As always, Del was at a loss as to what to do when a female cried, but Sam moved his horse closer to her and pulled her into his arms.

Chris recovered herself quickly, then moved away from Samuel and, with clear eyes, looked back at her father. "Forgive me. I'm ready to go now." She was very aware of the men around her, all of them embarrassed.

"Look, if you want to stay here . . ." Del was awkward in trying to comfort her.

"She's fine now, aren't you?" Sam said. "I think we ought to go."

Chris looked at him with gratitude and minutes later they were on their way toward home.

Chapter Twenty-six

Chris put down her book and leaned back against the tree that grew behind the little stone bench. She'd been in her father's house for three weeks now and she knew that she wasn't going to leave it again. She wasn't going back to New York, wasn't going to write any more stories about what was wrong in the world. Instead, she was going to marry Asher Prescott and live in her father's house forever.

With a sigh, she closed the book. She'd already told Asher and now all that was left was to tell her father. For some reason, she hated telling him. Of course he'd be utterly delighted that she'd at last done something that he wanted her to do, but still, Chris hesitated.

"Might as well get it over with," she murmured to herself as she stood. "A lifetime of being Mrs. Prescott and I think this will 'get it over with,' " she muttered.

She straightened her shoulders and started walking back to the house, passing Samuel Dysan on the way. The man had stayed on after the rescue and had

318

become part of the family. Twice, Chris had considered telling him her problems, but each time, something held her back.

She knocked on the door to her father's study.

"Come in," he called and, as usual, he sounded angry. Since they'd returned, he always seemed to be angry, sometimes not talking to Chris—as if he were furious with her about something.

He looked up at her. "What is it?" he asked coolly.

"I have something to tell you. Something that will please you, I'm sure."

He didn't say anything, just looked at her with one eyebrow raised.

"I have accepted Asher Prescott's marriage proposal. We're to be married one week from today."

She expected a burst of happiness from her father, but his face blackened. Wasn't she doing what he wanted?

"You never could do anything to please me, could you?" he began, coming up from his chair behind the desk. "I wanted you to stay home, but you wouldn't. I wanted you to marry and have babies, but you wouldn't. I wanted you to marry a *man* but you won't even do that, will you?"

Chris stood there blinking for a moment. "I'm going to marry the man you sent to me, the man you *wanted* me to marry."

"Like hell you are! I sent Tynan to you. I wanted you to marry *him.*"

"Tynan?" Chris said as if she'd never heard the name before. "But you said that if he touched me, you'd send him back to prison."

Del heaved a sigh, went to a bookcase, opened a door, and withdrew a glass and a bottle of whiskey. He poured out a healthy shot and downed it. When he looked back at his daughter, he seemed to have gained control of himself.

"I know that you've never done anything I've ever wanted you to do, so I thought I'd be able to get you to do what you thought I didn't want you to do. I sent you two men: one a weakling that could barely sit on a horse and the other one a . . . a man in every sense of the word. I thought you'd have sense enough to choose the right one. All I did was put a few obstacles in your way to make it more interesting."

Chris wasn't Del's daughter without having inherited some of his temper. "Of all the lowdown, rotten tricks, this is the worst. Do you mean that you created that entire story just to make me more interested in him?"

"It doesn't matter what I did since it obviously backfired. You chose that . . . that . . . don't you know that he only wants your money?"

Chris took a moment to control her rising temper. "I most certainly *do* know what he wants from me. But for your information, it was your hand-picked Tynan who turned me down, not the other way around. Your precious *man* refuses to have anything to do with me."

"And what did you do to him to make him dislike you?"

For a moment, Chris closed her eyes in an attempt to keep from screaming at her father. "I did nothing to make him dislike me," she said softly. "In fact, the reason I am marrying Prescott is because I'm carrying Tynan's child."

That successfully closed Del's mouth. "I'll go after him and bring him back here. I'll—"

"You will do no such thing. I'll not marry a man who doesn't want me."

Del sat down in his chair heavily. "But Prescott—"

Chris sat in the chair on the other side of the desk. "Asher wants my money and I want my child to have a name. I think it's a perfect arrangement."

Del seemed to age before her eyes. "Sam and I thought we'd planned everything so carefully. I didn't see any loopholes. We couldn't have been more wrong."

"What has Mr. Dysan to do with all of this?"

"Sam is Tynan's grandfather. In fact, Tynan's real name is Samuel James Dysan the third."

Chris couldn't speak for a moment. "He's who? What in the world are you saying? Tynan knows nothing about who he is."

"Sam hasn't known it all that long himself."

"Would you mind explaining what you're talking about? How long have you known about Tynan? Did you know when you got him out of prison?"

"Of course. You don't think I'd trust my only child to an outlaw, do you? I've always known who he was."

He leaned back in his chair. "I don't guess it'll matter that I tell you now, now that all Sam's and my plans have fallen through. Sam has hopes that Tynan will return, but I think I gave up last week."

"And decided that he didn't return through some fault of mine," she said with disgust. "How did you first learn about Tynan?"

"You're too young to remember, but Sam and I knew each other many years ago. He was a suitor of your mother's." Del smiled. "Now there was a woman with sense. She knew which man to choose. Anyway, Sam married soon after I did and he and his wife had a son right away, named him Sam after himself. There wouldn't have been any problems except for that hellion Sam's brother married. Sam made all his money on his own, but whatever his brother touched, failed. Sam's sister-in-law screamed night and day at her husband, then at her son who was just like him. Both men died young. It was when her grandson was born that she saw some hope of ever achieving what she wanted."

"And that was Beynard," Chris said.

"Yes, the woman thought for years that Beynard was going to be Sam's heir because Sam the second didn't produce any children. But then he and his wife decided to go to Washington to see about buying some timberland and they never returned."

"They were killed," Chris said softly. "Ty said that his mother had three bullet wounds in her back."

"All Sam could do was guess what had happened. He heard that his son and daughter-in-law had been killed in a boating accident and never made it to the coast of Washington. For years, he thought that he was going to have to make Beynard his heir, even though he disliked the boy. But six years ago, a friend of his daughter-in-law's came to visit and asked Sam what had happened to Lilian's child. Until then, Sam hadn't even known she was going to have a baby." Del gave Chris a hard look. "Sometimes fathers are the last to know what's going on in their children's lives."

Del folded his hands on the desk. "So, for six years, Sam's moved heaven and earth to find out if she had a child and if it lived. He found him three years ago. He's your Tynan. We think his mother must have said, 'Dysan,' and the old miner misheard it as 'Tynan.' "

"Who killed Tynan's parents?"

"Sam could only guess that his sister-in-law hired

someone to do it. Maybe she found out there was going to be a rival for her grandson's place as Sam's heir."

"So this is why Beynard wanted us. On the hill that day, at Hamilton's, he was talking about Tynan when he mentioned Sam, wasn't he?"

"Probably, but Beynard never had a chance. His grandmother was crazy and she poisoned his mind against Sam's family. She made him as crazy as she was. Sam made the mistake of telling the boy that he thought he'd at last found his grandson. Beynard broke into Sam's office, stole the papers on Tynan and came to Washington to find him. Several of the things that happened to Tynan over the last few years were caused by Beynard."

"So, actually, he kidnapped Pilar and me to get to Tynan?"

"We have no way of knowing for sure, but Sam and I think he knew Tynan . . . cared for one of you but he didn't know which one, so he took both of you."

Chris was silent for a few minutes as she digested this information. "So why did you come up with this elaborate scheme with Tynan and me? Why didn't Mr. Dysan just get his grandson released from prison and take him home? What did I have to do with this?"

"Sam only knew of his grandson by reputation. He'd heard of every gunfight, every time he got thrown in jail, the banks he robbed when he was a boy, all the scrapes he got himself into, and all the women." Del was watching Chris but she didn't say anything. "Sam wanted to know what his grandson was like. He was afraid he was like Beynard. And, too, we both hoped for an alliance between our families."

"So you used me," she said, her jaw set. "You used me in your matchmaking experiment."

Del's voice rose. "I thought maybe you could benefit by meeting a man, something besides those city slickers you'd met in New York. Give a job to a woman! Of all the stupid—"

"I don't think we'd better start this again," Chris said. "If you'd wanted me to meet him, you should have invited him to the house and introduced him to me. But no, you had to concoct an absurd farce to get us together. You had to threaten him with a return to prison if he so much as came near me and you also had to send that man Prescott who was drooling over me at every opportunity."

"And now you're going to marry him."

"I *have* to! That *man* you chose for me won't have anything to do with marriage. He's scared to death of the idea. And he'd rather do anything than go back to jail."

"Is that what he told you?"

"Yes, he did. I begged him to marry me, but he refused. You'll be happy to know that your little scheme worked on my part. I fell in love with Tynan—or Sam, whatever his name is—practically from the moment I saw him. But all he wanted from me was . . . what he got, so now I'm carrying the consequences of having fallen in love with him."

"He walked out on a woman carrying his child?"

"I most certainly did not tell him."

Del stood. "Well, we'll find him and make him marry you. He can't do this to my daughter."

"You do that and I'll walk out of this house and you'll never see me or your grandchild again. I'll not force myself on a man who doesn't want me. I've talked to Asher and told him about the baby and he's agreed to marry me and raise the child as his own. I think it'll work out nicely."

"Nicely," Del mocked. "I never would have thought this of Sam's grandson. I thought he had more guts than this."

"He said he was doing this for me and I think some of him believes what he's saying. He says he's not husband material and that I'll be better off with some man who's housebroken."

"But he could learn. *I* learned, didn't I?"

Chris looked at the floor. "I don't want to talk about this anymore. Tynan didn't love me. As much as you and Mr. Dysan wanted it to happen, it didn't. I'm going to marry Asher in a week and I'm going to stay here and raise my child and I'll probably never even see Tynan again. Besides, with his propensity for trouble, he'll probably be back in prison by the time of the wedding. Now, I think I'll go lie down and rest."

With that, she left the room.

Chapter Twenty-seven

"Do you really think you have the right to wear white?" Asher asked Chris as she sat in her father's garden. "I mean, isn't that asking for gossip?"

Chris didn't answer him. Since she'd, in essence, asked him to marry her, he'd started showing what he was really like. He was deeply angry that she'd spent a night with "someone like that gunfighter," and never lost a minute telling her so. They'd agreed that the child was to be known as his, so he could act proudly modest when the baby came three months too early. He didn't mind people thinking he'd seduced the rich Nola Dallas, but he refused to let anyone know that there'd been another man. He'd been angry when she'd told her father the truth.

"Won't you be showing soon?" he continued.

Chris closed her eyes for a moment. "How would I know? I've never had a baby. Doesn't my father have some work for you to do? I thought you were going to learn some of his business so you could help him."

"I can't this morning. There's a divine mare being put up for sale at Frederikson's and I need one more look at her before I buy her."

"But you've bought two horses already this week."

He stood back and looked at her and Chris knew what he was thinking. He'd taken Del Mathison's pregnant daughter off the man's hands and, because of this noble deed, he expected to be given the keys to the kingdom. He did no work and Chris suspected that he never planned to, that he was quite willing to go on living there, taking all her father had worked for and contributing nothing in return. And her father couldn't have cared less what Asher did. He was too angry at Chris to think of anything else. And Samuel kept looking at her with the saddest eyes.

"I thought maybe I'd buy this horse for you," Asher said. "You'll need a horse after his child is born."

She tightened her lips. In public, the child might be theirs, but in private, it was only "his."

"Yes, of course," she mumbled. "Of course I'll need a horse." She knew she'd say anything to get rid of him. As she watched him leave, she thought that after the baby was born, she'd probably leave Washington and return East. Her baby'd have a name, and she wouldn't have to deal with Asher every day.

She tried to bury herself in her book, but nothing could keep the tears from coming. She ran back to the house, tears pouring down her face, ran past Samuel, and up to her room where she spent yet another day crying.

The day of the wedding was overcast and looked as if it would rain. Mrs. Sunberry helped Chris to dress and there was never a more dismal dressing of a bride in history. Mrs. Sunberry kept crying, letting out little statements like, "He's not the man your mother would have wanted for you," and "He's already spent twice as much as your father does in a year," and "It's not too late to change your mind."

Chris had to grit her teeth each time the woman spoke. She had taken an instant dislike to Asher because he'd started giving orders the minute Chris told him about the baby.

Chris smoothed the white dress, put her chin in the air and left the room, Mrs. Sunberry sniffling behind her.

Her father was waiting for her at the foot of the stairs, and he managed to offer her his arm without so much as looking at her. His anger at her showed in every line in his face. Samuel walked behind them and he tried to put on a smiling countenance, but Chris thought he looked miserably unhappy.

It was on the tip of her tongue to scream at both of them that if they hadn't interfered, maybe this wouldn't be happening. If they hadn't told Tynan he'd have to return to prison where he would be beaten and starved, maybe he'd have considered marriage.

Quick tears came to Chris's eyes, because she didn't believe that for one minute. It wasn't the threat of prison that was keeping Tynan from marrying her, it was the fact that he didn't love her.

The church was packed with people she hadn't seen since she was a girl, and many people she'd never met before. There were some of her mother's relatives, the Montgomerys, standing there and watching her as she slowly walked down the aisle on her father's arm. Asher waited for her at the altar, smiling triumphantly.

"Probably thinking of the herd of thoroughbreds he's

going to buy tomorrow," Del said under his breath to her. "Do you know why that business of his failed?"

"I don't want to know," she hissed at him. "He's the man *you* chose."

"As contrast. I thought you were smart enough to know that."

"I was. Tynan wasn't."

"You could have—"

"Borne him twins?" she asked, glaring up at him as she reached the altar.

It was only as the preacher started the ceremony that Chris realized the full extent of what she was doing. She was promising to love, honor and cherish this man for the rest of her life. Tears welled up in her throat and closed it so that the pastor had to ask her three times for her answer. She was aware of Asher looking at her as if he meant to strike her if she didn't give her answer soon. Behind her, she could hear the people beginning to get restless.

It was then, while she was trying to answer, that all hell broke loose. A shot was fired outside the church and, suddenly, the building was overrun with men bearing arms. Men came in the windows, through the back door, from the door behind the altar. Two men must have been hiding in the balcony and they now rose, rifles aimed and ready.

"I wouldn't try it if I were you, mister," said a man with a pistol pointed toward one of Chris's Montgomery uncles who had his hand to his vest.

Everyone stood still, looking at the twenty or so men who surrounded the interior of the church. The big double doors in the back were open, three men guarding the entrance.

Chris watched with widened eyes as she heard a

horse approach the back doors. The rider seemed as if he had all day.

Through the doors rode Tynan on top of a big chestnut stallion, his gun sheathed, looking for all the world as if he were out on a Sunday stroll. He halted about halfway down the aisle, then, with everyone watching in open-mouthed astonishment, with twenty guns aimed at the guests, he took the makings of a cigarette out of his pocket and began to roll one.

"I don't guess I can let you do this, Chris," he said softly, licking the paper to stick it around the tobacco.

Chris took a step forward, but her father was there before her.

"You aren't taking my daughter without being married to her," Del said. "You're not going to make a whore of her."

"I never meant to. That's why I came to church." He hadn't yet looked at Chris, but kept looking down at that cigarette that was taking a long time to roll.

Del stepped back. "You can get on with it. The boy's marrying my daughter."

"But—" Asher began but Del grabbed him by the ear as if he were a little boy and pulled him to a pew.

"You can all sit down," Del bellowed out to the congregation as if it were the most normal thing in the world that the bridegroom was sitting on top of a horse in the middle of the church. "And you men," he said to the gunmen around the periphery of the room, "take off your hats."

They did as they were bid.

Chris heard chuckles from the congregation, then they sat down. She turned back to the pastor who looked a little pale and didn't seem to know what to do.

"Perhaps you should hurry before the horse spoils the church," she whispered. "His name is Samuel James Dysan III, also known as Tynan."

"Yes," the preacher said and cleared his throat.

This time, Chris didn't have any trouble answering his questions. Her hearty "I do," caused the congregation to laugh. When the preacher got to Tynan's part, she turned back toward him. She wanted to watch his expression when his name was said.

Tynan blinked a few times, and hesitated, and glanced at Samuel, saw the man nod once, then looked back at Chris—for the first time. "I do," he said and the congregation broke into applause.

Chris let out a yell of "hallelujah," tore off her veil, sent it flying toward Asher and ran toward Tynan on his horse. He caught her arm, heaved her behind him and backed the horse out of the church amid cheers and yells and guns being fired in jubilation.

She held onto him with all her might as he thundered across the countryside.

It was twenty minutes later that he stopped and hauled her around to the front of him and started kissing her. Her dress was unbuttoned to her waist after the first kiss.

"Wait a minute," he said, drawing back. "Is anybody going to come after us? I mean, is your father planning to send a posse out after us?"

"Maybe to send his thanks," she said, trying to continue kissing him.

"What was all that back there? Why did that man say my name was Dysan?"

"Because it is. Oh, Tynan, I have so very much to tell you. I know who you are and about your mother and father and Sam is your grandfather and I'm going to have your baby and what made you come back for me?"

He sat there looking at her for a moment, not able to take in all of it. "Is your father going to have me sent back to jail?"

"Only if you desert me."

"Ow," he said as she ran her hands along his ribs. "Stop that."

"You've been hurt. What happened?"

He grinned at her. "Lester Chanry found me again."

"And what did you do to that poor man this time?"

"I gave him a piece of the old miner's gold and told him where the mine was."

"So poor Lester will go up there and be met by that old man?" she asked, smiling.

"They deserve each other." He began kissing her neck again. "If nobody's chasing us and we just got married, does that mean we can go somewhere and start the wedding night?"

"This early in the day?" she asked in mock alarm. "Shouldn't we wait until night?"

"It'll be night by the time I get through kissing your pretty little body."

"Oh, well, that's all right then."

"Tomorrow you can tell me all about my—" he grinned, "grandfather, but now I have more important things to think about."

Holding her onto the horse, he kicked it forward and started down the road at a breathtaking speed.

Three minutes later the countryside rang with Tynan's shout of, "A BABY!?" Chris's laughter followed close behind.

Turn the page
for an excerpt from

Legend

by Jude Deveraux

Now Available from Pocket Books!

It was eleven p.m. and Kady was exceptionally tired as she entered her boring little furnished apartment. She'd chosen the place because it was close to Onions, the restaurant where she was working as head chef. There was even a maid service available that came and changed sheets and towels—so she didn't have to worry about those either—so the place was convenient, if not likeable.

For the life of her she couldn't figure out what had been wrong with her tonight. In theory everything had gone very well. Gregory, her fiance, had been at his most charming, and she appreciated the effort he'd made to entertain her friends. Even her friend Jane had been impressed, telling Kady that her own husband felt no obligation to talk to her friends and, instead, often spent his days with his face behind a newspaper. As for Debbie, she was so starry-eyed from eating Kady's cooking and having a man as handsome as Gregory pay attention to her that she could hardly speak.

"You're tired," Gregory had said abruptly after Kady had suppressed her fifth yawn at the dinner table. "You've been on your feet all day. You should go home and rest."

"I don't think freedom agrees with me," Kady said, smiling sleepily. "I should have spent today in the kitchen."

Gregory turned dark eyes to the other two women. "Can

either of you do anything with her? I have never seen anyone work as much as she does. She never takes time off, never does anything except work." As he spoke, he took Kady's hand and caressed it, then gave her a look guaranteed to melt her knickers.

But when Kady gave another yawn, he laughed. "Come on, baby, you're going to ruin my reputation as a lady-killer. What are Debbie and Jane going to think of me?"

Kady laughed, as Gregory always seemed able to make her do. Turning to her women friends, she smiled. "He really is the best man in the world—very exciting and all that. It's just me. I don't know what's wrong with me tonight. I seem to be drained of all energy."

"Probably from thinking about having to choose furniture," Gregory said as he stood, then pulled Kady's nearly limp body up out of the chair. He was quite a bit taller than she was and his face was as sharply chiseled as hers was soft planes.

Gregory turned to the other women, smiling. "I'll take her home, then return for whatever Kady's made for dessert."

"Raspberries with kirsch and—"

She broke off when all three of them laughed, making her blush. "Okay, so I'm just tired, not dead."

Holding on to Gregory's strong arm, Kady left the restaurant, and he walked her home, saying nothing, just keeping his arm protectively around her. At her door, he put his arms around her, then kissed her goodnight, but he didn't ask to be allowed to spend the night. "I can see that you're exhausted, so I'll leave you." Drawing back, he looked down at her. "Still want to marry me?"

"Yes," she said, smiling, leaning her head against his hard chest. "Very much." She looked up at him. "Gregory, I really am hopeless at buying furniture. I don't have a clue about curtains and sheets and—"

She broke off as he kissed her. "We'll hire someone. Don't spend another moment thinking about it. I have a deal going in L.A., and as soon as it's closed, we'll be able to afford anything." He kissed the tip of her nose. "All the copper pots you want."

With her arms about his waist, she hugged him tightly. "I don't know what I've ever done to deserve a man like you. I can't wait until we're married. After that we'll run Onions, I'll write my cookbooks and we'll produce a dozen babies."

Gregory laughed. "They'll certainly be well-fed little crumb-crunchers, that's for sure." Putting his hands on her shoulders, he set her away from him. "Now, go to bed. Get some sleep. Tomorrow your friends are going to take you to a carpet store to look at rugs to buy for the house."

"Oh no!" Kady said, clutching her stomach. "I can feel an attack of bubonic plague coming on. I think I must stay in the kitchen tomorrow and brew an herbal remedy."

Laughing, Gregory used his key to open her apartment door, then pushed her inside. "If you don't behave I'll hire a bridal consultant to 'organize' you. You'll find yourself being asked to register for trash cans and monogrammed toilet seat covers."

He laughed harder when Kady turned white at the very thought of such horror. Still laughing, he closed her apartment door, leaving her to get some sleep.

So now, Kady stood with her back to the door and looked about the boring, characterless apartment. She really was grateful that Gregory understood her total lack of talent in choosing furnishings. It wasn't that she didn't want a nice place to live, it was just that she had no idea about—and okay, no interest in—choosing chairs and such.

"I am the luckiest woman on earth," she said aloud, as she had twice a day since she'd met Gregory.

But oddly enough, as she stepped away from the door, her energy seemed to revive. As she felt the tiredness leaving her, she thought she might make herself some cocoa and read a book or see if there was a late-night movie on.

But even as she thought it, her eyes drifted to the big tin box setting smack in the center of her living room. She wouldn't allow herself to admit this but, truthfully, all evening the rusty old box she'd bought earlier today had been in the back of her mind. As she'd deglazed the roasting pan, she'd thought, *I wonder what is inside that box?*

She absolutely refused to think that her tiredness had been an excuse to get away from the others and get back to the box and its hidden treasure. "Probably a rat's nest inside," she said aloud as she went to her tiny kitchen to take a short, strong offset spatula and an ice pick from a drawer. It was going to take some work to get the lid off the rusty box.

Thirty minutes later, she had finally scraped away enough rust to pry the lid off enough to get her fingers under it. Her tugging made her fingertips hurt and she was thoroughly disgusted with herself for her frantic pulling and scraping. After all, just as the woman at the antique shop said, the only treasure inside was probably flour, complete with dead carcasses of weevils.

With her fingertips jammed under one edge of the lid, Kady gave such a great pull that she went tumbling back across the room, the lid clattering to the floor. Pulling herself upright, she leaned over the box and peered inside, and saw yellowed tissue paper.

On top was a tiny bouquet of dried, faded orange blossoms, obviously put there with loving hands and undisturbed for many years.

Immediately, Kady knew that what was under the paper was something very special. And something very private. Sitting back on her heels, she looked at the flowers. They were pinned to the paper and had not been dislodged in her frantic attempts to pry the lid off.

For a long moment, Kady hesitated with indecision. Part of her cried out that she should replace the lid and never open the box again, put it on top of her kitchen cabinet and look at the outside; forget about the inside. Or better yet, get rid of the box and forget she ever saw it.

"You are being ridiculous, Kady Long," she said aloud. "Whoever put this in here has been dead a long, long time."

Slowly, disgusted to see that her hands were trembling slightly, Kady unpinned the flowers, set them aside, then peeled back the tissue paper. Instantly, she knew what she was looking at.

Folded carefully, untouched by light or air for many years, was a wedding dress: perfect white satin with a deep, square neck edged in a white satin ruffle. Rhinestone buttons twinkled up at her.

Kady still had a feeling that she should replace the lid on the box and close it forever. But the fact that just today she'd had such a dreadful experience trying to find a wedding dress and now seeing that the old flour tin she'd bought on impulse contained a wedding gown, was too extraordinary to let pass. Almost lovingly, she put her hands under the shoulders of the dress and lifted it out.

It was heavy since there seemed to be many yards of the beautiful white satin, all of it aged to the most perfect color of heavy cream. The bodice ended just below the waist, and below that was a skirt, smooth and straight in the front, then yards of fabric pulled to the back in a heavily ruched train that would extend three feet behind the wearer. Hand-knotted silk fringe graced the skirt and the top of the train. Below that were little pleats and the dearest handmade silk roses.

Holding the dress up to the light, Kady marveled at it. Today she must have tried on a dozen modern wedding dresses, but she'd seen nothing like this. Compared to this dress, the modern gowns were peasants' clothes, with no embellishment, no thought to the design: mass-produced versus one-of-a-kind.

Kady couldn't seem to take her eyes off the dress. The long sleeves ended in buttoned cuffs, tiny piping about the edges, then what had to be handmade lace spilled from the bottom edge.

Shifting the dress in her hands, Kady glanced down into the box and caught her breath. "A veil," she breathed, then, with reverence, she spread the gown across her sofa and knelt before the box.

If a whisper could be made into fabric, then that was what she was looking at. Reaching toward the gossamer lace, she drew back, almost afraid to touch something as lovely as this, then, taking a deep breath, she slid her hands under the lace. It was so light, it seemed to have no weight, no substance, as though it were woven of light and air. Standing, she let the lace drape over her arms, feeling the divine softness on her skin. It didn't take a costume historian to recognize this lace as handmade, the flower-and-vine pattern worked by tiny needles, and if Kady didn't miss her guess, it had been made with love.

Very carefully, she spread the lace on her sofa, feeling that it was almost sacrilege to allow that fairy fabric to touch modern, plastic-based upholstery fabric.

Turning back to the box, she slowly and carefully began to empty it of the rest of its contents. It was as though she knew exactly what she was going to find inside it: shoes, corset, petticoats of fine cotton, hose with embroidered garters. More dried flowers.

Reverently, she set each item aside as she returned to the box to look at the rest of the treasures. In the very bottom of the box was a satin case, sewn with white ribbon and tied into a bow. As Kady lifted the case, her heart was pounding, because, by some instinct, she knew that what was inside this case was the key to why this beautiful dress had been stored away so long ago in such an ordinary old tin. As she lifted the case, she could tell that there was something heavy inside.

Leaning back against the couch, she put the case on her lap and slowly pulled one end of the ribbon to untie it, then even more slowly, she lifted the top flap of the case, put her hand inside, and withdrew an old photograph. It was a tintype of a man, a woman and two children: a very handsome family, all of them fair haired with sweet, happy-looking faces.

Kady couldn't help smiling at them. The man was very stern-looking, as though he was uncomfortable in the high, stiff collar he wore. Sitting to his left, his hand on her shoulder, was a small, pretty woman with an impish gleam in her eye, as though she found the whole idea of photography a great joke. Standing to her right, in front of the man, was a tall, handsome boy, about ten or eleven years old, with some of his father's sternness, as well as his mother's devilish gleam. On the woman's lap was a little girl of about seven who was a beauty-in-the-making. It was obvious that when she grew up she was going to break some hearts.

Turning the photo over, on the back was written a single word: *Jordan.* Carefully, Kady put the photo aside then fished inside the case and pulled out a man's heavy gold watch. The watch was so big, it filled the palm of her hand. On the worn cover was the word *Jordan* and along one edge, just above the hinge, was a deep crease as though the watch had been dropped onto something very hard.

"Or shot," Kady said, then wondered why she'd said that. "Too many westerns on TV," she muttered, but as she ran her thumb along the crease, it did seem to have striations, as though it had been grazed by a bullet.

Because of the deep indentation, the watch was difficult to open, but with persistence, she managed to make the hinge work. Inside, the face of the watch was beautiful, with ornate Roman numerals and elaborate hands. On the left of the watch case was another photo, this time of the woman alone. There was no mistaking her with her sparkling eyes and happy expression. Even in the photo she looked like a woman in love and happy.

Closing the watch, Kady smiled. What in the world had made her nervous? she wondered. Obviously, this was the wedding dress of a woman who had been very happy. She'd had a husband who loved her and two beautiful children.

Smiling, Kady put the watch beside the photo, then looked to see if anything else was inside the case. She pulled out a pair of amethyst earrings, the purple stones glittering in the artificial electric light.

Carefully, she laid the earrings on the silk case, leaned back against the couch and looked at everything.

Whatever am I going to do with all this? Shouldn't these things be in a museum? she thought.

One second she was asking herself what she was going to do with all this, then the next she could envision herself walking down the aisle of her own wedding wearing this heavenly gown. With renewed energy, she leaped to her feet and picked up the dress, holding it at arms' length.

This dress was not like modern clothes, so it hadn't been made for a woman five feet ten inches tall who had miles of legs, no hips, no breasts, and a boyish waist. At this thought Kady allowed herself a smug little smile. There had been several men in her life who had made some extraordinarily pleasant comments about her hourglass figure.

"This would fit me," Kady said aloud, turning the dress to hold it against her and seeing that it was indeed the perfect length.

Right away she knew that the sensible thing to do would be to go to bed now, then tomorrow she'd talk with Debbie and Jane about this dress. It was great that they were here and could give their opinions on something as serious as wearing a hundred-year-old dress to a modern wedding. Kady had no idea about these things. Was it done? Would she be laughed out of the church?

Even as she was thinking these very sensible thoughts, she was on her way to the bathroom, where she got into the shower and washed her hair. While she was conditioning her hair, then blow-drying it, she told herself that she couldn't wear a dress with a bustle to her wedding. It was really too outrageous to consider.

As Kady stood in her robe before the mirror, she began to arrange her hair. At the restaurant she pulled it back off her face and into a bun so it wouldn't fall into the food. She had never been very adventurous with her hair, nor actually very vain about her looks, but now she wanted to look her best. Using a comb, a round hairbrush and about three pounds of hairpins, she managed to sweep her hair into a high pouf off her face, then allow long curls to tumble down her back.

When she'd finished, she looked in the mirror and gave a little smile. "Not bad," she said as she touched up her eyes and lips with cosmetics.

When she'd done what she could with her head, she went into the living room and began to try to puzzle together the wedding outfit. There seemed to be an outrageous number of undergarments and it was difficult to figure out what went on in what order.

She put on a pretty but shapeless cotton slip next to her skin, along with a big, long pair of underpants. Bending, she pulled on the hose made of finely knit silk, and fastened them just above the knee with garters embroidered with pink rosebuds. She thought she'd better get the shoes on now because she guessed that once the long corset was on, she wouldn't be able to bend.

Feeling like Cinderella, Kady slipped her feet into ankle-high, cream-colored kidskin shoes that fit exactly, then used a buttonhook to fasten the little pearl buttons up the front.

After she'd managed to buckle herself into the boned corset, which took a bit of breath holding, she caught sight of herself in the mirror by the front door. "My goodness," she gasped. The corset had managed to shove her breasts practically under her chin, and, looking at herself, she had to admit that corsets did have their advantages.

There were a couple more cotton half slips, then a little camisole that seemed to fit on over the corset.

By the time Kady got to the dress, she was wearing more clothes than she did when it snowed.

Once the dress was on, she carefully avoided looking in the mirror until she was completely dressed. After putting on the earrings, with reverential hands, she picked up the lace veil and pinned it in place on her head. The lace was as light as a soufflé, reaching almost to her knees, concealing the long dark hair down her back, but exposing it as well. Lace gloves went on last.

When she was fully dressed, she turned and took a few steps toward the full-length mirror. As she moved, she wondered why the dress and the many undergarments didn't feel strange. The weight of all the clothes she had on should have felt burdensome or at the very least constrictive, but somehow they didn't. Somehow the dress felt right.

With her shoulders back, her head straight and managing the train as though she'd been born wearing it, Kady walked to stand in front of the mirror.

For a moment she just looked at herself in silence, not

smiling, not thinking, really, just gazing. She was not the same person she usually saw. Nor was she a twentieth-century woman playing dress-up in antique clothing. It was as though she looked the way she was meant to look.

"Yes," she whispered. "This is what I will wear to my wedding." She didn't need to ask anyone's permission, for she knew without a doubt in the world that this was the dress she was meant to wear to her own wedding.

Smiling slightly, she walked back to the couch and picked up the photo of the Jordan family. "Thank you," she said softly to the woman in the photo, for she knew that it had to have been her wedding dress, a dress she must have loved and stored carefully away so that another woman in another time could wear it.

With the photo in one hand, Kady picked up the watch and unfastened the lid so she could see the second photo of the woman. "Thank you very, very much," Kady said, smiling at the whole family. "Thank you, Mrs. Jordan."

As Kady held the two objects, and as she said the name Jordan, she suddenly felt dizzy. "Must be the corset," she said as she sat down heavily on the sofa, the photo and watch falling to her lap. "I should get out of this dress. I should . . ."

Trailing off, she felt as though she were falling asleep but at the same time her weakness felt different. She felt that this dizziness was something she didn't want to give herself up to. At all costs, she thought, she *must* fight this. She must open her eyes!

"I say, let's hang the bastard," she heard a man say.

"Yeah. Get rid of him once and for all."

"Here that, Jordan? Make peace with your Maker, 'cause these are your last moments alive."

"No," Kady whispered weakly. "Don't hurt a Jordan. Such a nice dress. You shouldn't hurt one of them." For a moment she almost succeeded in opening her eyes and sitting up, but then she heard another voice, a man's voice.

"Help me, Kady. Help me."

Kady could see only blackness inside her closed eyelids.

"Yes," she said and quit struggling to sit up. "Yes, I will help you."

In the next second Kady collapsed against the sofa, unaware of where she was or even who she was. Limply, her hand fell to her side as she gave herself up to the deep swirling sensation that overtook her.

Look for
Legend
Wherever Books Are Sold